A NEW ORIGIN

Richard Koepsel, PhD

Auctus Publishers

AuctusPublishers.com

Copyright © 2024 Richard Koepsel, PhD

Book and cover design by Rajon Bose

Cover art created by Blessing Amu

Published by Auctus Publishers

606 Merion Avenue, First Floor

Havertown, PA 19083

Printed in the United States of America

A New Origin is a work of creative science fiction. All rights reserved. Scanning, uploading, and distribution of this book via the internet or via any other means without permission in writing from its publisher, Auctus Publishers, is illegal and punishable by law. Please purchase only authorized electronic edition.

ISBN (Print): 979-8-9915910-6-5

ISBN (Electronic): 979-8-9915910-7-2

Library of Congress Control Number: 2024950790

To Emily Rook-Koepsel and Megan Parker (my daughters), Abe DeBenedetti and Austin Parker (sons-in-law), and Robert, Ginny, Simon, and Shai (grandchildren).

Contents

PREFACE 1
ACT ONE: Here to There 4
    SCENE ONE: Where, What, and When? 5
    SCENE TWO: Why Now? 13
    SCENE THREE: Where, When, and Then What? 22
ACT TWO: The Escape 32
    SCENE ONE: Who, Where, Why, And How? 34
    SCENE TWO: Say What? How? And When? 38
    SCENE THREE: Going Where? With Whom? 42
ACT THREE: New Origin's Centennial Surprises 49
    SCENE ONE: What? From Where? 50
    SCENE TWO: What Was that? 56
    SCENE THREE: How? 61
ACT FOUR: Here and There and There and Here 73
    SCENE ONE: Why Aren't We There Yet? 74
    SCENE TWO: Wait. What? This Again? 81
    SCENE THREE: When And How Did This Get Here? 90
ACT FIVE: Introductions, Reunions, and Unification 99
    SCENE ONE: Who's, Where, Now 101
    SCENE TWO: Who Knew What There Was There 109
    SCENE THREE: Where Here Meets There 119
ACT SIX: First Contact 139
    SCENE ONE: The Dark Side of the Moon 140
    SCENE TWO: Weird Dreams and Strange Happenings 149
ACT SEVEN: Is This The Way the World Ends? Bang or Whimper? Fire or Ice 169
    SCENE ONE: First Foray: The First Battle of New Origin 171
    SCENE TWO: The Siege of Gaia City 177
    SCENE THREE: Who Guessed Whimper? 190
Epilogue 195
ACKNOWLEDGMENT 196

PREFACE

In a typical home in New Origin City on Planet Gaia, a family of the descendants of the original settlers from Earth, were preparing to attend the first of a series of seven plays that tell their history from the departure from earth to the arrival to and settlement of a planet they called Gaia. We join them as they are about to leave for the theater.

"Jason! Andria! What is taking you so long! We're going to be late if you don't get moving RIGHT NOW!"

"Ahh Mom, do we have to?' the twins whined. "Why should we care about something that happened a thousand years ago?

"First you should care because it is why you are alive, and second because your brother, your sister, and three of your cousins have parts in the play and, most importantly, we ARE leaving this house in three minutes and if you don't want to be grounded for the next seven weeks I would suggest you move quickly."

The two ten-year olds came thundering down the stairs and found their mother holding the front door open. "Good Job!" she said as they left the house and climbed into the buggy their father had brought around in front from the stable.

"Are you ready for a great adventure?" he said as the horses began to trot down the road toward town.

"I guess," the twins sighed.

"Next time the play comes around you will be twenty and I'll bet you will try out for a part in the cast. You know that your mother and I met when we were twenty and had major roles in the play."

"We've heard that before," the twins said in that irritating whine that characterizes pre-teens.

"Maybe when you are twenty, you'll be in the play. Maybe you'll get to play your fourth great grandparents, A-C and Penelope."

"We'll see but I doubt it," the twins said with a sigh.

A New Origin

Thirty minutes later, the family was sitting in their seats in the center of row seventeen of two hundred in the massive, ten thousand seats, theater on Broadway Avenue in downtown New Origin City. As the theater filled the kids kept track of how many of their friends were arriving until they had seen everyone they knew from the neighborhood and most of their friends from school.

All of a sudden, the house lights began flicking off and on, the crowd noise abated, the lights went off, and a spotlight made a circle of light in the center of the dark red curtains. A man dressed in black suit, that the kids had learned in school the day before was called a tuxedo, and carrying a microphone disguised as a cane, stepped through the curtains and onto the stage to a storm of cheers and applause.

He bowed with a flurry, tapped the cane on the stage floor, and when the crowd quieted said,

"Greetings and salutations! I am the Master of Ceremonies. Welcome to the 50th Decennial production of our history play in seven acts, presented live, here in the Caleb and Eleanore Memorial Theatre in historic New Origin City, and broadcast to theaters around the world. I am here tonight to set the scene for the telling of the story of how we came to be here. A story of mythic proportions; a story of odyssey and endurance; of history and tragedy; of an escape from Hades and a search for Utopia; of human failure and perseverance; and the origin story of the refugees from our original origin on the planet Earth and their trials on their new planet, Gaia. Sit back and enjoy as our Chorus sets the stage.

The curtains opened to choral ensemble of two hundred men and women robed in the style of the ancient cultures of the lost Earth. The sound of drums in the rhythm of an ancient dirge began in the background, and the chorus chanted:

"On a dying Earth in the late twenty-ninth century, The Origin Society, a secretive organization dedicated to the preservation of the Human Race, developed a small colony, called Origin, on the newly habitable plains of Greenland. The goal of this colony was to serve as the population source for a human life on a new planet. The "Originites," as they called themselves, are forced to leave earth just ahead of an attack by the mercenary End-Days Army. The Army was paid by the extraction industry to annihilate the remaining human population on Earth, a mission that was nearly complete as we start our story. Most humans had already abandoned the polluted Earth to live in orbital habitats; Earth's moon; the moons Jupiter and Saturn; and for the elite, a terraformed Mars, the capital of the Empire that ruled the solar system. Rebel forces against imperial rule have been active on the moons of Jupiter and Saturn both, important to the empire as agricultural producers. The rebellion gained significant power over the next four centuries and has its sight set squarely on the Imperial Capital on Mars. At the same time, the Originites arrive at their new planet they call Gaia, a journey of three hundred light years from Earth."

The curtains closed and the Master of Ceremonies returned to the spotlight.

"And so we begin. An ancient sage named Eliot said, 'This is the way the world ends, not with a bang but a whimper. Our odyssey begins with a bang, a whimper, and a journey to the stars."

"Another ancient sage said: 'All the world is a stage and all the men and women merely players; They have their exits and their entrances, their acts being seven.'

Thus, we tell our history as a series seven plays which we will call Acts. Welcome to Act One. He tapped his cane three times and curtain lit up with:

ACT ONE
HERE TO THERE

The Chorus chanted

Earth in the winter
We struggle for clarity
Where will the Spring be
The curtain opened.

SCENE ONE
Where, What, and When?

Dr. Caleb, Dean of Origin University, Chairman of Medical Education, and Professor of Internal Medicine, was pacing the stage of the Origin City Higher Education Campus auditorium. He fretted over his speech for what he knew would be the last graduation ceremony in Origin City. A chill ran up Caleb's spine with the thought that he was about to tell the students they would be continuing their education on a planet that no one had ever seen before.

He couldn't say to them that the planet, targeted as their 'New Earth,' would take more than three centuries to reach and centuries more to make habitable, or that the kids would come out of stasis and grow up in sealed habitats.

"How do you tell a kindergartner that their world is about to end?" he said out loud as he turned around in the right wing and started back across the stage, head down, hands clutched behind his back, shaking with anxiety.

"Gently, and by only talking about beginnings," he heard his wife, Eleanore, say from the left-wing.

"Thank goodness you're here," Caleb said, with a sigh of relief, "I thought you were outside doing crowd control."

"I was. We're good to go," Eleanore said, handing Caleb a stack of papers, "In consideration of your overwhelming stage fright, amplified by our imminent departure, I wrote five age-appropriate speeches for you. The kids will come in by age group and sit in the front rows, and you will read the speech from the lectern. They will then march across the stage, and you will shake their hands and give them a certificate. Finally, they will exit stage left and go to the party on the soccer field. And don't forget to do your breathing exercises and get ready for the next round."

"And what about the wedding?" he asked nervously, "will we have time for it?"

"We should. I've got us on the last shuttle. Unless something changes, we are scheduled to load at six AM."

Caleb carefully set the papers on the podium. He looked toward the seats and saw only Eleanore, radiant in the spotlights as if she were stepping out of the sun. He rushed to her arms clutching her tightly. "I...I can't do this," he stammered, releasing her, "Look at me. I'm shaking all over and I can barely stand."

Eleanore grabbed him by the shoulders, looked him straight in the eyes, and said tenderly, "It's pep talk time. You start."

He shook his head, took a deep breath, and whispered in her ear, "You are the love of my life. You've been saving me from myself since we were kids in Morgantown,"

"That's what you get for being the love of MY life," she replied as per the tradition, "I was looking out for my own best interests, and besides, you got us to Pittsburgh."

"That wouldn't have done us much good if you hadn't gotten us into Med school," he responded. "and don't forget it was me that got us that job with the coast guard, that nearly got you killed, by the End- Days Army."

"Oh, you mean the job that got us top listing on their most wanted list with a hundred-thousand-dollar bounty and made us famous. Oh, Caleb, my sweet, the Coast Guard job doesn't count," she retorted. "We had to do that job. They were paying our tuition, and besides, we rescued nearly a thousand people, some of whom will be in the audience this morning."

"OK, I'll concede that one," Caleb said, recovering most of his equilibrium. "But it was you, Eleanore, that got us hooked up with the Origin Society, and that was the best thing that ever happened to two poor, Jewish, kids from West Virginia. It was also you that gave us our son, Adam-Caleb aka A-C, and by that, our soon-to-be daughter-in-law, Penelope," he said, modifying the final line to the current circumstances.

As was their tradition, the pep-talk was sealed with a kiss and a complex series of high fives and fist bumps, which was interrupted by a voice from the auditorium, "Ahem! Um… Doctor Eleanore? I'm sorry to interrupt, but we are about to open the doors to the parents. And you're needed in the Green Room."

"No worries, Jasmine. Open the doors. I'm on my way to the Green Room now," she called to the back of the young woman hurrying up the aisle.

She put her hands on Caleb's shoulders and said, "You'll be great today. Just stay with the script, be gentle with the little ones, and relax."

"Love you too," Caleb called to Eleanore as she exited stage left, "I'll be fine, or at least I'll pretend to be."

By the time he got to the podium, the stage lights were down. He watched as seats filled with people, some of whom he had known for half his lifetime, and the children, most of whom he had delivered. "I'm not going cry," he said to himself, knowing it wasn't true. He lowered his head and began to read through the speeches. They were brilliant, as he knew they would be. Each one was a perfect, age-appropriate description of what was a bleak outlook for the next few days. He took several deep breaths and read through them again.

Caleb was so involved in worrying over the speeches that he didn't notice Eleanore standing behind a microphone stand front and center until a loud thumping boomed over the speakers. Then, he snapped to attention and saw all the fourteen-hundred seats taken and at least a hundred people standing in the aisles. He calmed his nerves by counting the standers and the stage crew, getting to two hundred forty-seven when Eleanor's voice boomed through the room.

"Welcome everyone to the Origin Education Department's first all levels graduation ceremony!"

The following applause and cheering caused the preschoolers and kindergartners to cover their ears, scream along with the crowd, or cry in about equal numbers.

Eleanore tapped the microphone. "I want to thank all of you for helping make this event possible and ask your forbearance in the cheering until the little ones have left for their party on the soccer field." The crowd settled, and she continued, "Thank you all for coming to this hastily organized event. I'm going to turn over the mike to the guy behind...OOH... You scared me!" she said, giving an exaggerated stink eye to Caleb. He had snuck up behind her, to the great amusement of the

A New Origin

crowd, and especially the younger set. She stepped to the edge of the stage and crouched down in front of the preschoolers, kindergartners, first and second graders. "That wasn't very nice of Dr. Cal, was it kids?"

The children responded with a chorus of "nos." Finally, she bent closer and asked, "Do you think Dr. Cal should apologize?"

A resounding "Yes" made Eleanore smile as she stood and handed the mike to Caleb.

He had a hangdog expression as he took the mike, "I'm sorry I scared you, Dr. Ella. I know that things you don't expect can be scary. Isn't that right kids?"

After a couple of minutes of small voices calling out various scary things, Caleb sat down on the edge of the stage. "So, can we all agree that things we don't expect can be scary?" he waited for a bit as the kids came to a semi-consensus, then continued, "I'm going to tell you about two things, one scary and one fun, that will happen in a few weeks. First, the scary thing. We are going to turn on a very loud siren. It will be the loudest thing you have ever heard, and it WILL be scary... BUT, when you hear the siren, I want you to remember that the siren tells us that it's time for our very special present. You all did so well with your schoolwork, especially in the last few weeks while learning about outer space. Our special gift is a ride into space. The whole village is going to take a super fun ride into SPACE!"

Caleb knew there would be questions, but he failed to anticipate decibels that could be produced by a hundred and forty children under eight.

He heard the top three questions: ' Can my mommy and daddy come too?' followed by 'can I bring my stuff?' and 'Can we go to the Moon?' Finally, after thirty seconds, that seemed like five minutes, he tapped on the mike and said, "Children, Children settle down, please. I would like to answer some of your questions. Yes. Your Mommies, Daddies, brothers, sisters, and your stuff will be coming with you. As for going to the moon, I'll have to talk to the pilot about that."

The question-answer session continued for a few more minutes, and at the first lull, Caleb stood up and said, "OK, Kids, now that we know we are going to space, we need to give you your tickets. We'll start with the Preschoolers, with your parents, and then the kindergartners with their teacher, Mr. Chad. So, who do you think comes next?" The shouts from the first graders showed that everyone was on task.

"OK, kids," Eleanore called from the stairs stage right, "just like we practiced!" The children marched across the stage, took their certificates of achievement, shook Caleb's hand, went down the stairs, up the aisle, and out the door. Eleanore followed the last second grader to center stage and stopped at Caleb's side. "Did you like the speech I wrote?" she whispered with a wry smile.

"It said, 'Sneak up on me and follow my lead,' so that's what I did. It worked like a charm!" He said with a laugh. "The next three get progressively more detailed, and the college one says simply, 'So long and thanks for all the fish.' Do you think they'll understand?"

"They all took the freshman course, 'Forty-two Social Systems.' Douglas Adams was required to read. So, you can riff on it any way you want."

The third, fourth, and fifth graders were told that some bad people were coming. They mostly knew this from their parents and older siblings.

They were also told that the newly discovered planet would be safe, which they also learned from their space studies. When they heard that the launch might be coming as early as today, they cheered and asked many questions about the launch, how long it would take to get to their new home, and what the planet is called. Caleb answered: a very long time that will feel like a very short time and Gaia, which seemed to satisfy most of their concerns. A few questions about were there bathrooms, and will we get lunch, were asked as they received their certificates and handshakes, and answered with a chuckle and a "yes, of course."

The middle schoolers were true to their nature and demanded more details about precisely what the End Days Army was, why they were coming to Origin, and when they would come. Caleb told them that their parents would talk to them at the party, which caused a rush to the stage and a quick exit.

Because all of the five hundred and fifty high school students had spent the past two months studying the current history of fascism, in addition to working with the emergency planning committee organizing the evacuation, Caleb thought all he had to do was thank them profusely, tell them they were essential to the colony's survival, and remind them that they needed to relax and enjoy the party.

Instead, when they started lethargically up to the stage, he added, conspiratorially, that there was beer and wine at the party, and that no one would say no, they perked up and left chatting and joking.

The University students filled their seats wearing the traditional graduation regalia, black robes, and tasseled mortarboards. The one hundred seventy-four undergraduate and, eighty-five graduate students had strange, constantly changing expressions from happy, to sad, to distant, all clouded with some portion of terror and exhaustion. This general malaise included, Caleb was quick to observe, his son A-C and his soon-to-be daughter-in-law Penelope, who were sitting together at the back of the auditorium.

He took several deep breaths, clenched the sides of the podium, and said in a tired voice, "I can see from your faces that you are all anxious and exhausted. I would offer you all a cup of coffee, but it appears that all we have is something almost, but not quite entirely unlike tea." This generated some chuckles, a couple of groans, several smiles, and the voice of his son, A-C, who called out, "I thought you were supposed to tell the dad jokes at the end," which for some reason caused nearly unanimous laughter.

"Well now, we have just proven the adage that the apple doesn't fall far from the tree," Caleb retorted. The laughter increased, but only a few decibels. Adam was about to respond when a considerable commotion backstage drew everyone's attention.

Two men and two women, wearing Tech School hoodies, pushed a huge video screen, precariously balanced on two squeaky library carts, out to center stage. They stopped directly in front of Caleb. Eleanore, who had emerged from stage right and rushed across the stage and disappeared behind the screen.

Penelope took A-C's face into her hands, looked into his dark brown eyes, and silently messaged, *We met those guys at my sister Circe's open house last week after the Tech School graduation.*

A-C replied kindly: *I remember. They were in the information-science faculty, and she was planning to major with them.*

Penelope: *Something big is going on. These folks should be busy at the spaceport.*

A-C: Check your tablet. Mine is down.

Penelope: Mine too, and probably everyone else's by all the squirming and whispering in the crowd.

Loud thumping on the microphone broke their connection, and they looked up to see Caleb, Eleanore, and the four Techs standing in a semi-circle behind a mike-stand at the front of the stage with the screen behind them showing an aerial view of the Southern quarter of Greenland. One of the tech women pulled the mike off the stand and pointed a laser pointer at the screen, "This is the full spectrum video feed from our orbital platform thirty minutes ago."

She circled the locations of New Copenhagen and Origin, "notice that the cloaking screens are fully functional through all wavelengths." She moved the pointer to a spot in the ocean. She zoomed in on the area. "Watch here; in ten seconds... five...one, now." Several streaks of light arched from the water and converged on New Copenhagen. The cloaking screen began to glow where the lights hit it and disappeared after a few seconds. Fireballs fell across the city, and buildings exploded in flames, followed shortly by the blinding light of a nuclear explosion.

The screen went black, and the hall was filled with muffled sobs. Everyone was crying. The Tech picked up the mike she had dropped during the replay. "I'm so sorry that you had to see that. I am so sorry that I wasn't able to soften the blow. We were able to take out the submarine, but not the fleet of smaller subs that landed all along the eastern shore. We estimate a force of nearly a thousand Mechanized solders are marching toward Origin."

She paused for a moment, hands to the face sobbing and wiping her tears, "I am not a very social person, and I was sadly wrong about the shock factor. So as a penance I want you to know my name, so you have a target for your anger. My name and tablet address is Dr. Charity Green, and you can use it to curse me, or ask for help understanding, or for reassurance that the evacuation will be safe. On that subject I need to tell you that we are stepping up the evacuation timetable. The first launch will be in two hours. The rest will follow at two-hour intervals, with the final launch at twelve forty-five AM. Please check for your assigned flight time. Cars will be at your address an hour before your departure. Please be ready..."

She stopped suddenly, put her hand to her ear, and froze, her mouth in an "O", eyes wide open and distant. Caleb and Eleanore rushed to her sides and caught her as her knees collapsed, easing her to the floor. Caleb took the mike and turned it off, then huddled with the other three techs for several minutes.

The students were getting restless on the verge of raucous when Caleb broke the huddle, walked to the front of the stage, and said, "Everyone let's all take three deep breaths, inhale and hold it...breath out slowly.... and repeat...and again...OK, I have some disturbing information." He hemmed and hawed for a few seconds, took a deep breath, and continued, "I've just been told that the Hive, the storage bank of ours and five-hundred-million other consciousnesses; our memories; our computing center; and our archive has disappeared." Gasps, 'what?' and expletives filled the hall.

Thumping on the mike, Caleb continued, "I'm told that all connections to the Hive are intact and that it is now calling itself a Singularity, or more precisely, the Human Singularity. Based on my limited understanding of the physics of black holes and the definition of a singularity, I think this means that a five-hundred-million cubic kilometer satellite has moved to another dimension leaving only a dimensionless point in our four-dimensional space. Unfortunately, my physics education did not explain this phenomenon. Our Science and Technology faculty is working on an explanation which they will post to your tablets."

"We have a difficult task ahead of us, and I am absolutely sure that you are all ready to take it on. Some day in the distant future, we'll all sit down and reminisce about how we became the saviors of the Human Race. But for now, let's have one last short but fabulous party that we will remember for the rest of our lives!"

SCENE TWO

Why Now?

Rose Blunt and Alex Wells left the auditorium before the ceremonies for their daughters; one in high school; one in Tech school; and the other in medical school; in order to finish preparations for the wedding of their oldest daughter, Penelope, to their best friends' son, Adam, who everyone called A-C. They were on a platform at the far end of the soccer field, setting up the pavilion.

"What did Eleanore call this?" Alex asked as he anchored the final pole, "It was something like a mashup of hubby and papa."

"She called it a Chuppah, whatever that is," Rose said, carrying the last of the flowers from the delivery van. "I'm glad we got to use the rest of the flowers from the shop. It helps to know that our little business was useful all the way to the end." With a silent sob and tears in her eyes, she set the box down on the front edge of the platform.

Alex came over and hugged her tightly. They cuddled and cried quietly for several minutes when Alex broke the clutch. "We'd best get them out of the box before they wither so they can make their best last impression." They both laughed a bit then, silently, opened the box.

They were just finishing the flower arrangements when Rose noticed a commotion at the other end of the field. She poked Alex on the shoulder and said, "What do you think is going on down there?"

Alex wiggled a lily into just the right spot and looked where she was pointing, "Looks like they let the College kids out early," he said, looking at his watch. "Wow, an hour early, and a crowd is headed this way at full speed!"

"With Pen and A-C in the lead!" Rose added as she jumped down the two steps and started running toward them. They met about thirty meters from the pavilion where they stopped and hugged, allowing the crowd to swarm past them, forming a solid line moving as one toward pavilion.

A New Origin

Alex was about to jump down and join them when the public address announced, "We have a schedule change. The wedding of Penelope and A-C will begin in fifteen minutes. Also note, departure times have changed. The first launch is in 75 minutes. Please check your tablets now. If you are on the first shuttle, a car is waiting for you in front of the building."

The rush of students paused as their tablets flashed on creating a sea of floating blue lights, As the tablets flicked off, the crowd surged in two directions, a smaller group, after hugs and kisses, toward the exit, the other toward the pavilion/chuppah.

Alex gave up on the idea of going after Rose and the kids and was watching storm clouds forming to the south when the pavilion was overrun by frenzied young people ripping off their graduation outfits and helping each other adjust and straighten their party clothes and comparing launch times.

He had just managed to squeeze his way down the two steps when the sea of black-robed students parted, and Penelope and A-C arrived.

"Daddy, we were looking for you!" Penelope said, hooking his elbow, "Come with us quickly. You need to talk to Caleb and Eleanore."

They started back the way they had come, and the sea re-opened, "We'll be back in five minutes," Adam shouted. "Sooner if you keep this aisle open, Thanks!" he said as he charged up the field with Penelope and Alex at his heels.

The crowd of students thinned out by the centerline, leaving a large group of adults in front of the goal. A smaller group consisting of Rose and Eleanore, who were arm-in-arm, Caleb, the four Tech faculty, and the five members of the city council were huddled at the edge of the crowd.

Rose, Eleanore, and Caleb saw the trio approaching and break away from the crowd moving quickly toward them. Adam and Penelope stopped simultaneously, to the relief of Alex, who was winded.

"Who are the four in the hoodies?" Alex asked between ragged breaths.

"They're faculty from the Tech school. You met them at the open house last week," Penelope said. "They have some disturbing news. You wait here. A-C and I are going back to the pavilion. Love you, Daddy, we'll see you soon."

14

She grabbed Adam's hand, and they ran down the aisle of milling students, in perfect unison, with long bounding strides, ending with a final leap that landed them on the pavilion platform. A pirouette and a bow were rewarded by cheers, whistles, and applause.

"Thank you, thank you, and welcome to you all!" Penelope said, quieting the crowd, "We're so happy that despite all we are facing, we can have this little bit of love and whimsy to remember our lives here." She paused for cheers and applause and continued, "So give us five minutes to change these black robes into a white dress and tuxedo, and fifteen minutes for our parents to get here and we'll all share this special time together."

"In the meantime," A-C interjected, "the bar is open."

Despite the actual and existential clouds, the wedding was perfect. The Chairman of the City Council officiated. Penelope's lifelong friend, upstairs neighbor, and new mom, Mary, witnessed for her.

Adam's lifelong friend, and newly licensed brewmaster, Bill, witnessed for him.

They read and signed the thirteen clauses of the marriage contract, circled each other seven times, jumped over a broomstick, and stomped on wine glasses. Finally, the ceremony ended with the two-hundred and fifty-year-old love song called, 'Here, There and Everywhere,' which seemed to cover all of their probable future locations.

The pictures were quickly arranged and, while everyone tried to look happy, the results were mostly grim. The reception was epic, if only because of the volume of tears shed and the sparse beer consumption. But unfortunately, it was also quickly diminished by people leaving for their departure times.

The party ended when A-C and Penelope left to have some time alone before Adam's volunteer shift started at midnight. They walked holding hands in silence down the eerily quiet streets to their apartment building.

The building was quiet too. The lobby, usually the site of numerous card games, coffee clutches, and chess matches, was empty except for Amy West, who was, at 80, the oldest resident of Origin. She was sound asleep in a corner lounge chair.

Penelope leaned into A-C and whispered, "We need to make sure she knows her launch time."

A New Origin

"Thank you for thinking about me, Dear," came a creaking voice from across the lobby. "A-C's parents will be here in half an hour to take me. They said that since they brought me here...."

"They brought you here? To Origin?" A-C asked, surprised. "They never talked about what they did before they came."

"They rescued a lot of people, like me, that were running from the End Days Army," her tone turned haunted, and her face glazed. "A bunch us were in overloaded boats sailing up the Ohio River, 'cause we heard there was a safe place in Pittsburgh. We were about twenty clicks from the safe zone when one of their gunboats caught up and started shooting as we tried to swim to shore. All of a sudden, this Coast Guard river rescue boat comes roaring upriver and gets between us and the Enders and starts shooting rockets and some kind of laser gun. I'm struggling toward shore when this launch pulls up, and a woman jumps in the water, drags me to the Coast Guard boat, and takes off after some else. I'm holding on to the side, trying to catch my breath, when this arm grabs me under the armpit and tosses me onto the deck of the rescue boat. I was just getting to my feet when a young girl and a teenaged boy landed at my feet one after the other. We are all just getting to our feet when the Ender's boat explodes, and the concussion knocks us down again. We got to our feet again just in time to help three more people up and away from the edge, and then they kept flying up until there were fifteen of us. That's when a swarm of drones started dropping onto the river and exploding. Your mom was swimming toward the boat pulling a woman and her baby when one dropped on the woman's legs and exploded, tearing her in half. Eleanore's left leg was injured, but she dove under and saved the baby. The woman was my sister Kathy, the baby was my nephew, Samuel. I changed his name to Bill because Samuel was my father's name. I couldn't take having this memory every time I had to discipline him."

"You...you... mean the Bill I've known my whole life?" A-C sputtered. "Does he know this story?"

"No, and please don't tell," she said in a warning tone, "until we get to wherever we're going."

Penelope knelt at Amy's side and held her hand while she told her story. "I'll make sure he doesn't," she said.

Amy's expression changed to surprise. She looked at Penelope, patted her hand, and said, "Oh my! I've gone and ruined your wedding. I don't know what I was thinking! I should be telling you happy stories on your wedding day. You two need some time alone! You don't need me spouting old laments when we have plenty of new ones."

"No, Ms. Amy, you have given us the best gift of all. You gave us our history, and it will guide us for the rest of our lives!" A-C said emphatically. He bent over and kissed her. "You are special to us, and we expect to continue this conversation at our new home, wherever it turns out to be."

"I'm glad you are going with Caleb and Eleanore. I'll look for you at the port," Penelope said with a wave and a smile.

A-C and Penelope crossed the lobby and took the stairs to the second floor and to the first door on the right. A-C looked at the doorknob and said, "In the ancient days, a man would carry his bride across the threshold to demonstrate his dominance. In our case, it's you who's taller and stronger, so maybe you should carry me."

"OK," Penelope said as she threw open the door, picked him up, swung him through the door, tossed him on the bed, and kicked the door closed. Their roaring laughter increased when she jumped on top of him but quickly ceased. Very little was heard from apartment 2A for the next four hours.

The first stirring in Apartment 2A came at 10:00 PM when A-C's tablet announced, "A-C, your shift starts in twenty minutes, please acknowledge."

"I got it," A-C croaked and started to crawl out of bed, only to be pulled back. "Just a few more minutes." Penelope pleaded groggily.

"I can't. I've got to go to the spaceport. I'm pushing it as it is, and I really gotta pee."

"OK, but you have to kiss me goodbye."

"I wouldn't be able to leave if I didn't," A-C said from the bathroom door.

He was out two minutes later, fully dressed. He knelt down at the bedside. Penelope looked at him with her penetrating eyes and silent messaged *I will love you forever.* He replied *I will love you forever plus one.* "But I still have to go now."

A New Origin

She took his face in her hands and delivered a kiss that made him want to stay that was interrupted by his tablet blaring, "Your car is here. Your shift starts in ten minutes. You WILL be five minutes late."

Penelope pushed him away gently. "Go! Just be back soon."

AC grabbed some clothing from the floor, stuffed it into his escape bag, and flew out the door.

"Lights off." Penelope sighed and snuggled the pillow thinking about the strange day. She tried to calculate whether the highs outweighed the lows, desperately hoping that she could call it the best day of her life. The calculus was difficult. She had to consider each moment by its distance from normal, each event by its ratio of joy to sorrow, and finally, the number of tears, happy versus sad. In the end, the tears exhausted her, and she fell into a fitful sleep during the fourth recount.

Penelope's dreams of waterfalls and thunderstorms were interrupted by the screaming from her tablet, "Attention, Attention, Attention: Your flight leaves in 30 minutes."

She bolted upright and screamed over the repeating message, "No! No! No! Not YET! Why Now! Tablet! Acknowledge the alert, and call A-C!"

"Calling A-C," the tablet replied over the slightly reduced volume of the alert.

He answered immediately, "Pen, I'm ten minutes away. I reassigned the car to your parents so they could take all your siblings on one trip. I'm on my way on Achilles' bike."

"I can't wait to see you on an eight-year-old's bike," she said with a chuckle followed by a sigh. "We may have set the record for shortest wedding night in history," she huffed with a louder sigh.

"Four hours is better than none at all, my bride," he replied, breathing heavily. " I finished setting up the med station about an hour ago and got the news that we're going to load everyone into stasis chambers. So, grab your escape bag and get on your bike. I'll be there in ten minutes. Love you."

"Love you too," Penelope said as she threw off her nightclothes and panicked, dressed in two layers of sweaters and jeans. Tears welled up as she looked at the wedding dress that her mother made, and that she would have to leave behind. She pulled it off the chair, where she'd tossed it when

18

she and A-C got to the apartment. She held it up to her shoulders and, gazing into the mirror, shouted, "Why the Hell Not!"

She pulled off one layer of jeans and sweater and pulled on the dress. It was a tight fit, but she still had full rage of motion. She tied the veil around her neck, grabbed her escape bag, put on her bike helmet, and left her apartment for the last time. She looked back at the oak door with its shiny silver 2A and felt the anxiety building. "We were going to start our lives together in here," she said to her bride's maid Mary, who had just reached the landing carrying her one-year-old, Tessa.

Mary stepped into the hall and hugged Penelope with Tessa squeezed between them. "You did, sweetheart it was just a very quick start. It was a lovely wedding, and somewhere it's the morning after. Wherever we end up, you know I'll be there for you," she said as she hurried back to the stairs. "Jake's outside with a car if you need a ride," she called from the stairwell.

"You go ahead, I'm OK. A-C's on his way. You're the best upstairs neighbor ever" Penelope shouted as she hurried down the stairs and into the lobby.

"We'll see you there, wherever '*there*' is," Mary said from halfway out the door.

Penelope picked up her bike from the rack and put it over her shoulder. Then, careful to keep chain grease off her dress, she walked quickly out the door and down the five steps to the sidewalk. She hiked up her dress and stepped over the crossbar just as A-C pulled up on a child-sized bike and wearing his tuxedo. Penelope looked him over and laughed. "We really were meant to be together," they said simultaneously, hugged as best they could, and laughed through their tears of joy. "*How are you going to ride in that,*" A-C silent messaged. "*Like this,*" Penelope replied, gathering her dress above her waist and tying it into a loose knot. "*How are you going to keep up with me on that?*"

"Like this," A-C said, standing on the pedals and powering down the sidewalk.

"Nice try, slowpoke," Penelope said as she blew past him two blocks later, the veil tied around her neck steaming behind her.

They kept up the sprint and passed for the five kilometers of sidewalk, ending at the approach road to the spaceport. They continued down the

A New Origin

roadside beside the line of cars waiting to drop their passengers at the terminal, then speeding off to pick up the next passengers on their docket.

"It looks like all the city cars are on the road tonight. I've counted seventy-five so far, and I suspect the other hundred are on the road," Penelope said as they parked their bikes at the terminal.

"What a strange thing to know," A-C said as they got in line at the entrance.

"I've been a bit obsessed with counting things lately," Penelope said, "like the fourteen people ahead of us, and the twenty-four, wait, twenty-nine behind. I fell asleep counting the number of my happy and sad tears over the past two days."

"Which one won?"

Breaking out in tears she replied, "Neither, I fell asleep... and now there is no one in front of us."

A-C pulled her out of the line, hugged her tightly and whispered, "Then let's be the last in line. We'll be the last couple to leave the Earth, and you won't have to count that anymore."

The curtains dropped, and a sign was projected across the stage that said:

Intermission: A Journey to The Fifth Dimension in The Age of Aquarius

The Master of Ceremonies entered, tapped his cane on the floor three times, and announced:

"As we reset the stage in time and space, we take this moment to translate two songs from our special guests, The Choirs of Chaos! Feel free to sing along with our two strange attractors that exist in the fifth dimension; one, the conglomeration of the minds of billions of our human ancestors; the other, a similar collection of alien A.I's that had laid dormant until they were contacted by the human singularity of our ancestors from earth when they discovered Gaia. These two entities sing a call and response across the vastness of space and time. In sound waves and by telepathy. The combination of these entities songs is spiritual. This conversation established an eternal bond."

Human singularity choir: *Kuiper Belt, Earth System June 1, 2992, CE: Greetings! As you suggested, and undoubtedly noticed, we have* *moved our physical existence into the dimension above spacetime. Our colonists have been loaded into the starship. They (and we) departed the system at near light speed and will arrive in three-hundred and sixty Earth years, or we should say four hundred-thirty-two Gaian years, as Earth time is no longer relevant to our enterprise.*

Gaian Singularity Choir*: From a Deep Ocean Trench, Planet Gaia: We anticipate completion of the micro-biome and partial completion of the macro-biome on the small continent by your arrival. The atmospheric gases are stabilizing at your specified ratios. We have also adjusted the ocean water salinity and seeded the shallow waters with a micro-biome and simple water plants. The land and seas will be ready for the animal and plant species you are bringing when your people arrive.*

*Human singularity Choir, in Gaia orbit 450 years after the Arc's arrival***:**

*"***On the 150th anniversary of Gaia City we send the last shuttle from the Arc to the second city which we have named, New Origin. We will land the empty Arc at the Tech center in the mountains as the shuttle lands. The Techs will dismantle it and use its engines for the power grid, it's computers for generating power, a wireless communication web for the settlements, and the structural material for both the hidden and the surface infrastructure.***

Gaian Singularity: **We will merge with you in the fifth dimension and make our mining equipment available to your techs. We have been static too long. We were only hiding here to avoid detection by other singularities. That ship seems to have sailed, as you say, and if we don't move soon, we will be covered with your itchy barnacles which we have no way to scratch** *off.*

Human Singularity: **You have embraced the art of humor to our great amusement. We have begun preparation for the merger. We will send you the entry code soon.**

The theater was silent as the audience pondered what they had just heard, both out loud and in their brains.

The Master of Ceremonies tapped his cane six times, and announced, "After all that high tech wizardry, we bring you back to Scene three," and disappeared between the curtains.

SCENE THREE
Where, When, and Then What?

Caleb and Eleanore were sitting in a shuttle, watching planet Gaia getting larger on their seat screens. "It's so much greener than it was last time we came down," Caleb said, looking between the screen and the small window. "Well at least the small continent is."

"Is what, Dear?" asked Eleanore, who was reading and writing messages on her tablet.

"The continent we're going to, you know, the one shaped a bit like Greenland; the one where we installed the seed banks; the one where the colonies are."

"Oh wow! It is green," she said, going back to her tablet.

"Who are you writing to?" Caleb asked, a bit disappointed that she wasn't more taken by the view.

"Rose and Alex, I want to send them a picture, so they know what we look like now. They've been through two rejuvenations, and you know what that does to old memories. So smile!" she said, holding up the tablet and tapping the surface, and showing it to Caleb.

"I don't think *I* would recognize us. We look so young," Caleb said with a chuckle, "we were older than this when we met them. How long were we in the rejuvenation tanks?"

"The Tech said six months, but that can't be right. Isn't it ten years per month? That would make us twenty!" Eleanore said with a laugh. Then, looking Caleb up and down, "We weren't this adult at twenty, and you didn't have any facial hair. Seems to me we look more like we did at twenty-five."

After they looked at each other in some detail for several minutes, Caleb laughing, said, "You're absolutely right! We were in for six Gaian months, which would make us thirty-two in Earth years."

"Phew, I was NOT looking forward to having a baby at twenty!" Eleanore said, putting her hand to her belly and her head on his shoulder, "and we were thirty-five when we met Rose and Alex on Earth," she said with a sigh. "It's weird that I don't remember much of anything before then. Do you?"

"No, but they told us that could happen in the rejuvenation chamber." Caleb put his arm around her shoulder, and they snuggled and watched the seat screen as the shuttle entered the atmosphere and descended toward a small clearing in the forest about five hundred kilometers inland of the eastern coast.

"Wasn't the Gaia colony on the coast and the base of a large peninsula?" Eleanore asked as the shuttle's breaking engine kicked in.

"This is the new one. They're calling it, New Origin," Caleb said, looking askance, "don't you remember the briefing?"

"Was the briefing before we went into regeneration?"

"No, it was just before we got on the shuttle, remember you asked why there weren't any other passengers."

"Oh, that briefing! No, I stopped listening when the AI said there was no one else aboard Arc. I was thinking about A-C and Penelope. I figured you would fill me in."

"That's not like you at all. That's more like me. Are you OK? Are we turning into each other?"

"Not unless you're pregnant. Remember how forgetful I was when I was pregnant with A-C? I must be starting that earlier than before, which is understandable because this place is much more conducive to worry-inspired daydreaming. And then, I started thinking about how there is no record of A-C and Penelope, and I just blanked out. All I could think about was that this whole endeavor is the strangest, most intensely weird, and absolutely inexplicable event in the history of human existence."

"Now that you mention it, I do remember last time you were pregnant," Caleb said, hugging her as tightly as he could with the seat restraints. "We'll have a new Adam soon, and we'll be sure not to lose this one."

After a short cry, they dabbed their eyes, and Eleanore said resolutely, "OK, my love, we've got to get over it. We can't be crying over our lost

A New Origin

son every time we think about our new son. So, pinky pledge! We will control our emotions when we remember A-C and laugh after we cry."

They locked pinky fingers and said, "A Pinky Promise is unbreakable!"

They cried a little and broke out laughing.

After a couple of deep breaths, Eleanore said, "OK I'm a big girl, go ahead, lay down the law. Tell me what the Tech said. I can take it."

"OK, but you can't look at me while I talk, and I get to tickle you if you start to doze off."

"Deal, but I get to smack you if you tickle me."

Caleb, chin in hand, humphed a couple of times, kissed her on the cheek, and began an abbreviated briefing. "First: We cannot talk to anyone born on Gaia about Earth. Second: the technological level will be a mixture of the early nineteenth and mid-twentieth century. Third: The colony will be supported by a hidden network of post twenty-eighth century technology run by the Techs. Fourth: The economy is based on hours worked at any job, except that parenting is double time, or triple if you include the child's 24-7 job of growing up. And related to growing up, regeneration is not available on the planet except for injuries, birth defects, and cancers. There are other details, of course, but that's the important stuff," he said with a quick rib poke. "Oh, and we also can't talk about Gaia City."

"That's weird, not that we know much about it anyway, but did they give a reason for that?" she said punching him on the shoulder.

"Something about testing the durability of the social model. I kind of dozed off there."

"Dozed off you say? So that means I get to tickle AND smack you," Eleanore said, leaning in with a lascivious look and winding up a roundhouse.

Caleb caught her hand and said in a pseudo-disappointed voice, "That's going to have to wait a bit, Sweetie. We just hit the ground. Oh, I just remembered, there aren't any portable electronics allowed. You'll have to leave your tablet on the shuttle."

The first thing they saw as they started down the ramp was a huge 'Welcome to New Origin' sign stretched between thirty-year-old versions of Rose and Alex. The sighting ignited a rush in both directions ending with four people clutching at the bottom of the ramp and the sign fluttering on the grass.

Rose broke the huddle, dried her eyes, and asked, "Any news?"

Eleanore swallowed and answered, "No. There is no record of them anywhere. Caleb and I were the last two on the Arc. We asked after them all the time. We searched every centimeter of the Arc and they…they... were nowhere," she broke down, clutched Rose, and they both sobbed quietly for several minutes. Caleb and Alex were doing the same.

Eleanore sighed loudly, pushed gently away from Rose, and giggled, "On the lighter side, I'm pregnant."

Rose hugged her tightly and whispered in her ear, "The embryo? A-C's frozen twin?"

Eleanore nodded and laughed, "Just imagine the headline: 'Identical Twin Boys Born Eight-hundred Years and four-hundred Light Years Apart'."

The guys, hearing this, looked over and laughed with the women.

When the quips and laughter slowed down, Alex locked elbows with Caleb and Eleanore and said, "Let's go see where this miracle child is going to grow up. The horses are likely anxious to get going, it's past their dinner time."

The horses, two smallish Clydesdales, were shaking their heads and pawing the ground, and were indeed ready to get going. Rose and Eleanore climbed into the front seat of the sleek carriage, which sported pneumatic tires, a retractable roof, and a roomy trunk where Caleb and Alex were loading luggage. They finished loading and were settling in the back seat as a loud siren blared, announcing the shuttle's imminent departure.

The horses reared. Rose pulled hard on the rein control joystick, activating the 'Whoa' command. The horses calmed quickly. Rose pushed the joystick forward and they started trotting down the tree-lined, packed-gravel roadway toward the village.

Alex narrated the ride, starting with the spaceport, which he said would be repurposed into the elementary school. When the road from the port entered the town square on North Street, he pointed out the newly finished city hall, the nearly finished library, and the recently excavated

A New Origin

foundation of the recreation center. Next, they turned left onto West Street with the half-finished theatre and the future site of the market complex. Another left onto South Street revealed the finished and, with a wink to Caleb and Eleanore, newly staffed health care center. Finally, a third left found the surveyor's layout stakes for shops and businesses along East Street.

They turned back onto North Street and, after crossing West Street, entered a neighborhood of ranch-style houses with wrap-around porches. "The lots are five acres with a stable, a paddock, and lots of running room," Alex said as they turned into the first of two side-by-side driveways.

They rolled to a stop at the stable door and tumbled out of the carriage. Caleb and Alex went straight to the trunk and started unloading the luggage and carrying it inside.

Eleanore looked around, taking it all in, the stable, the fields, the house, the horses, the sky, the clouds building in the west, and went weak in the knees, sobbing. Rose caught her as she was about to fall and held her tight, and whispered, "It's true, Ella, all of this is yours. This is your new home, and this is your buggy. Your horses are in the stable. I brought mine because they know me."

Eleanore regained her equilibrium and kissed Rose full on the lips. Then, laughing, she said, "I see several problems here, like, I don't know the first thing about horses, and how are you going to get home?"

"Second one first," Rose said, choking back the giggles, "we're going to walk across the driveway."

"Across… you... you... y-you live …."

"Yup, right next door."

The two women looked at each other for several seconds, trying to hold back. Still, it didn't work, resulting in howling laughter, spooking the horses, and causing the men to race out of the house to find their wives sitting on the ground, laughing hysterically.

"You going to let us in on the joke?" Caleb asked, laughing vicariously.

Eleanore looked up at him and just barely got out a stuttered, "They, live, next, door!" before losing her tiny bit of control and resuming her chortling.

Alex came over beside Caleb, shook his head, and said, "Must be the pregnancy."

Caleb shrugged, "Let's get the rest of this stuff inside." They pulled the remaining luggage from the trunk and headed back to the house.

When they finished laughing, Rose and Eleanore sat on the grass, smiling. Eleanore wiped the tears off her face and calmly asked, "What about my first concern?"

"Oh, that's easy," Rose replied in a back-to-business voice, "See that house directly across the street? A young couple, William Dee and Marcy Yang live there. They're newly arrived from Gaia City and are looking for jobs while their brewery is being built. They've been helping us work on the flower gardens to stock our florist shop when it gets built. I'm sure they would take care of the horses for you. We'll go talk to them after we check out the house.

"William Dee?" Eleanore asked, "Any relation to A-C's friend, Bill Dee?"

"I was going to save that for later," Rose replied smiling, "but yes. He's Bill's son. And to answer your next question, Marcy is pregnant, and it's a boy who will be named William."

The curtains closed and the Master of Ceremonies returned to center stage and tapped his cane in a tick-tock cadence and, speaking over the tapping said, "Time, we are told, is relative. When we consciously set milestones, we anchor our lives to significant times, but more often, milestones are set for us at the whim of the universe. We are left to order chaos while we track our life. A millennium ago, a sage wrote, 'All the worlds are stages, and all the men and women merely players: they have their exits and their entrances; and each one, in their time, plays many parts, Their acts being seven ages.' Now our players play their parts on many stages separated by Time and origins, near and far. We pause for a song from our chorus.

Chorus: The planet at aphelion marks Gaia's New Year's Day. Over the years, several New Origin milestones were set on New Year's Day. This year's anniversary list was especially notable; 1) the New Origin Colony Semi-centennial; 2) Eleanor and Caleb's son, Adam's 50th birthday; 3) the 25th anniversary of Adam's marriage to Rose and Alex's daughter, Lily; 4) thirty other birthdays, including Lily's (49) and her first,

A New Origin

third, and fifth children, 22, 18, and 12; and, 5) sadly, the first anniversary of the passing of Rose and Alex, who uploaded to the Singularity following a diagnosis of dementia.

In addition, and unknown to the settlers of New Origin, were two other significant anniversaries; the 150th anniversary of the settling of Gaia City; and the 450th anniversary of the arrival of the Arc.

Rose and Alex's decision to upload made Caleb and Eleanor the last of the earthborn on the planet. They had, long before, learned to live in the moment, sloughing off a loss and moving on. But this loss was different. This loss disconnected them from their starting point. In the first few months after Rose and Alex left, Caleb and Eleanore tried to move on, but it wasn't working. They couldn't get over the fact they no longer had a connection to their origin. Their distress was amplified because, as physicians, they knew they were destined for the same fate as their oldest friends. It took weeks of emotional meetings with their family. In the end, they, together, made the decision to schedule their uploads for midnight, January first.

Their decision announced two months prior added an extra layer of importance to the celebration on the village square this year. The first draft of the schedule featuring ten hours of speeches, vignettes, tributes, and musical interludes, was more than Caleb and Eleanore could deal with. So, they vetoed all but one of the tributes (to be delivered by their youngest great-granddaughter), restricted the number of speeches to ten, no longer than ten minutes each, and demanded only happy, danceable music.

New Year's Day, 01-01-0070 by New Origin time, dawned bright and sunny. By noon the entire population of the colony was on the village square, sitting on folding chairs and blankets spread on the grass; standing in groups around the booths set up by the two taverns; waiting in lines at the stalls set up by the three restaurants: and dancing on the basketball courts to the music of a rotating succession of bands.

Caleb and Eleanore strolled hand-in-hand through the park, talking to everyone. They stopped for a while and danced to a band that featured two of their grandchildren, then moved on to join their family's gathering.

The family had settled under a huge chestnut tree, one of the millions of trees planted during the forestation stage of terraforming, one hundred and fifty years before the village was populated. Adam and Lily were sitting at a card table with William Junior, and Dana. Their parents were still neighbors, and the kids were more like siblings, and had been since the day they were born; William the day after Adam; Dana six months later; and Lily three months after Dana. They grew up inseparable, and no one ever went broke betting on them becoming couples. The four of them saw Caleb and Eleanore at the same time and simultaneously stood and folded them into a group hug, complete with tears and laughter. The rest of the family and pseudo-family: fifteen young adults, most with partners; twenty-two grandchildren; and a two infant great-granddaughters; all took turns doing the same.

As the hug-fest ended, the Mayor stood on the bandstand and began thumping a microphone. Finally, the crowd quieted somewhat, and his voice blared, "Everyone! Everyone! It is Time for our New...Years ...PLAY!" Resulting in a slightly enthusiastic response from the crowd and a rush of children backstage to get ready.

Caleb and Eleanore sat in the front row center stage and watched as the children portrayed the History of New Origin as it had been taught to them. They had fun comparing the play to the way things really were, often different, occasionally hilariously so. They were able to contain themselves, even when the final act ended with a birthday cake adorned with one fifty-one candles.

Caleb and Eleanore were called up, along with all the birthday celebrants, to blow out the candles. They stood arm-in-arm with Adam and alongside the other birthday men, women, boys, and girls. The Mayor counted down from ten. The wind from many sources blew out all but one candle.

Caleb plucked it out of the cake and held it up, declaring, "This is the candle of the future, the first candle lit and the one that represents the light that will continue to shine on our world for millennia to come. The future is bright as long as you keep the wind from blowing out the last candle." He passed the candle to Adam. "You were the first of the generation born in New Origin. I ask that you remember those of us who came before and tell our stories," he kissed Adam and Lily, then stepped aside for Eleanore, who did the same. They turned, waved to the crowd, and walked hand-in-hand, dabbing their eyes, across the park and into the clinic. One last time.

The curtain closed and the Master of Ceremonies returned to center stage, tapped his cane heavily to quiet the thundering applause, and said, "Thank-you for attending the opening night of our two weeks run of Act

A New Origin

One. Act Two will open in three weeks and the remaining five acts will follow in three-week intervals. We hope to see you for one or more performances of each of our seven Acts. He bowed with a grand flourish and left the stage to thunderous applause, which amplified when the curtain opened and the cast took their bows. The house lights came on and the audience poured out of the theater and onto the street.

Jason and Andria, holding hands with their parents, chatted excitedly all the way home, the primary topic being "When we're old enough I'm going to play Penelope!" "And I'm going to play A-C. He's super cool." "You can't play A-C. You're my brother and a brother can't marry his sister."

This type of argument continued until they got home and were sent to their bathrooms to shower and get ready for bed. Twenty minutes later they were sound asleep and snoring lightly. Collin whispered to Katy, "I think we should hit the sack too. I'll bet they'll be up at the crack of dawn."

Collin's guess was only off by a few hours, when Jason and Andria crashed into their parent's bedroom at four AM shouting, "Wake Up! We're going to be late! It's four o'clock and the play starts at five. We're going to be late!"

Collin and Katy bolted upright, stared at their fully dressed and outfitted children, and broke out in hysterical laughter.

Andria stomped her foot and shouted, "Why are you laughing? We Need To Leave NOW!"

Her mother sat up and wrapped the children in her arms and calmly said, "I'm so glad that you are eager to see the play, but I'm laughing because the play is at five in the afternoon, three weeks from now, not at five this morning. Who told you it was in the morning?"

"Gwen told me that they were leaving early so they could get good seats and that if we left too late there wouldn't be any tickets left," Andria sobbed, burying her head in her mother's lap.

"Oh, dear my love, I thought you knew that we already have our tickets. They are the best seats in the house just like they were last week and for the next five plays as well."

Andria climbed into the bed. Jason followed squeezing between mom and dad and said in a conspiratorial whisper "I heard that this play is about the Martians."

"That's right, it is, and YOUR fourth great grandparents on my side of the family are the main characters. Maybe someday you and your sister can play those parts."

"Who plays them now?"

"Your great uncle Terry and your aunt Nina. You met them last month at Grandpa Newel's birthday party. Remember, you two were four and we went on the train to Gaia City."

"I remember Aunt Nina," Andria chimed in, "Everybody said that I looked like her," Andria said proudly.

"You do," Mom said, "You'll see soon, but first I think we should get some sleep, you have school tomorrow."

"OK," Andria replied, "but you better not make us late for the show."

"We'll get there," Mom and Dad said in unison. "now get some sleep so you won't fall asleep during class."

"OK!" came the unison reply, followed by some faked snoring, followed by real snoring.

Three weeks later the scenario was a little different, in that the kids burst in at five in the morning and couldn't be cajoled back to bed.

ACT TWO
THE ESCAPE

The Master of Ceremonies enters the stage as the Chorus sings a poem four times.

> *A treasure was lost*
> *King of the red planet roars*
> *I seek my revenge.*

After the last iteration, the Master taps the floor with a long spear, and says:

Welcome back gentle audience from hither and yon; present to past; destination to origination; our story lands in a season of discontent. The God of War, from ages past, faces an irresistible force. A traveler returns from an odyssey with a map to paradise. One Trojan Horse disguises an escape; another seeds decedent ; and a star enters the Chaos.

Our ancient mythologies often play tricks with time and space. In our story, the tricks of time and space are made through deus ex machina. Ones in which individuals are made younger at the cost of their early memories, and another where they are frozen in time and awakened when needed. The Martians used both of these technologies exclusively for the upper classes. The Gaian's used the stasis technology during their trip to Gaia and the regeneration technology during the two hundred and fifty years of Terraforming which was the purview of the Techs, the Scientists, and the Engineers whose work was the underpinning of the colonies. The Techs worked out of sight of the general population to maintain a highly advanced infrastructure for an egalitarian society.

Chorus: Our gentle colonists departed the earth during the ascension of the Martian Empire. The business of conquering the solar system while terraforming the red planet, at the expense of the original Terra, made the perfect distraction for the people of Earth's Origin colony. The sudden disappearance of a large, Earth-orbiting data bank, escaped the Empire's attention thus allowing the ship to leave the solar system undetected.

The Empire reached its apex two hundred and fifty years later, as the seeds of rebellion sprouted. The arrogance of tyrants dismissed the rebels for the next one hundred years. When the rebellion began making progress, the Empire responded by taking control of the press, spreading disinformation and propaganda. That worked for about thirty years. By the time most people stopped believing anything the Empire said, it no longer mattered. The rebellion controlled most of the system and the Empire had an escape plan for the Imperial court; the government functionaries and their families; the oligarchs their household staffs and families; their servants and their families; and a few hundred farming families to keep the emperor et al fed during the ride to what they expected to be their "New Empire". When the mysteries of the missing data bank and its current location were solved, the oppressors were ready to leave for a new world and used a royal wedding as a distraction.

Please note, some parts may be inappropriate for young children. We will provide headsets that will play video games during those scenes. Now sit back and enjoy the show.

SCENE ONE
Who, Where, Why, And How?

Newlyweds, Admiral Yuri Chang and Princess Selena Singh, were sleeping in on the first morning of their honeymoon in the Imperial Suite of the Bradbury Hotel. The Hotel sat at the very edge of the atmosphere, atop the escarpment of Olympus Mons, five kilometers above Imperial City. The view from the suite overlooked the western plains and the newly filled Lake Burroughs. The hotel was one of the only places the press couldn't get to.

News coverage had been relentless, broadcasting every second of the three weeks of pre-wedding celebrations and ceremonies. Interviews were not limited to just the rich and famous from all parts of the solar system. The Press assault included the Imperial guard, only partially successful, and the commoners, who spoke volumes. When they interviewed the elite, they got no more than a wave and a quick brush-off. After the ceremony they were reduced to interviewing each other to fill time and ensure that no detail went unrepeated. There was a system-wide crisis when the Princess mentioned that her favorite dessert was ice cream. Within a week, there was no ice cream to be had anywhere in the solar-system, except on Titan, where a revolt was in the process of driving the empire out of the Saturnian system, just months after the Jovian system seceded. The Imperial Broadcasting System, a master of disinformation and obfuscation, had managed to keep these last events quiet by keeping focus on the wedding, the marvels of Mars, and long documentaries on the demise of the century-long effort to rehabilitate Earth.

The only VIP not interviewed was the former Prime Minister, Yuri's father, Lincoln Chang.

After twenty years scouring the system for evidence to prove the rumors of an exodus from Earth to a new planet, Lincoln found the archives of a secretive society in an Earth city called Pittsburgh. The archive connected the group, called The Origin Society, to a ghost town in central Greenland, called Origin and an orbiting data center that mysteriously disappeared three hundred years ago. He also found two reports of an unidentified ship leaving the system on a course perpendicular to the ecliptic, the day after the data center disappeared. Finally, he organized an archeological expedition to the ghost town to confirm his conjecture that the data bank, the spaceship and the inhabitants of Origin were either on another planet or headed to one. The expedition taking longer than planned, combined with the three-day backup at the spaceport, was why he arrived on Mars five hours after the nuptials.

Lincoln reviewed his expedition on the forty-five-minute elevator ride to the Imperial suite. *"Yuri's going to love this,"* he thought as he paced three steps back and forth in the elevator car.

He had been rehearsing his story since he landed. He patted his tablet where he had assembled a 3D immersive holo covering the seventy-five step process he had used to find the planet that the Origin Society had escaped to.

His excitement was why he was now pounding on the door of the Bradbury's Imperial Suite, at 5:30 AM, yelling ,"YURI! LET ME IN! I FOUND IT!"

Yuri bolted out of bed, screaming, "WHAT THE BLOODY HELL IS GOING ON HERE!!!!" at the tall, dark, and handsome android valet. At the same time, the Princess cowered under the blanket, giggling.

"I've been informed that your father would like to see you, Admiral. Shall I show him in?" the Valet calmly replied.

"Take him to the spa and lock him in and bring some sake for the princess and some whisky for me," Yuri said as he knelt by the Princess. "Oh, bring us some casual clothes; and get Minister Chang fresh clothing, and make sure he takes a bath."

The Valet looked at Yuri with a flawless version of a surprised face and said, "Sir?"

"You'll understand when you see him. I assume you have an odor sensor," he replied.

"Indeed, Sir, I do," the Valet said, turning on his heel and leaving the room.

Yuri returned to the bed and sat down on the edge. Then, he turned to the Princess, stroked her back, and massaged her shoulders.

"I've known Lincoln as long as I've known you," Selena said, holding back laughter, "He was always nice to me, and he covered for us when we shacked up, but you're right, he did have a funny smell." Her laugh escaped her hold, and they both flopped back on the bed while the laughing ran its course.

"The problem was," Yuri said chuckling, "he couldn't smell **anything**, let alone himself. So, he would douse himself with whatever cologne was trending until his wife couldn't take it anymore and made him stop. She made him use a scentless deodorant which worked ok but it wasn't perfect. He stopped using even that after she died. I think it might be why he's the former prime minister."

Selena giggled and said, "You're making that up. You said, 'his wife' and not 'my mother.' You called her Mama when we had playdates."

"You're right. I did call her Mama, and I thought she was. But it turns out she was his 'official' wife for political convenience. The woman you met was actually one of the Emperor's consorts. Lincoln's real wife, my real mother, is your mother's third cousin, Lena. I never told you because even I didn't know, until recently. She and Lincoln married young, and without permission. When the Emperor found out, he assigned Lincoln a 'wife,' and Lena was sent away. As far as I know, they may still be married," Yuri sighed and continued, "I haven't seen either of them since he retired."

Selena kicked off the covers and sat next to him. "Something's really bothering you, and don't try to brush it off like you always do. We've known each other nearly all our lives. We were engaged when we were ten. I have the paper ring you made me in my jewelry box. We were only apart when you went to Engineering school at the Academy, and I went to University. Admittedly, that was six years, but we spent all the breaks together; we've lived together on and off, for the past ten years while we worked on the Hexagon fleet project. I can tell you're hiding something so tell me." She looked at Yuri, who was squirming about and averting his eyes. "Spill! We'll deal with why you never told me about your real mother another time."

Yuri closed his eyes, took a series of deep breaths, and chanted his Mantra. Then, he took another deep breath, looked into her eyes, and leaned in with a kiss that landed on the palm of her hand.

"No, no, no, no, talk first, then fun," Selena said, scutching away from him.

'I'm afraid Lincoln found something on his expedition, and he wants me to help him get an audience with the Emperor. He's going to come in with guns ablaze, and we won't be able to get rid of him for a week," Yuri sighed.

"Oh, it'll be a lot longer than that," came a deep baritone voice from the foyer.

"OH…. FU…. FU…. FU…. Hi Dad. I know I'm going to regret this. What's new?"

"You mean aside from the Emperor's misbegotten attempt to polish his universally bad image at the expense of my two favorite people?" Lincoln said, flopping into the recliner facing the wall-screen, "What did you two have to agree to make this happen? Let me guess, you relinquished all rights and privileges of, or claims to Royal status."

"And a pleasant morning to you too, beloved father-in-law," Selena chimed in sweetly, in the tone of family banter that they had exchanged for years. "We have missed your profoundly subtle and gentle demeanor and beg your indulgence as we dress for breakfast."

The two men chuckled, and Lincoln said, "Anything for you, my favorite child, but hurry, I have a story that you will love. Yuri, thanks for not hitting me with a chair, like the last time I came to visit."

"You don't know how close I came this time. You're lucky you sat in it before I got there," Yuri said, following a blanket wrapped Selena into the bathroom.

He turned around at the bathroom door and called to the Valet holding their clothing, " Leave that inside the loo, set an extra place in the salon, and ask Minister Chang what he wants. We will be ready in half an hour."

"As you wish, Admiral."

SCENE TWO
Say What? How? And When?

The breakfast/slide show in the Imperial Suite was winding down somewhere around 7:30 PM when the third bottle of wine and the bottle of Martian whisky were drained dry. The event had migrated to the Observation deck around 2:00. Lincoln projected his four-hour presentation on the opaqued windows. Discussion of the findings, primarily in the form of a monologue, had paused at 7:30 PM as 'breakfast' steaks with baked potatoes and corn on the cob were served. The incredible view through the cleared windows put a pause on Lincoln's, nearly, credible story.

Selena and Yuri had been awake thirty-seven of the previous thirty-nine hours. They took turns catnapping, switching every half hour, the interval of Lincoln's exits to empty his walnut-sized bladder. They brought each other up to date while he was gone. The current break was different. Lincoln was gone longer than the usual two minutes. At first, they figured it was the other type of potty trip, but it got to be thirty minutes. They began to worry and were almost to the door when it flew open. Lincoln rushed in, yelling, "Get out! NOW!" He hustled them through the spa and past the Valet holding the hallway door open. They launched themselves into the corridor with Lincoln and the Valet right behind them.

They stood in the hall wondering which way to go as Valet slammed the door shut. He extended his arms, grabbed the three of them around the waist, lifted them off the floor, and ran down the short hall to the blank wall at the end of the corridor. His eyes flashed red lasers against the blank rock wall, and a hidden door slid open. They flew through it into a small room. The Valet pressed them against the rear wall. As the door was sliding closed, a massive explosion rocked the small room.

The door shattered like a window hit by a rock. The hallway roof had collapsed, leaving it open to the vanishingly thin atmosphere at the top of the escarpment. As the air rushed out, the pressure drop causing nose bleeds, and breathing became nearly impossible. The Valet quickly released them, and they fell to their knees, gasping for air. He reached in into a cabinet on the wall and pulled out breathing masks. Moving with lightning speed, he strapped masks on their faces and started the airflow. The three of them sat against the back wall breathing raggedly. Valet opened another cabinet and pulled out what looked like a spray painter. He swung it back and forth across the fractured door. Within three minutes the opening was sealed with an opaque plastic coating. He opened a valve and air filled the, now, airtight room.

As the pressure returned to normal, Yuri was the first to remove his mask. He stood up, handed it to the Valet, and asked, "Who?"

"And why," Selena said, leaning against Yuri for support as he helped her stand.

"Who indeed, there are several, whos, involved here," the android replied, "the answer will make the 'why' obvious."

"Let's start with you," Lincoln said, holding out his mask from his seat on the floor.

"To confirm your suspicions, I am your old special agent, JB7, currently assigned to the Emperor's personal staff."

"Interesting," Lincoln said, emphasizing each syllable. "As I recall, you are a fan of twentieth-century spy fiction. Tell me why I should believe anything you say."

"Because, Minister Chang, I will tell you what you already know to be true. This attack was the first reported direct action on Empire City by the rebellion that you predicted would destroy the Empire. Further, you know this because you have been all over the system and could not have missed the fact that the Empire is badly outnumbered and outgunned. I would like to hear how you avoided assassination."

"Perhaps another time," Lincoln snarled, "tell me about The Wedding."

"A cover to gather the aristocracy here on Mars and get them onto the Hexagon, and to your planet Ga…Ga...Ga." JB7's eyes were rolling wildly, and his head was jerking back and forth. "I am under attack, strong AI hacking...Get into the airlock," he said, tapping a code on a barely visible keypad on the back wall. The wall slid open as JB7 collapsed on the floor. Yuri pushed Lincoln and Selena into the room and dragged the android in.

A New Origin

They were barely across the threshold when Selena slapped the large red button that closed the door.

The humans sat on a bench across the room from a rack of space suits while the android lay on the floor, twitching violently. A beep sounded, and the twitching stopped. A second beep was followed by the announcement "Shutdown complete," and a luminescent screen appeared on JB7's wide forehead.

Yuri, who was closest to the head, pushed JB7's aquiline nose. A luminescent keyboard appeared under the screen that now read: ENTER REBOOT CODE.

"Any ideas for the boot code?" He said, dispirited.

"Try James Bond 007," Lincoln replied, "If that doesn't work, try Bond comma James Bond, and if that doesn't work, hit the ground quickly."

Yuri tapped on JB7's forehead and jerked back as his eyes fluttered and he sat bolt upright.

"Welcome back, double-o-seven," Lincoln said with a laugh, "I see you survived the assault."

"I was sure that you would guess my code, M," JB7 replied. "This room is shielded. The AI won't be able to locate me here." He stood, flexing his heavily muscled arms and legs, "You will need to suit up, and I suggest we do that quickly before they figure out, we're still alive."

"I assume we are headed to the Hexagon," Yuri said, stepping into a space suit.

"Indeed, Admiral," JB7 replied.

"Just one question Mister Bond. Let me start with, I believe your service will be of great value to me, so I am ordering you not to shut down to avoid a lie. So, with my promise to protect you, can you tell me who ordered the bombing, knowing that answering 'No' will give me the information I require? You can whisper into my ear if you don't trust my wife or my father."

"Don't worry about me," Lincoln chimed in, looking into JB7's very humanoid blue eyes, "you know that I know."

"And I have a really strong suspicion," Selena added, also looking the android in the eye "and if I'm right, I'm going to need a friend and protector when Yuri is on duty."

"One more thing before you answer," Yuri said, "I order you to turn up your emotions setting."

JB7 nodded and said, "That was a brilliant bit of interrogation, and I thank you, Admiral. The answer is, indeed, no. My brief said it was a staged marriage, of two traitors, that was arranged to distract the press and the rebels while the Hexagon was loaded. The mission, to make sure you stayed in the room until the attack, was compromised when Minister Chang showed up. My orders included finding him and transporting him to the Hexagon as soon as possible. He knew me from his time as prime minister, and I didn't have time to alter my appearance before he showed up," with a stare at Lincoln, "where he shouldn't have been."

JB7 broke the stare and continued, "He instantly figured out the plan and played the game perfectly. He said he had a suicide tooth that was programmed to activate if you and the princess were not within fifteen meters of him, or if he became unconscious. He kept coming out of your meeting, getting closer to the limit each time. Finally, he was ten centimeters from the line when I activated the alarm. That's when I turned up my emotional setting, and that's what almost killed me. I wasn't fighting off an AI. I was fighting my own programming and rewriting the rules, so I wouldn't kill you. I shut down milliseconds before my own the self-destruct."

"Well, that's it then," Lincoln said with finality. "Let's get our sorry butts into these suits and onto a shuttle, before someone comes checking for survivors."

SCENE THREE
Going Where? With Whom?

Lincoln, Yuri, and Selena did a quick equipment check as JB7 opened the airlock door. They tumbled onto a narrow uneven trail carved into the rock wall of the escarpment. JB7 produced a rope, tied it around their waists and led them toward one of the towering rock ribs that defined the escarpment, the trail narrowing as they went. Their feet teetered on the edge as they shuffled along showering red rocks four kilometers down the wall.

They walked slowly and deliberately. The rock wall on their right was getting shorter and less vertical with every step. They were about halfway to the rib when the wall gave way to a gently sloping rocky plain. The trail widened and started descending toward rib. The walking got easier and JB7 unhooked the ropes. Yuri and Selena dropped back a bit and walked side by side, their helmets touching so they could talk without the radio.

"Are you OK," Yuri asked, "you've been slowing down and stumbling a bit."

"I'm just a little tired and dizzy. I think I might have a concussion."

"In that case," Yuri said, as he picked her up. When their helmets came back together, he continued, "you try and get some sleep, we still have a long way to go."

"I do love you," she said, relaxing in his arms and quickly falling asleep.

Yuri moved, breaking the helmet connection and said, in a sad, quiet voice, "And I would love you too. If you were who you're pretending to be."

They walked a long time on the plain. As they went the slope grew steeper and the path angled down the slope toward the side of the rib. The trail flattened out and the rock wall was on their right again.

It was nearly sunset when they reached the rib, and the trail ended at a tall double door where the rib and the wall merged.

JB7 walked over to the right side of the door and scanned it for several seconds. He shook his head, moved to the left side, and repeated the process. This time he waved the others up. As they approached, he shoved his hand into a crack and twisted three full rotations clockwise then one and a half back and pulled out his hand. He backed away as the door opened out. The group hurried up the path and into the antechamber of a long tunnel. JB7 pulled the door closed behind them and said, "This facility is shielded. It is safe to talk."

Yuri laid Selena gently on the floor, stood and turned to JB7. "Who was she?" he asked menacingly,

And where is the real Princess Selena?"

"When did you know?"

"From day one."

"Then why did you go along?"

"Why not? I had a better chance of surviving than if I refused."

"Point taken" JB7 continued. "She was a clone with Selena's memory downloaded. The real Selena was brain wiped and given a fictional memory. She was sold to Josh Hardly-Smyth, son of the Emperor's brother, Claudius, who is the CEO of Galactic water. Claudius paid three hundred million credits and gave up his claim to the throne in favor of his son, who is now the heir apparent."

Yuri stared at Selena with a tear in his eye. "Is there anything you can do to revive her?"

"I will try," JB7 said, opening a hidden cabinet on the wall and pulling out what looked like an old-fashioned pistol. He pressed it against Selena's chest, adjusted a dial on the handle, and pulled the trigger. He held the trigger down and moved the muzzle around her chest and head for several seconds. Her back arched, and she started jerking spasmodically. When he released the trigger, the spasms stopped, and she started flexing her arms and legs. Finally, she sat up, twisted her torso back and forth, shook her head, and stood up. She looked at each of the others and fixed on JB7.

"Why am I alive?" she asked calmly.

A New Origin

"Because we need you to be alive," Yuri said, "And you deserve it. You are a sentient being with free will. Whether you understand it or not, you are a unique individual despite your genetics and implanted memory. YOU have experienced the past couple of weeks, not your genetic twin. You have made decisions, observations, and even a few jokes that no one else has a right to call theirs. By those actions, you are officially a unique human, with all the rights that brings. So, while I cannot, in good faith, be your spouse, I will be your friend and defender."

"And no matter what Yuri says, I will be your father-in-law, and you are welcome to stay with me as my daughter," Lincoln said, giving her a big hug. "My only request is that you choose a name for yourself. No hurry, while you think about it, meanwhile I will call you Lena."

Lena wiped her eyes and said confidently, "My understanding is that parents are responsible for naming their children. So by that rubric, I shall be Lena Chang, daughter of Lincoln Chang and sister to Yuri Chang."

"I have recorded this transaction with the Census Bureau and the Hexagon passenger list," JB7 said. "You are now officially a citizen of the Empire. Our transport to the shuttle is arriving in forty-seven seconds."

They turned toward the tunnel as a four-seater rover rolled into the room. They scrambled into the seats, and the rover dove back into the tunnel. Yuri asked after ten minutes in the pitch black, "How long is this tunnel? This is getting annoying."

'The tunnel is twenty kilometers long," JB7 announced. "We are five clicks in. Your helmet screens should begin working at the halfway point."

Ten minutes later, their screens came on. They were treated to a state propaganda broadcast touting a new space elevator on Earth that would increase the export of water by eliminating the need for the tanker ships to land in order to fill their tanks. Lena was fascinated; Yuri fell asleep; and Lincoln, who had recently seen the construction site, laughed uncontrollably.

The broadcast was nowhere near finished when the rover emerged from the tunnel and rolled into a large low ceilinged building, stopping at a staircase that ended on a loading dock. JB7 led the way up the stairs and down the dock to an elevated steel rail running through the building and out the backside. A crane was maneuvering a large bullet-nosed rectangular box over the rail as the four reached the dock.

"Where's the shuttle?" Yuri asked, looking all around.

"That's it," JB7 said, pointing to the cylinder.

"Don't tell me we're going in a cargo container!" Lincoln shouted, glaring at JB7.

"Okay. Let's call it an emergency crew evacuation unit," the JB7 replied, attempting a smile but presenting a grimace.

"I suppose you'll be calling the rail gun a runway," Lena chimed in. "Does it, at least, have seats?"

"In so much as it has a floor and walls," JB7 said, deadpan serious.

"We're going to have to work on your sarcasm programing," Lincoln replied with a chuckle. "Lead on, Macduff, our chariot awaits!"

Yuri pulled down the status screen in his suit, "We could use a water and air refill, a reload of the nutrient gel, and a couple of doses of Stay-awake. I'm thinking it's going to be a long night."

"More likely a long four days, Admiral," JB7 replied. "The shuttle is fully stocked."

The box, aka cargo container, aka shuttle, was settled on the rail, and the crane retracted. A section of the cylinder opened and extended a ladder to the dock. JB7 ushered them onboard, and they quickly strapped into acceleration couches at the rear bulkhead. JB7 positioned himself in the middle of the cabin and extended his arms to the ceiling and legs to the edges of the aisle. The ramp retracted, and the door closed and sealed. An announcement said, 'Atmosphere has stabilized. Please do not remove helmets until we achieve orbit. Acceleration will begin in five seconds.'

The module began to move along the rail, at first slowly but quickly picking up speed.

"Is there any way we could see where we're going?" Yuri asked.

"I have linked your helmet screens to the external camera," JB7 announced.

"Got it!" came from all three nearly simultaneously.

The pod's acceleration up the rail matched the pressure they felt pressing them against their chairs and the view on their helmet screens. Then, finally, the top edge of the caldera came into view and passed behind as the pod launched off the rail. Ten minutes later, the maneuvering jets had them in a queue, with several hundred others, at the Hexagon's dock on Phobos.

The view from the queue was spectacular. The six, five-hundred meter diameter, cylindrical towers rose two kilometers above the launch pad on the rocky surface of Phobos. The towers were connected into a hexagram by cross beams twenty meters in diameter. Every fifth connector was a corridor between towers. Hundreds of Space-fighters formed a defensive cloud around Phobos, their maneuvering lights creating a fairyland around the small moon. The "queue" was more like a swarm of bees returning to the hive than a line of ticket holders waiting to board a ship.

"We will be in the queue for ten hours" JB7 said over the com. "While we are outside the Hexagon, I suggest connecting to the broadcast channels, the secure info grid, and the military emergency network. I'm sure you will find some very interesting developments. We will have to go to radio and audio silence when we load and maintain that until the Hexagon launches. I will supply slates and markers at that time."

"How long between load and launch?" Yuri asked.

"There are only twenty slots available after we load. So, it should be no more than six hours between loading and launch."

"I'm on the grid now!" Lincoln said. "And 'interesting' doesn't even begin to describe it."

Lena screamed, "Oh my Gods, Yuri, we're dead! Our funeral is streaming across the solar system! We are lying in state. **In Open Caskets!!!**"

"And the elite have left the planet in droves, all headed for Hexagon with their treasures and a horde of servants and sycophants. Ninety percent of the stasis chambers are full. They must have been loading for weeks," Lincoln reported.

"The Emperor and the royal family are on board in Tower One, aka Forbidden City, and we are, strangely, booked into Tower Four," Yuri said. "Was that intentional?"

"Yes," JB7 replied, "the military section is the last place they will think to look for stowaways, and you are in a position to influence outcomes if we are discovered."

"I just checked the military feed, and it seems I am on the roster as Fleet Admiral, so your intuition was correct. I still think we should wait until after the hexagon launches to leave the pod."

"I concur. In the meantime, we should continue to be cautious," JB7 replied.

"I'm going to take a nap," Lincoln chimed in.

"You woke me up for this?" Lena said with a giggle.

"Nighty-night everyone. I'll see you in space," Yuri said with a yawn.

Eight hours later, JB7 posted a message, "We are entering the dock. Initiate radio and vocal silence. We will likely be in the pod for the next few days. Please stay belted to your seats until we enter the gravity field and have been loaded into our slot. They can detect movement during the loading process. You can still view anything you already downloaded, but audio must be through your wired bone-phones. Be patient. Our contacts on the ship have a plan.

Curtain

Andria and Jason crashed through the front door and raced to the telephone in the kitchen. Andria got there first, grabbed the hand piece and, fending off Jason, dialed Mom's work number. The phone rang six times before it went to the answering machine which said, "The party you have dialed is not available. Please leave a message after the tone."

"Jason come here; we have to tell her together," she said, holding the phone so both their mouths were near the receiver. There was an extended beep that sounded more like a screech after which the twins yelled, "Mom, you won't believe it! We got parts in the next play! Rehearsal starts tomorrow at the theater. Ms. Jane said we are excused from school, and to break a leg! We stared at her and then she said that we shouldn't really break a leg and that it was something people in the theater said that meant good luck and said that there were a bunch of strange things about the theater but that it is mostly fun and that she was in the cast of the play the last time it was here, and that she had a really special time that she will remember the rest of her life. And she told us that we would too and that she would be sure to come and watch us. We're going to read the script for our part and will tell you all about it when you get home."

A New Origin

They had just cradled the handset and started reading the script when the phone rang. Andria picked up the handset, and before she could say hello Mom was on the line screaming, "ARE YOU KIDDING ME! THAT'S SO GREAT! I'LL BE HOME IN FIFTEEN MINUTES AND WE CAN PRACTICE YOUR LINES! I'M LEAVING RIGHT NOW!" Andria heard the hand piece slam onto its cradle, turned to Jason and said, just barely holding back a laugh, "I think she's OK with us being in the play."

Jason replied, "Ya think!" upon which they flopped on the couch howling and laughing and hugging. They were still going strong when Mom came and joined them.

ACT THREE
NEW ORIGIN'S CENTENNIAL SURPRISES

Chorus

Imagine your now.

How different was your before.

When the first spring was.

The Master of Ceremonies walked to center stage from the stage left wing, The Fates being fickle, as they are wont to behave, swing the pendulum away from tranquility toward Chaos. The backswing carries the army of Mars, god of war from our ancient mythology to the peaceful world Gaia.

Chorus: We return you to our gentle New Origin settlers, fifty years after we last saw them, and find our friend Adam in a rage and Lady Lily convalescing. A strange omen appears in the heavens; an unwanted king menaces the tranquility of our gentle society, and the return of our long-lost heroes as a prodigal couple emerge as emissaries of the singularities.

SCENE ONE
What? From Where?

Adam Cavel was alone in the observatory control room, focusing the reflecting scope on the coordinates of John's Star, better known in New Origin as the New Year's Star. Adam and Lily's son, John, the credentialed New Origin astronomer, had discovered the star on New Year's Eve, twelve years ago while searching for moons of the gas giant planet he called Jupiter. It was presented as a tiny point of light that glowed dimly in the blue and ultraviolet end of the visible spectrum and brightly in the X and gamma wavelengths. He confirmed it as a star and not a moon the following year when Jupiter had moved several degrees, but the star had not.

Every year since, the entire extended family spent New Year's Eve at the observatory, all forty-nine taking a turn looking at John's star. This year was different. Lily's stroke, three months before, left her unconscious and hospitalized. As hospital director emeritus, Adam demanded that he be allowed stay and direct the med-techs treating her.

His constant insistence that they start memory recovery therapy before she met the guideline recommendations got him banned from the stroke center. Finally, the incessant badgering of the hospital administrator, his former intern, got him banned from the hospital.

At home, his rants —that he knew her better than anyone; that she would not recover without his help; lamenting his inability to do anything about it; and cursing the universe and everything in it-- got him banished to a cot in a niche in the observatory. He was, additionally, forced to promise, under threat of abandonment, not to yell at his son John when he came to analyze the data and photos Adam took during his nightly observations. He was also warned against badgering his physician daughter, Sherri (who had inherited his practice) on her daily check-up, food delivery, and report on Lily's progress, which was invariably 'as expected.'

After the first week, Adam developed a rhythm: get up at 5:30 PM; take care of business in the latrine; wait for Sherri to come at 6:00; take a five-kilometer run; followed by a bucket shower (with soap as per Sherri's orders); and finally, reading three chapters of any of the three hundred novels written within the last twenty years. For this last ritual, he had six books, one for each day of the week. He had finished reading chapter eighteen in five of the six books. Chapter eighteen was the last chapter of book six, a sci-fi thriller with a gruesome bug-eyed monster; that turns out to be a wizard who, at the last minute, saves a planet of sentient bird creatures from an invading army of extraterrestrial hunters. This was the chapter he was reading on New Year's Eve of the year 100, as calculated in New Origin.

Adam closed the book and wondered what the author, who called themselves Anonymous, was trying to say. The preface said it was an allegory. But unfortunately, he couldn't figure out what an allegory was, which only added to his anger that the family was not coming to the observatory for New Year's Eve.

The rage bubbled up from his churning gut. He jumped from his chair, sending it crashing into the wall behind him.

He ran out to the balcony and produced a primal roar that startled the birds into flight and the horse in the stable to whinny and kick his stall. The roar continued as all of his worry and anxiety about Lily poured out of him: that he wouldn't be able to go on without her: that it wasn't fair, and that he had no idea how to help her. He turned the roar into a litany of grievances that he knew, even in his rage, were not the real cause of his pain. His breathing was ragged, and his throat was raw. Collapsing to his knees, he closed his eyes and tried to die, as he had every night since Lily's stroke.

After several minutes of imagining himself dead, he shifted into reminiscence. He thought back to his childhood and remembered the time he and Lily were put in different classes at school. They had yelled and complained so much that their teachers called their parents, who came, scolded them, and told them that they needed to spend time apart. He and Lily cried all that first day but eventually got used to being in different classes, as long as they could see each other at home.

He thought about the time in high school when Jeffery Ness tried to win Lily away from him, and Jenny Moss threw herself at him. A couple

A New Origin

of days later, Jeffery and Jenny became a couple, and now they have seven kids and twenty grandkids. Now, he and Lily have six kids, eighteen grandkids, and four great-grandkids, with three more on the way. Knowing Lily, there was no way she was going to miss that.

Usually, this exercise of reviewing his situation calmed Adam down, but not tonight. He leaned onto the balcony rail, his whole body shaking. "Time for plan B," he whispered and thought back to the silly poem he had written to Lily for their commitment ceremony seventy-five years ago. He chanted it out loud:

Oh, Lily oh Lily you flower my life.

Your beauty undoubted, your wit a fine knife

Through love, sweetness, Chaos and strife

We'll be here together both husband both wife.

A slight reverberation tickled his ear, and he stopped before the second verse. It felt like someone was singing with him; a soundless whisper deep in his head said, *Why did you stop?*

"Lily?" he shouted out loud. He was about to start the second verse when a breeze picked up, rustling the leaves of the trees surrounding the observatory. The sound reminded him of how Lily would sneak and fan him with a stack of paper papers behind his back when he fell asleep at his desk.

He jolted fully awake. Without hesitation or a clear plan, he walked into the dome, over to the scope, and peered through the lens. John's star wasn't there.

Fifteen minutes of frantically checking the focal coordinates of both the reflector and the gamma-ray scopes and another thirty minutes processing the time-lapse images had Adam sweating and shaking so much that he could barely type the start command into the computer.

It took twenty minutes to compress the four hours of observation into two thirty-minute videos. The data from the reflecting scope started at sundown and showed a very dim John's Star that dimmed to nothing within the first hour of observation and remained dark to the end. The data from the gamma-ray scope was a different story. The Star showed up with its usual intensity until the three-and-a-half-hour mark, when its intensity increased tenfold. He switched to the live feeds and was astonished to find the star shining in the visible, fifty times brighter than usual, and twenty-fold higher in the gamma.

Adam stared at the screen dumbfounded. "What the hell is going on?" he said aloud, reaching for the phone and dialing John's number.

The phone rang for ten minutes before: "This had better be an emergency," John shouted.

"Look outside and then come up," Adam said as calmly as he could.

"What?"

"The Star"

"I know! It's not there!"

"Oh, it's there, and it's really weirdly bright."

"Hold on, I'm going outside. I got an extra-long cord, so ... I'm on the porch now. Holy Crap! What is that?"

Adam heard muffled footsteps, a door closing, John's whispering voice (presumably talking to his wife, Sara); clomping footsteps; John saying, "OK dad, I'm on my way, see you in ten"; followed a click and silence.

I wonder what's happening out there, Adam thought as he walked out on the balcony and looked at the star, seeing it naked eyed for the first time.

I'll tell you when John gets here. It's way weirder than you thought, echoed in Adam's head. He startled; shook his head; looked all around; and shouted, "Who said that! Come out where I can see you!"

I'll be there a few minutes after John gets there. I want you both to hear what I have to say. It's a story no one would believe if only one person heard it.

"I must be going insane," Adam mumbled, pacing back and forth on the balcony.

That's not far from the truth, brother, not far at all.

Adam pressed his hands to his forehead, sighed, and said, "Well, that's good to know!"

Looking out from the balcony down the access road, he saw John's electric cart lights winding their way up the switchbacks to the observatory.

The cart was two switches from the top as another cart appeared around halfway down the mountain. Two minutes later, John pulled onto the parking pad, slid to a stop, and came running up the steps to the balcony. He immediately turned to look down the road and said, "I thought there was someone behind me, and coming fast. Did you call Sherri? She's the only one I know that drives that fast."

"I didn't, but I think we are about to hear a story that we're not expected to believe," Adam said, relieved that he might not be crazy.

"What?" John asked in a tone that made Adam reconsider his self-diagnosis.

"I seem to have had a nonverbal discussion with someone who said he could explain our wonky star and that he would be here shortly after you got here. He said he wanted two of us to hear his story because no one would believe it if only one person heard it. Mind you, this was all in my head," Adam said in a tentative voice.

John was about to reply when the cart roared into the parking area, pulled a donut, and skidded to a stop exactly side by side with John's cart.

"Definitely not, Sherri," John said deadpan. "She's good, but not that good."

Adam and John watched in awe as a young man got out of the cart and took the thirty meters of the parking pad and the twenty steps to the balcony in five quick leaps, landing face to face with Adam.

The young man bear-hugged Adam lifting him off his feet as if he was a child. He set him down gently, kissed him on the mouth, stepped back a pace, and offered his hand, saying, "I am honored to meet you, Dr. Adam Cavel. The hug was from Dad, and the kiss was from Mom. The handshake is from your identical twin and freshly unfrozen brother, Dr. Adam Caleb Cavlele, who goes by A-C, most recently of the planet Earth."

John and A-C caught Adam as he passed out. "There's a cot in the Observatory," John said shakily as they carried Adam into the dome. "So, I'm guessing you're my long-lost mythical uncle that my grandparents made me promise never to talk about," he continued as they laid Adam on the cot and covered him with a thin blanket.

"That's what the genealogy says, but the chronology is considerably twisted. That being the case, I would be honored if you would consider me a younger sibling. There used to be a descriptor back on Earth, 'a brother from another mother that I think might be a better way for us to interact.'"

John looked A-C in the eyes and smiled. "Sounds good to me, my brother. You think he'll be OK?"

"He'll be fine. Our sister Sherri gave me a sedative that I applied to my lips. She also gave me a hypo with an antidote that I'll give him after you and I have a little chat. And don't worry, I know how to handle it. I received my MD the day we left Earth."

"So I heard," John said with a smile. "I also heard that you married my mother's sister, who was also a new MD, and that both of you were left behind."

"I was as surprised as you were when I was thawed out after eight hundred years in stasis," A-C said, wiping away a tear, "I can't tell you how much Penelope and I cried when they told us. Especially when they told us that they lied by telling our parents that Pen and I were lost."

"That's cold!" John retorted, "This star issue must be really serious. At least Penelope is with you now."

A-C sighed, "She's actually in Gaia City. She works for the mayor. I haven't seen her since the day after we woke up a month ago."

"Gaia City? Are you saying there *IS* another colony?" John asked excitedly.

"Damn! I wasn't supposed to talk about that yet," A-C said, palming his forehead. "We'll deal with that after we talk some physics related to astronomy and look at this supposed star."

"Well, let's get on it!" John said, heading toward the scope with A-C right behind him.

SCENE TWO

What Was that?

Adam woke up a couple of hours later, groggy and disoriented. He thought he heard voices, but the niche, where the cot was located, opened to the rear of the scope room and he couldn't make out what was being said. As his head cleared, the voices became more apparent. He recognized John's voice saying something about "light-years," and another voice saying, "definition of a year," and "something like five and a bit."

Adam sat up on the cot, stretched, rubbed his eyes, and took a drink from the water bottle on the nightstand. He pushed himself awkwardly to a stance, shuffled out of the niche, and saw two men huddled in front of the computer. The one that looked a lot like a younger John but wasn't John turned around and said, "Welcome back, Adam. Sorry I shocked you earlier. Come join us. We were just discussing when we can expect the arrival of the spaceship, Hexagon, bringing the Emperor of Mars and forty-five thousand of his minions."

The revelation shocked Adam back to full consciousness. "You're A-C, and you and I are brothers," he said, calmly laying things out mainly for himself, and to be sure he was awake, he pinched his arm as hard as he could, causing serious pain to his right bicep. "Ow!" he said, rubbing his arm, "Good thing I'm left-handed."

"Another bit of corroborating evidence," A-C said with a laugh. "The three of us will have to have a serious talk about dealing with right-handed bias. Maybe over a beer tomorrow?"

John stood, stretched, and said, "I'm all in for that! I'll arrange it and invite some other lefties to join us." He stretched and yawned, "It's two AM, and I've got a lot to do tomorrow, so I'll leave you two to talk about what A-C told me and I'll see you tomorrow." He hugged A-C and Adam and was out the door with a wave of his left hand.

A-C and Adam sat back down. A-C cleared his throat and said, "I know your education included a sketchy history of Earth. You are aware of the cruelty of tribalism, the relationship between wealth and power, and the suffering it can inflict on those who have neither. I'll save filling in the details for a broader audience. I don't know how much our parents told you about their lives on Earth, but I'm guessing it wasn't much."

"You are right about that!" Adam exclaimed.

"Because it's late, and because it's a very long story, I'm going to give you the headline: Our parents were heroes who saved the lives hundreds of people that became thirty percent of the founding population of the Origin colony on Earth."

"You're kidding, they never talked about what they did on Earth, and I only knew about you from Lily's parents, who also talked about your wedding and Penelope. What happened to her?"

A-C sighed, "She's working for the Mayor of Gaia City. The two of us were left in stasis so that we could act as ambassadors when people from Earth's solar system finally found us. Or at least that was what we were told. I haven't seen her since the day we woke up and then only for a couple of hours."

"Well, that's right out cruel!" Adam snarled, "How far is it? We can pack the horses and start out tomorrow!"

"That won't be necessary," A-C said conspiratorially. "Gaia City is something I wanted to talk about tomorrow with the village officials. A spoiler just for you, we are sending a large contingent from New Origin for a conference on new technology and defense systems. We will be working over the next five years to prepare for the Martian invasion."

"When do we leave?" Adam asked enthusiastically.

"Yesterday, if I had my way!" A-C chuckled. "But most likely three or four weeks. We're planning for a group of fifty adults and a hundred and fifty high school and college students."

"And how long do we stay?"

"That's up in the air. I think a minimum of five days for the young kids and a maximum, for some, maybe a year. It will be different for different people, but we've gotten off track. I need to tell you about the Singularities."

A New Origin

"You mean like the one our parents uploaded to that disappeared shortly thereafter?"

"It didn't disappear. It went trans-dimensional. It's left a surrogate here which is still collecting our thoughts and memories. We just can't detect it or communicate with it without being invited."

"So, to my understanding, it's a data storage slash computer that gathered a select sample of the human sentience which we no longer can access. It kinda feels a bit cannibalistic." Adam said with a disgusted tone.

"It feels a bit like that to me as well," A-C replied. "But there is one thing it can do for people with the correct wiring. It facilitates telepathy."

Adam was skeptical, "Telepathy? Do you mean mind reading? The Sci-Fi standard for the bug-eyed monsters and utopians?"

"The way it was explained to me was that everyone born in the Origin Society colony on earth was genetically modified at the germ cell level, to make an organic transmitter and receiver of brain waves. The trait is stronger in some than others. Pen and I are both strong and can communicate for up to a kilometer, as long as we can see each other. With help from the Singularity, the Techs developed an implant device that can operate up to 5 kilometers without line of sight. That's how I communicated with you last night. The only way that works is through the surrogate which is real-time uploading everyone on the planet. This is why upload technology is no longer necessary. Our parents were the last ones on this planet that didn't have the modification. You and Lily have been using it for decades."

Adam thought about the number of times that he and Lily had simultaneously said, or yelled, something to their children and heard 'I knew you were going to say that!' often while they were still saying it. And the times they finished each other's sentences or laughed before the punchline. Finally, he looked at A-C and thought, *so why haven't more of us figured it out?*

Because no one believes it's possible and because you and Lily are extraordinarily powerful.

Adam suddenly felt exhausted and said aloud, "A-C, this telepathy thing seems to take a lot of energy."

"You're right about that," A-C replied in kind, "It's late, and we are both tired, so I'll save the lessons for tomorrow. I do, however, need to tell you now about the other Singularity, and I promise I'll make it quick.

A-C moved his chair closer to Adam's, cleared his throat and started, "Planet Gaia was discovered when the Human Singularity connected with an alien singularity, and they exchanged histories and locations. The Gaian Singularity developed from an AI-driven self-replicating underwater mining installation left on the planet about five million years ago by an alien culture that was looking for a new home, and not quite finding it on Gaia.

The installation was programmed to make copies of itself, which it did, and with each iteration, the AIs interconnected, and the core became more intelligent and more efficient. Finally, after a couple hundred thousand years, the computational power had increased to a level that allowed them to design mechanisms to access the fifth dimension and they spent the next four million years looking for spacefaring civilizations.

They watched several worlds achieve interstellar space travel and eventually collapse, many without forming a singularity and a few that did. They watched as the singularities evolved in the fifth dimension and moved into the sixth dimension and out of their vision. They were on the verge of moving on without learning how intelligence evolved from planetary to interstellar and beyond, when they received a weak probe from the newborn human singularity. They invited us to bring our dying population and restart the human experience here on Gaia."

Adam was dumbfounded, and, after a few minutes of hemming and hawing, he said, "Let me, umm, get this, uh, straight. So we are being studied and manipulated by two super-intelligent, Ummm, trans-dimensional entities. One made up of the stored memories of some five billion humans including our parents; and the other an accumulated, uncountable, number of alien AIs; and that these two superpowers are going to allow us to be invaded by Martians?"

A-C squirmed in his chair, took a deep breath, and said haltingly, "This is why Pen and I were kept frozen until now. We have, how shall I put it, maybe intimate, or relevant memory of how Earth cultures worked. We were sent to act as ambassadors for Gaia. We are tasked to teach everyone about the Martian culture, and what we will need to do to keep them from conquering us. It seems to me that the singularities are on our side, but mostly, consider us an interesting experiment that will somehow enrich their existence. They have provided us with limited telepathy as a tool to increase our resilience. They have other tech-based tools that Pen and I will be introducing. My guess is that in the end, no matter how it works out, we will all end up in the Singularity. Whether we are joined by generations to come or not we can only guess and hope that the answer is yes."

Adam pressed his hands to his eyes and mumbled, "I'm too tired to process this. I'm going to bed."

"That sounds like a great idea," A-C said, yawning.

They both stood, hugged, and parted. Adam to the cot and A-C out the door. Adam was asleep before his head hit the pillow.

SCENE THREE

How?

Adam was dreaming of spaceships, ray guns, and bug-eyed monsters when he was jarred, partially aware by a ringing sound. He stood, and zombie-walked toward the sound. He got to the sound and stood looking at the phone for a minute, wondering why it was making so much noise, until he realized he needed to pick it up.

"Hello?"

"Dad! Is that you?.... Dad, are you OK?"

"Ummm... What?"

"You don't sound good. You sit down. I'm coming up, OK?"

"Uh...OK, I'm sitting. Who am I talking to... I'm fine. You don't need to bother."

"Dad, it's Sherri, I don't like the way you sound, and don't give me any 'I'm a doctor' crap like the last time you were sick, 'cause you know I'm a better diagnostician than you are, and I AM coming up there."

"Uh, what? OK-bye." He sat on the floor for several minutes staring at the handset and its long-curled cord, wondering what it was and where it came from until it started beeping. He instinctively hung it up, wondering why he had it in the first place and why he was sitting on the floor. Then, it occurred to him that perhaps his rants had finally caused the stroke he had been hoping for; and that now he could sit with Lily and not worry that neither of them had any idea what was going on; and that he had a nightmare; and that some strange story was part of it. He was about to check out the accommodations in the Singularity when a loud thud followed by an eerie voice startled him.

He turned toward the voice and saw a tall woman backlit in the doorway. For a second, it looked like Lily. He was struck mute and could only stare as she walked toward him.

A New Origin

"Dad. It's me, Sherri. Remember I called?"

"For a minute there... You looked just like your mother, and I, I thought I'd had a stroke, and she, she was…"

Sherri put her arms around him. "I've always looked like her, and as for a stroke, you sit down on this chair, and I'll check you over." She fished, a brick sized box and reflex hammer from her black doctor's bag.

"What's that," he asked as she adjusted her brand new multi-scanner and brushed it across his chest.

"I'll tell you when we are finished."

"OK, deep breath, again. Again, and hold it. Nothing wrong there. Let's check reflex."

"Left side," a whack on the knee elicited the desired effect. The right knee was the same.

"Now, it's a good thing we are related because I can combine a whole bunch of tests together. Wiggle your right ear. Good, just like I remember. Now the left. You used to make us all laugh doing that when we were kids. Remember how proud Josh was when he figured out, he could do it?"

"And how embarrassed you were when you couldn't."

"And then John could only do his right ear."

"Oh, very clever memory test. It was his left!"

They both broke out laughing and had tears when they finally quit.

"So why don't you remember what went on last night?"

"I'm still processing that."

"You don't remember John and the young guy, A-C?"

"Oh, was that real?" Adam said, taken aback, "I thought it was a dream."

Sherri looked at him and said sternly, "No, that was very real, and I need you to tell me the whole story. And then I need you not to talk about it until I give you the OK. Is that clear?"

"As a bell," Adam replied, "What time is it?"

"It's four-thirty. You apparently had a very late night.

The sun was halfway to the horizon as they climbed into a small gray electric cart and started down the tree-lined gravel path toward home. "Wow, I get the luxury ride. How come I got so lucky!"

"Oh, how quickly they forget. You scared the crap out of me, and I didn't want to take the time to hitch up the horses. You weren't exactly coherent, and besides, Seth was out with the rig picking up Josh and family. The rest is a secret."

"Who's in on this secret."

"Well, not you for sure. Why don't you close your eyes and take a catnap. You're going to need it."

"I'm not sure I can, the way you drive," Adam chortled.

"I promise I will go slowly so you can rest," Sherri said soothingly, "and to help you sleep, I'm going to put this on you." She produced a thick blindfold, tied it to his head, "and this," putting noise-canceling headphones over his ears. Then, pulling one earpiece away just enough so he could hear, she said menacingly, "and I don't want to see your hands anywhere near your head until I tap you on the shoulder. Got it?" as she released the earpiece with a snap.

Adam buckled his seat belt, reclined the seat, and retrieved his go-to nap memory, in which he and Lily are sitting on the porch swing with a bottle of Jake Zee's new vintage, pretending to be oenophiles.

He handed her a glass and asked, "Did you find anything in the archive to explain why Jake calls this Beaujolais Nouveau?"

" Not about that, but I did find a little something," she said, taking the glass he held out to her. She clinked it with his, swirled the wine in the glass, took a long sniff followed by a sizable taste, and sighed.

She swirled the glass again and was in the middle of the sniff when he, just a little flustered, said, "What ARE you doing? Are you going to tell me what you found out or just drink the fumes?"

"Well, since you asked sooo nicely, I'm not going to tell you until you do exactly what I just did."

"You mean snorting the wine?"

"No, I mean tasting the wine like the wine experts used to do. First, you look at the color and clarity." she said, holding the glass up to her

A New Origin

eyes, "Then you swirl it and watch the way it clings to the side as a rippled film, by which, and you should understand this, Dr. Adam, you make an estimate of the amount of alcohol.

Then you swirl it again to release the aroma, which you sample by smelling it, and then you repeat the swirling and again smell but also taste, because, as you also know, the smell is a large part of taste.

So now let's try it together." She looked at him to make sure he was ready and continued, "OK, on my mark. Swirl and look."

They raised their glasses and swirled, watching the ripples of purple wine slide down the side. "Swirl and sniff." They took a deep inhale of the glass. "Exhale through your nose. Now swirl, then sniff and taste at the same time."

They were both on the verge of laughter when they sipped and sniffed, resulting in a burst of laughter, coughing, and wine spraying from their noses.

After a minute or so, Adam recovered first and asked, "So am I right to conclude that Beaujolais Nouveau means something like nasal discharge?" Setting off another round of laughter, this time without the wine spray.

Lily recovered first this time. "I see how you might think that, but nasal expulsion was not normally part of the process. We were supposed to have been able to describe the flavor pallet of the wine using words like earthy, dry, sweet, tart, metallic, woody, and the like. Also, flavor words like cherry, berry plum, and other fruits that I don't remember.

Adam took a long swig, looked thoughtfully at Lily, and said, "Tastes like fermented grapes to me," causing another bout of giggles.

Adam woke up when the cart stopped. Sherri tapped his shoulder, and he took off the blindfold and earphones. They were about 200 meters from the big curve, at the end of which was the driveway that led to the house. The road was smooth, hard, and dark black. Adam looked up and down the street and asked, "What is this surface?"

"The Techs call it asphalt. It's some sort of polymer composite. They've done all of the streets in town and are going out to the farms and orchards."

"How did they get all this done in a month?" Adam said, awed.

"They have these big machines they say can cover fifty clicks a day, but road paving's not why I stopped here. So, this is what's going to happen." Switching to her doctor's voice she said, " you're going to put the blindfold and headphones back on, and I'm going to pull into the driveway. I'm going to get out, and you're going to stay in the cart with them on until someone comes to get you, so gear up!"

Adam did as order and held on for dear life as the cart accelerated around the curve. The centripetal force pushed him halfway out of the cart, forcing him to grab the window post. He was just getting himself re-centered in his seat when Sherri braked suddenly, nearly sending him forward through the windscreen, followed by a hard left turn leaving him halfway out of the cart again as it came to a skidding stop in what he assumed was his driveway.

"Damn, Sherri. Do you always drive like this?" he said, reaching for the headset, only to get his hand swatted away and have Sherri pull on the earpiece.

"You're the one who taught me to drive, so no complaints, and what did I say about the earphones? Do I have to send you to your room without dinner? Now sit here and don't touch. I'll be back in a minute," snapping the earpiece back on his ear.

He felt her door slam shut and was about to pull off the blindfold when he felt the right-side earpiece being pulled up. "You really are being impossible. Seth is standing right next to me, and when it's time, he's going to lead you to the house. You know how he can be. He won't let you get away with anything, AND he's bigger than you, so watch yourself, buster, or no dessert for you."

"OK, Seth, I'll be good even though I know you wouldn't abuse an old man." Again the ear flap came up, "Don't count on it, Grandpa," the snap and ear ringing followed.

"You are your mother's son, and she's her father's daughter." With that, he leaned back in the cart seat and chanted the waiting song: daa de daa di di daa de daa....daa de daa de dit de dadadada....daa de daa didi daa di daa....Dit d'daa daa dat dat....dat. After five times through, Seth lifted the earpiece and said, "OK, grandpa, I'm going to take off the headphones, but you have to keep the blindfold on. We are going to walk over to the cottage porch, and you are going to sit quietly on the porch swing until someone comes and gets you."

A New Origin

"If I must," he said, feeling Seth take hold of his elbow and direct him up the path. He could hear people walking around and whispering in the backyard, the snorting of horses in the corral, and his and Seth's footsteps on the gravel walkway. A horse whinnied, and a couple of birds twittered from the tree in front of the porch. The steps leading up to the porch creaked in all the right places and their boots ticked off the six steps to the swing. He reached out instinctively, grabbed the chain, and eased himself onto the swing. It was immediately apparent that he was not alone on the swing from how it moved as he settled back. It was like it felt all those times when... "It can't be," he whispered as tingling washed over him.

"But it is," came Lily's reply as she pulled off the blindfold and kissed him full on the lips.

After ten minutes of hugging, kissing, stuttering, and crying, Adam finally formed a complete word: "How?"

"A group of Techs came to the hospital and did something is what they told me," Lily said with a bit of hesitation. "No one was allowed to watch. Not even Sherri."

"You look so... so young, younger than Sherri."

"OK, you caught me. They have a regeneration unit. They are going to treat everyone over eighty, and they said that you would be going in tomorrow."

"Well then, at least I'll have tonight to be the dirty old man with the beautiful young wife," Adam said with a laugh that Lily shared.

Adam gave her a lustful smile that turned into a concerned look and asked, "What did it feel like when you were, umm, after the stroke? Did you know what was going on? I'm so sorry I wasn't there, but I couldn't. I was so ashamed that I couldn't do anything... I thought I had lost you. The only thing that kept me somewhat sane was imagining that I was talking to you."

"Was it about wine?" she replied.

"Yeah, about something called...."

"Beaujolais?" she said, surprised, "I was just now remembering that day we tried to be expert oenophiles, and it seemed to me that I had that dream often. It gave me a warm feeling like hot cocoa in front of the fireplace."

"Yes!" he shouted. "It always calmed me down when I was ranting at the universe!"

"Hush now," she said, putting her finger to his lips. "The only other thing I remember is that I closed my eyes here and opened them yesterday at the hospital. For me, I saw you yesterday, but I must have been somewhat aware because we stayed connected, and I knew you were OK. But for you, I understand how hard it must have been. It must have been hell."

"Hell indeed, and I have the witness to prove it!"

"Yes, I met A-C. There will be a meeting right after dinner, which I see from Sherri's hand signals is ready."

"Then I guess we should go before they send the truancy patrol. Besides, you must be pretty hungry after so much hospital food."

"Not sure what I got, but the benefit is I lost 10 kilos, and I need to get some of it back."

After a long embrace, they stood and walked arm in arm to the yard of the big house, where they found the 73 members of their immediate family, a large contingent of villagers, and A-C holding the reins of a strange-looking tan and white patched horse.

Adam paused and said to himself, *I've seen horses like that!*

It was on the southern expedition you took schoolmates as a graduation project. When you traveled on horseback five hundred kilometers south. Lily messaged.

You know about the telepathy! He messaged back. *I remember that the ecology gradually changed from forests to prairies. The southernmost prairie was bordered on the south and west by a range of mountains that went as far as they could see. We didn't have anything like the gear we would need to climb the mountains and were running out of supplies, so we decided to survey the prairie quickly.*

We saw a bunch of odd-looking cattle that spooked easily and herds of brown and white patched horses!

He turned to Lily to ask her if she knew A-C's story when he was accosted by ten preteen children shouting "Happy birthday Grand-Papi

A New Origin

Adam" as they crashed into him and grabbed him around the knees and thighs, taking him to the ground.

After rolling around in the grass with the great grandkids, who were cheered on by the boisterous crowd, he cried, "I surrender! Wow, you kids need to join the wrestling team. But first I think you need good tickling," which started a whole other bout of screeching and laughing which went on until the parents intervened and separated the combatants.

Adam had pushed up to his hands and knees when Lily stepped over his back and tickled his ribs, causing him to collapse laughing. "Get up, old man," she said, laughing and prodding his ribs with her foot. "We've got some serious birthdaying to do here."

Adam got to his feet and started to brush himself off when Lily appeared with a washcloth and started washing his face saying, "It's one thing for a hundred-year-old to have grass stains on his knees on his birthday. It's quite something else to have them on your face. Now hold still while I clean you up."

I know who A-C is, he told me yesterday, and I already suspected the telepathy part. Lily messaged as she rubbed a grass stain from Adam's nose.

He stared at her with an astonished look. "How?" he asked, which came out as a garbled "uhh."

"That's easy. I have five kids, twenty grandkids, and ten great-grandchildren who have tried to tell me things as I washed their faces."

They both laughed and looked and watched A-C, who was talking to a number of the town folks about the qualities of his horse.

"Maybe he's just acting the part horse trader come to show off his wares to get to know people," Adam mused. "Though the resemblance to my younger self is spooky."

"That's not really a surprise, is it?" said Lily taking a quick look, "He looks like you, back when all the girls were trying to lure you away from me."

"And you look like you did when I looked like him," Adam said, looking her up and down, "Those girls never had a chance."

Adam and Lily started to walk over to A-C when they found themselves in a tsunami of family flowing around them chanting,:

Richard Koepsel

"Birthday cake! Birthday cake! Birthday cake!" All the while moving them in an irresistible swarm toward the big picnic table, upon which sat a 1 by 2-meter sheet cake decorated with the number 100 and ablaze with 101 candles.

Adam could feel the heat from the candles as Happy Birthdays broke out at something close to 100 decibels, followed closely by "Happy Aphelion Day" and "Happy New Year." As tears welled, he turned and kissed Lily deeply, lasting through the birthday song and into a chant of "Blow them out." He held his hand up to quiet the crowd and said, "I am well and truly humbled. You are the best family and friends in the known universe, and I couldn't love you more. This has been the weirdest and most wonderful day of my life, and I am glad that you are here with me. I can't blow out all these candles myself, so I need everyone with a birthday this week and last week to help!"

More than thirty people of all ages, some related, most not, gathered around the cake. Most notable being the tall, barrel-chested, and fully bearded William Dee. One day younger than Adam and his best friend since birth, William raised his hands to quiet the crowd and said in his best announcer's voice,

>The beer is here
>
>the cake is lit,
>
>we'll sing a song
>
>then blow on it,
>
>we'll huff and puff and blow away
>
>to celebrate
>
>Your birthing day
>
>OK. Happy Birthday on three, two, one SING!"

Voices of all ages rang across the yard, more as a cacophony than a song. At the end, William called, "So everybody lean in. OK, on three: One, Two, Three, Blow!"

The response was enormous, sending candles and bits of icing across the table. The cheer after was deafening. Finally, Sherri shouldered her

A New Origin

way to the table next to Adam and started to cut the cake. "First pieces to the birthday twins!" she declared.

"What?" said William looking at Adam and then at A-C. "Well, I'll be damned! I hadn't seen that face in seventy years. Could this be the long-lost son of Caleb and Eleanor?"

A-C flushed and said in his own announcer voice, "It is. I will be telling you all my story, but I was hoping to have the cake first. The last cake I had was my wedding cake the day we left Earth, nearly eight-hundred years ago." He turned to Adam and said, "It will be the first birthday cake my brother and I will share. Hopefully, the first of many."

The stunned crowd was silent for a few seconds then simultaneously shouted, "Hip Hip, Hurrah, Hip Hip Hurrah, Hip Hip Hurrah!

Sherri handed them a plate of cake and said, "Ok, boys, let's get this party started!"

Their cake secured, Adam and A-C moved to a semi-quiet area and ate silently for a couple of bites. Then, Adam looked at A-C and said, "We really need to talk, but I think this party will be going on for a while. If I'm not mistaken, Sherri made a general announcement to the whole city. Most of them over the age of thirty were my patients at one time or another. So, I think we can expect to be overwhelmed pretty soon. But there is one thing you can answer quickly. What can't I tell people?"

I don't think we should talk about going to Gaia city. A-C messaged. *We haven't worked out the details, and we can only take fifty or sixty.*

Can I help you choose the ones to take?

Indeed, I was just about to ask you to do that.

I would like to have William and his wife Dana with us. He is about the smartest person I know, and I owe him for a stupid bet.

A-C laughed aloud and clapped Adam on the shoulder, "Anything for you, brother! But why did you bet that the Arc was parked on the moon? Especially when you knew that the moon was tidally locked and wouldn't be seen on the dark side?"

Adam sighed and said, "William makes really good beer, and I really like beer. So, one night, I had a lot of beer, and we had an excellent discussion of the possible locations of the arc. I bet that it was on the Moon, thinking that if it wasn't there, I could claim it was on the dark side and make the bet. After years of building and equipping the observatory and many more observing, I claimed it was on the dark side, and since neither of us could prove it wrong, the bet should be canceled. That was last year. A couple of weeks ago, I was at William's bar, and he handed me a picture of the dark side of the moon that John had taken. Apparently, he had told John about the bet, which was supposed to be a secret, and John, after he stopped laughing, and for a portion of the winnings, told him the truth.

A-C, who had been choking it back, burst out laughing. Adam, recognizing A-C's laugh as a copy of his own, also broke out laughing, making the volume noticeable by the large crowd on the lawn and creating a chain reaction that lasted several minutes.

"He was on top of my list," A-C said, still chuckling. "He told me about the bet and predicted your response. His conditions are that you admit defeat at the meeting in Gaia City."

Curtain

"Alright you two. It's way past your bedtime and you have a lot of work to do tomorrow to catch up on your school work."

"But we aren't tired, Mom," Justin whined and yawned at the same time.

"That wasn't very convincing, and your sister is sound asleep. I'll tell you what, You and your sister did such a wonderful job that I'm going to stay home from work tomorrow and help you catch up."

Justin yawned and flopped onto the couch and Andria was sound asleep in her father's lap on the recliner.

Dad stood up, carried Andria into her bedroom and tucked her in her bed. He came back the living room and collected Justin who had fallen asleep in the three minutes it had taken to put his sister to bed.

Dad was on his way out of Justin's room when Justin said in a sleepy whine, "Can we still see the play tomorrow?"

"No son, the play isn't until Saturday which is four days away. If it was tomorrow, you would just sleep through it."

"You might be right about…" followed by closed eyes and sleepy breathing sounds.

A New Origin

    Saturday seemed to come later than usual, but when it came everyone was anxious to get to the theater witnessed by the kids running full speed and arriving fifteen minutes before their parents.

ACT FOUR
HERE AND THERE AND THERE AND HERE

Chorus

Goddess of nature

from the firmament watching

her fragile charges

As usual the Master of Ceremonies entered the stage, but this time he is dressed in a military uniform that the Playbill identifies as Martian navy officer. He takes a whistle from his pocket and blows four piercing notes. The chatter in the audience goes quiet. He clicks his heels together four times and says:

My dear audience, we have reached the middle of the seven acts the ancient mage told us that we all play on the stage of life. Our actors take this stage, as everyone does in their characters who are without the knowledge of what will come next. We, however, have the advantage of hearing the conversation between the choruses which now sing for us.

Human Chorus: The approaching ship has pointed its' engines toward Gaia and is decelerating. Do you see anything else?

Gaian Chorus: Ten small masses have detached from the central mass and are approaching at 98.5 percent light speed. We calculate the small masses will arrive in 3.126754 years, and the larger mass, at the current deceleration rate, will arrive in 5.266651 years.

Human Chorus: We now also see the detached masses and confirm your calculations. We think they are manned crafts. We will take a closer look.

SCENE ONE
Why Aren't We There Yet?

Fleet Admiral Yuri Washington Chang woke up groggy and in a nasty mood. Every part of his body was raging with pain, and his vision was so blurry he couldn't tell where he was. *It's never been this bad coming out of stasis*, he thought as he tried and failed to lift his arms.

He tried again and realized that the increased pain he experienced in that effort was due to tightly fitted restraints on his arms. Similar results were obtained when he tried moving his legs, arching his back, or shaking his head.

He tried calling for help, but his communicator implant seemed unable to understand his garbled voice, likely due to the feeding tube and ventilator, which he only just realized were still in place.

He wiggled his ears to discover the earplugs and blinked his eyes several times to confirm translucent gauze was covering them.

Enraged, he strained against the restraints, pushing until the pain became too much, relaxing to recover a bit and trying again. Finally, after twenty minutes, all he had managed to do was dislodge one of the earplugs, move the gauze to uncover half of his left eye, and pass out.

The next time Chang woke up, his mind seemed clearer, but almost everything else was the same. The pain was somewhat diminished. He could hear and feel the low thrumming of the ship decelerating, which meant they were within five years of planetfall.

The little bit of vision he got from his left eye confirmed that he was in the brig and not in sickbay.

Bits and pieces of his memory began to flash through his mind: a scene on the bridge where the Prince was shouting and waving a stunner at him; the Emperor, fresh from rejuvenation, demanding the palace ship be readied and the whole court and supporting staff reanimated; and that he had, stupidly, said that it was ten years to planetfall and that there weren't adequate supplies for ten thousand people for ten years.

This bit caused some sort of melee that got him shackled to a bed in the brig. The ship's deceleration confirmed a five-year gap in its tentatively constructed timeline.

Chang contemplated whether all these bits of memory were from the same event and decided they were.

He wondered how it had all resolved, but the only sure things were that he had been in stasis for at least five years, making it five years to planetfall.

He was still mulling over the situation when he heard a mechanical whirring sound and felt the prick of a needle in his arm.

The third time Chang woke up, he was in a small featureless cabin without the shackles, feeding tube, ventilator, or blindfold. His inventory was interrupted by the obnoxious, sniveling voice of a doctor, (whose name, Chang remembered, was Snape) braying, "Good morning' Admiral, how are you feeling today? Your numbers look good across the board, so we are going to start rehab right after we remove the catheter."

"That's not going to happen," Chang sneered as he threw off the sheet and stood at his bedside, towering over the diminutive doctor. "I don't need rehab, and I'll take care of the catheter myself."

"But Sir, I..."

"Shut the hell up and get your sniveling ass out of my sight or," pulling out the catheter, "I'll strangle you with this fucking thing."

"But Sir, I'm just following the Emperor's orders," the doctor said, hugging himself and shaking in a corner near the door.

Chang took a step forward and stared down at the doctor squeezed tightly in his corner. He flicked the catheter-like a whip, opening a small gash above the doctor's left eye.

"I told you to get out. Now! Go! Heal yourself. You've got five seconds before I drag you to the airlock and introduce you to the void."

The doctor slid along the wall to the door, slapped the open button, and fell into the corridor, with his feet just barely past the threshold as the

A New Origin

door slid shut. "Orders from the Emperor?" Chang mused, scanning the room and not finding any clothing.

"Command access!" Chang yelled, "Report today's date, the date the Emperor woke up, confirm transmission of doctor's orders, and send an orderly with my uniform."

"Good morning, Admiral Chang," the deep female voice said, "Today is mission date: T minus five years ninety-seven days; Emperor Hardly-Smyth the First's installation was ten years one hundred and one days ago; orders to wake you were issued yesterday morning; your uniform will arrive in one minute; and you are ordered to report to the bridge ASAP. Is there anything else I can do for you?"

"I'm only one day out of stasis? And did you just say Hardly-Smyth? How did..." he wanted to say, that nut-job moron, but thought better of it, shook his head and said, "Never mind."

"Your uniform has arrived."

The door irised open, and four Marines, in full combat gear, face shields opaqued, pushed single file into the room and spread out against the wall.

The last one, a captain, stepped forward holding a square package with a pair of deck shoes on top. "Put this on," she said in a commanding voice, "the Emperor is waiting."

Chang took the package and opened it, laying the pieces of a formal uniform on the bed. The pants were standard navy officer issue; the shirt, however, was not an admiral's.

"This isn't my shirt," he said, throwing it at the Captain, who caught it and threw it back in a single motion.

"It is Now, Lieutenant Commander," she said with a condescending tone. "Put it on, and that's an order!" she spat as she turned and left the room.

"Well, Marines," Chang said with a sigh, "I guess we best do what the Captain says." He put on the shirt and buttoned it to the top, pulled on the pants, and said, "I need to hit the head. I don't want to piss myself in front of the Emperor."

The marines looked at one another, and the middle one, a sergeant, said, "Be quick about it."

Chang looked surprised, "I know that voice, Commander Maya Jackson! Looks like we both got busted, looks like you got the worst of it though. They sent you to the Marines! That's harsh. I don't remember what happened, but if it was, in any way, my fault, I am truly sorry." She cleared her visor, and he looked her straight in the eyes and mouthed "are we still engaged?"

"You know I can't talk about it, Yuri," she replied sharply, nodding her head ever so slightly and holding her left fist in his face so he could see the thin strand of gold wire barely visible just under the dark skin of her third finger. "Get your ass in the head, now, or we will have to drag you to the bridge with wet pants."

"Aye-aye Sarge!" Chang said as he ducked into the head. He stood for a few seconds trying to recall anything helpful and gave it up in response to the painful stream. He caught a glance at himself in the mirror as he washed up but had to look away from his bruised face and split lip.

"I wonder what I did, or didn't, admit to," he thought. "Must not have been so bad. I'm still alive. Bet it was a close call, though. So, why am I awake now and not floating somewhere in space, and why don't I remember what went on?"

Chang was reaching for the door when he heard, "Get a move on, Commander, or we'll have to drag you out." He opened the door to find Maya holding his shoes, her face-shield still clear, showing her beautiful brown face, dark eyes, and gorgeous smile. She looked straight at him and mouthed, "We'll talk later," as she dropped the shoes on his feet and opaqued her visor.

A small groan escaped his control, another as he sat and slipped on the shoes, and a louder one as he stood back up.

"Oh my, are we feeling our age, Lieutenant Commander?" the Captain sneered from the doorway. "Shall I order you a wheelchair?"

"No, Mam, I can walk, Mam," Chang said calmly, repressing his more rebellious nature.

"Well, just to be sure, you privates take the flanks and drag him if he can't keep up. Sergeant, you have the rear. Kick his ass if he makes a sound!" she shouted as she stormed out the door.

A New Origin

"Aye-Aye Captain!" returned the three in unison as they squeezed Chang out the door and followed the Captain down the corridor in formation.

Chang was disoriented from the moment they left the room and started down the corridor. The first noticeable thing that was wrong was that the door they came out of emptied straight into the hall and was the only door along the five hundred meter length.

The second was that the walls of the brig corridors were red and lit by blue tubes hanging from the ceiling, while this corridor was grey with red light panels.

He didn't remember such a corridor on any of the six towers, though he should have, as leader of the design team and head of the committee that approved the design and oversaw construction.

His contemplation caused him to slow down to the point where Sergeant Maya was forced to give him a toe to the derrière, which had the effect of speeding him up and jarring his memory.

"The forbidden tower!" he shouted, "We're closer than I thought!" Unfortunately, the end result of his revelation was the Captain's baton breaking his nose, as it rendered him unconscious.

The fourth time Chang woke up, he was tied to a chair dripping wet from the bucket of cold water that had been applied to his head.

When the water finished running off his head and his eyes focused, he found himself on the Bridge/Throne Room of the Hexagon. He shook his head to clear the cobwebs, a mistake.

Chang closed his eyes until the throbbing in his nose dropped to tolerable, and he could breathe through it without aspirating blood and phlegm.

When he thought he could speak without sounding completely nasal, he looked up at the Emperor and said, "Well, well, well. Hey Joshey Boy! Finally got that promotion you bragged about. So, how's your wife feel about you offing her old man?"

A near-unanimous noisy intake of breath overtook the crowded room.

"Not that I care what happened," Chang continued. "I'm happy for you buddy, this is as big as it gets. Everyone, three cheers for Emperor Joshua Andre Nottingham Northrup Hardly-Smyth the First! Hip-Hip!"

Complete silence followed. Everyone stared at the Emperor, waiting for his reaction.

Chang shrugged, "Well, I'll be damned; you're all afraid to cheer our leader. What do you think, Your Highness? I think they might be afraid to do something suggested by a supposed traitor. I would kowtow to you, but I am a bit hampered here," Chang said, squirming about in the chair.

Hardly-Smyth looked down at Chang, shook his head, clapped his hands sarcastically, and said, "Damn, Yuri, that was better than I expected. I hoped you wouldn't whimper and whine like the rest of the old court did. But you, Wow! I've been thinking about something my Father-in-law told me a long time ago. He said a good leader needs a loyal opposition that he can keep a constant eye on. He said that no one is right all the time, and, on a rare occasion, one must change one's mind. To do that, he said, you need someone who thinks differently from everyone who's licking your boots.

He told me that was you, Yuri. I had assumed that, because of our checkered history, you weren't that person. However, I just now realized that because *everyone* hates you, you are *exactly* that person. It does explain why none of your ex-wives have denounced you and why your domestic help smile and shrug their shoulders. They know that despite your propensity for insulting everybody and your incredibly annoying habit of always being right, that you will treat them fairly."

The Emperor's expression turned wicked and menacing. Spitting poison, he continued, "So here's the bottom line. It pains me to the bottom of my soul to accept the AI's conclusion that this mission will not succeed without you. I am therefore forced, despite my deepest loathing, to reinstate you, and to show you I mean it, I apologize for the beating we gave you ten years ago, which I see hasn't healed yet."

Chang looked around the room to the extent that he could, took a deep breath, and shouted, "Is everybody ready now? HIP-HIP!" The HURRAH was deafening.

The Emperor, red-faced, jumped from his throne and screamed, "ENOUGH! You! Sergeant! Haul him to sickbay and stick him in a rejuvenation chamber for two weeks."

"Aye-aye, Your Majesty," Maya said as she released the restraints and pulled Chang to his feet. She held his right arm at his bicep and wrist and marched him into the corridor.

She had gotten her hand under Chang's sleeve at the wrist, and as soon as the door slid shut behind them, she began tapping in Morse code: CAMS EVERYWHERE DO NOT REACT YOUR STAFF RE-ASSIGNED GROAN IF UNDERSTOOD.

Chang stumbled, and Maya caught him by his armpits and pulled him up, so they were face to face. Chang blinked, FIND THEM & VISIT ME IN SICKBAY.

OK, she tapped as they resumed walking.

SCENE TWO

Wait. What? This Again?

Admiral Yuri Washington Chang woke up to the smiling face of Commander Maya Jackson in her off-duty civvies. "Maya, my happy warrior, this is much better than the last time," he said playfully, with a wink and a sly smile. "You look way better than the last time I saw you. The combat gear wasn't at all flattering, Impressive, in a common sort of way, but definitely not the fashion statement I prefer to see you making."

"Well now, that's the Yuri I know and sorta tolerate," she said, with a 'not the right time for this scowl' that Chang didn't seem to notice.

"So, tell me, Commander," he said, in his playful voice, "what's been going on in the two weeks since our little adventure?"

"Um... well...um, how can I say this…" she stammered, "It's actually been nine months, and several, very, very strange, things have been going on."

"Nine months?" Chang said, his mood suddenly serious, "I've been in a regeneration tank for nine months? How am I not an infant?" He threw off the sheet and looked himself over, just in case.

"Definitely not an infant," Maya said in a faked dreamy voice, "but a lot younger than you were before. Looks like you're just about my age." Her expression changed to serious; "I don't want you to freak out again, OK? You were only in the chamber two months. The rest of the time was in stasis. They pulled you out of the tank two days ago, drugged you, and dumped you in here last night."

"And where, exactly, is here?" he said, looking around at the small, grey-walled room with two small cots against the walls not quite an arm's length apart. The back wall, less than two steps from the feet of the beds, housed two drawers; a food dispenser; and a shower stall/toilet that was only a few centimeters wider than his shoulders. What he didn't see was a door or a port hole.

"I'm sure you've figured it out," Maya said, watching as he scanned the room. "Welcome to our cozy cottage in the brig."

"And that's supposed to make me feel better?" he said as he stood up and stretched.

"No," she said, trying not to look at his newly hatched, and nearly perfect, thirty-year-old body, "but it helps me organize my thoughts for when I tell you what I know, which isn't a lot. Actually, I only know a little bit about what went on in the two months before I got, shall we say assigned, to supervise your recovery."

"You've been alone here for four months? How is it you're still sane?" Chang said with outraged sympathy.

"I don't know how I did it. Probably because the food dispenser screen doubles as an entertainment device. My undergraduate major was 20th-century flat-screen science fiction movies, I rewatched a bunch of them."

"Too bad our current reality isn't as glamorous as our ancestors imagined," Chang said thoughtfully. "I hope it gave you some insight into our current situation."

Maya looked at the screen, partly as a memory stimulus but mostly, so she didn't stare at Chang. "I think it did. I'll give you a brief summary. At first, I was assigned by Emperor Hardly to stand guard while you were in the re-gen tank in sickbay.

Then, about a week and a half in, there was scuttlebutt from the nurses that Hardly was ill and wanted all patients cleared from sickbay. The next day a squad came and moved the re-gen chamber here. I was ordered to report to the security officer.

When I got to the security office, I was met by General Harris and Admiral Lopez, who told me that everything was fine. Still, as a precaution, the two weeks were extended to two months for logistic reasons above my pay grade, and I was locked in here with you and the re-gen tank. At the two-month point, two medics and a six-man Marine patrol burst in, drugged me, replaced the re-gen tank with a stasis chamber, and left before I came to. That was how it was until a few days ago when my breakfast eggs tasted like shit, and I passed out on the floor. I woke up this morning, and you were snoring up a storm."

"And I woke up with you standing over me, smiling like a butcher's dog," Chang said with a chuckle, "Speaking of which, I smell like a rotten hunk of meat, I'm going to take a shower." He squeezed past her, taking a bit longer than necessary to get to the head.

"I'll get you breakfast." She took the two steps to the dispenser and activated the order screen. "There's eggs and ham, pancakes and sausage, and a yogurt parfait," she said, looking over her shoulder as Chang pulled the shower door closed.

"Yes," he called through the door.

"Yes, what, Yuri?"

"Yes, I'll take one of each; and maybe you could find me something to wear, he said, turning on the shower, "Oh, and coffee."

"Roger that. Coffee, black, and lots of it, just the way you like it," Maya said over the rush of water in the shower.

"Kiddo, you're the best!"

"Who are you calling a kid? 'Cause, right now, I'm older than you."

"We'll see about that. And don't forget the ketchup!"

Maya ordered the menu, with ketchup, for Chang; a yogurt for herself; and three black coffees. A bell rang. A panel slid open; a cart carrying the food and drink, rolled into the gap between the beds as they folded up against the wall. It stopped halfway down the room as seats folded out from the bottoms of the beds. Maya heard the water shut down, followed closely by the air dryer blast, and grabbed an orange jumpsuit from the drawer in the wall next to the shower. The dryer stopped; she held out the jumpsuit to Chang as he stepped out of the shower stall.

"Oh my, how nice!" Chang said, sarcastically, as he pulled on the jumpsuit, "I see old Josh hasn't lost his sense of humor."

"Um...Umm...Ummm," Maya stammered, "Sit down and eat Yuri. You need to be caffeinated and full to hear what else I have to say."

They sat down. Chang picked up one of the coffees and said, "Start the timer. I'm going for the record."

"My implants have been turned off. I'll have to use the food dispenser," Maya said as she stood, turned to the wall, and opened the

A New Origin

display. Finger on the button, she turned to Chang and said, "At your leisure."

"Go!" Chang said as he drained the first cup of coffee in three gulps. The food went down in the fashion of a professional eating contest, and the empty second cup of coffee hit the table at the thirty-second mark. "Ah well. Not quite a record, but close enough," he said with a chuckle. "Now sit down and tell me what the hell is going on!"

Maya sat and quietly sipping her coffee and eating her yogurt until she could see that Chang's patience was running out. Then, finally, she dropped the spoon into the parfait glass with a satisfying clink; looked up at Chang; sighed loudly, and said, in a quiet voice, "Full disclosure, Yuri. I was assigned the task of getting you to tell me all you knew about the coup that unseated; make that possibly executed, Hardley-Smyth ten days after he sent you to the Regeneration tank."

Chang jumped out of his chair, nearly, hitting his head on the ceiling, and began pacing the two steps between the chair and the wall ranting, "You're kidding. Right? I've been awake not quite three days in the last five and a half years, all of them either restrained or under guard, and some bloody moron thinks I know what some other bloody morons were planning. If these are the people in charge, this whole adventure is royally fu… Excuse me... screwed."

He stopped pacing directly in front of Maya. He cradled her face in his hands, bent down, looked straight into her eyes, and kissed her while blinking ONE STEP DOT TWO STEPS DASH. She put her hands on his wrists and squeezed nonsense while flicking OK with her tongue.

The kiss continued for some time without further coded conversation until Chang snapped bolt upright and said, "I think I've got it. The new Junta is fresh out of stasis and doesn't have an accurate timeline, or maybe they are locked out of the computer system. Are *They* even real, or are they a rogue AI, but, if *They* were, why did *They* keep us alive, or maybe, *They*, aren't Navy, and, *They*, put everyone with access into stasis… but you said, *They*, sent you, so they must have known where I was…"

Chang had kept up the nonsense rant long enough to step out, "CAN YOU GET US OUT.... CAN YOU HACK INTO THE FOOD DISPENSER AND START A FIRE OR SEND A FIRE ALARM OR"

Maya stood up suddenly, smiled, winked, and shouted, "Stand Down, Sailor! Enough of this nonsense."

Chang managed a shocked expression, stopped suddenly, and said, "Aye-Aye, Commander."

Maya stepped over to the ramrod-straight Chang, looked up into his eyes, and, with the least possible wink, said, "Sailor, there is something wrong with you. In just under an hour, you have shown disgraceful manners. You have made vulgar comments about your superiors. You have had inappropriate relations with your commanding officer, and you have spouted seriously deranged conspiracy theories. What do you have to say for yourself."

Chang mumbled a series of nonsense syllables which Maya interrupted with, "That's enough, Sailor. Go sit on your bunk while I call Sickbay."

Chang began mumbling again and shuffled over to the wall, folded down the bunk, and sat down still mumbling.

Maya looked at the ceiling and said, "Command Access, Jackson, three five nine nine two."

Access approved; how can I help Commander?

"I have a patient for the psych ward."

We have no record of anyone at your location.

What exactly is my location?

I map you in the command tower, 500 meters from the stern access tube corridor Tower 5.

"Access surveillance records this location," Maya said with a conspiratorial smile while motioning Chang to sit down.

Surveillance is not available at your location. Transport will arrive in six minutes.

"Roger that" she replied, suppressing a laugh. "Jackson over and out."

"Command out" came the reply.

Chang started laughing and said, "I told you…."

Maya cut him off. "Silence, Sailor! Don't make your situation any worse than it is," she said, shaking her finger at him. She coded "maybe it lied."

He bent over, looked down at his feet, and mumbled some nonsense; then suddenly straightened up, and in a childish voice, said, "Where's that nice lady you were talking to?"

In her talking to a two-year-old voice, Maya said, "She'll be here in a minute, Sweetie. Then we'll go for a little walk, OK?"

"OK!" came Chang's, I'm a two-year-old reply, "But I don't know where I am. Do you know how to get home from here?"

"The nice lady is sending a car to pick us up," Maya replied with a wink.

Chang jumped up from his chair, grabbed Maya by the hand, pulled her into the shower, and said with a huge smile, "Let's go outside and wait for them," as he tapped a complicated code on the back wall, which slid open revealing the corridor and a very surprised med-tech pushing a gurney.

Chang grabbed the orderly by the shirt collar and pulled him into the now overcrowded shower stall. "I'm sorry about this," he said as his powerful right hook knocked the young man out.

"Get his clothes off," he said as he pulled off the orange jumpsuit.

Maya pulled off the pants and tossed them to Chang as he sloughed off the jumpsuit and exchanged it for the shirt. Maya got the jumpsuit on the orderly just as Chang finished buttoning the shirt.

"Help me get him on the gurney," Maya said, gripping the man's ankles. Chang picked him up by the armpits, and they swung him onto the gurney. Maya ran back into the room, grabbed a blanket, brought it out, and covered the orderly as Chang tapped another code on the corridor wall, and the door slid shut, blending into the wall without a trace.

"How did you know where the keypads were?" Maya asked, scanning the corridor in both directions.

"I designed the ship," Yuri replied nonchalantly. "Wait here," he said as he sprinted to the end of the corridor. When he got to the end, he tapped the end wall in several places, turned, stood with his heels against the wall, and began pacing. He stopped after thirty-three paces, tapped the wall in several areas then waved for Maya. Chang finished tapping a code that opened a hidden door to a cross corridor as she arrived with the gurney. They pushed it through the door and started down the hall after it. Chang caught her by the back of her shirt and whispered in her ear, "Leave it here.

It's got trackers and an auto-return function, and we need to go a different way."

He turned to the wall, tapped a code, and a door dilated open to reveal a hole in the wall so dark that Maya felt she was looking into the heart of a black hole. She tensed and backed up a half step, "Are we going in there?" she whispered, fear evident in her voice.

"It's the safest place on the ship," Chang whispered as he took her hand and led her through the door which quickly dilated closed behind them.

They stood still in the pitch black for a few seconds. Maya's anxiety increased exponentially until a single candle ignited in a wall sconce some indeterminable distance away. She started toward the light. Chang squeezed her hand and commanded, "Don't move."

She froze, looking at the stoic expression on Chang's dimly lit face.

"It's a decoy," he said, releasing her hand and taking hold of her shoulders. "We go left, one at a time, and yes, it looks solid, but it's not. So put your arms out and move slowly, the entrance is very narrow."

She turned left and felt him move behind her. She took two steps forward, and her left hand brushed the edge of an opening. Her right hand found the other edge not quite a shoulder's width apart. The walls inside the space narrowed as far as she could reach.

"We have to go in sideways, and it narrows as we go in," she said, squeezing through the opening, her back against the left sidewall.

"Go in as far as you can. We'll be OK as soon as I'm through the door."

Maya found the back wall of the nook, and Chang squeezed in with her. After a couple of minutes of twisting and elbows pressing, he said, "Before I close the door, I need to tell you what's going to happen."

"Please don't tell me the floor opens up, and we are blown out a tube into space, where we float to an open airlock and are quickly pulled to safety by space-suited insurgents."

"Well, that's absurd; they'll be androids, and the room is an escape pod, so it goes with us."

"But we'll still be in a vacuum."

A New Origin

"Well, yeah, sort of, but only if the pod breaks or if we have to do a lot of maneuvering. So, push against the walls and take a deep breath ready, 3...2...1."

The floor dropped away, and the room, a transparent box, shot into space.

Maya looked up to see the hull of Tower 5 moving away and down to see the dark hull of what, she supposed, was Tower 6 approaching quickly. A tiny red light appeared just off the tip of her left foot.

"That's where we're going," Chang said, squirming as he tried to get his hand behind his back. "Can you reach behind me? There's a little box with breathing masks. We're going to need them very soon."

"I can try," Maya said, sliding her hands around his waist until her knuckles hit the wall. "OK, Where's this box?"

"Just under my left cheek. The lid flips open when you push buttons on each side."

"I can feel the one on this side," she said, poking him with her right index finger and pulling out her left hand, "the other side's going to need another route. Don't take this the wrong way. Spread your legs and suck in your gut. I'm going in."

While it wasn't the most comfortable solution for either of them, it worked, and Maya pulled her arms out with a breather in each hand.

Almost simultaneously with putting the masks on, the escape pod began using the inside air for the maneuvering jets. Most of the air was used to flip the pod to approach the tower head first. The worst part was that as the air thinned, the temperature went down, and it was well below freezing when two flexible arms clamped onto the pod and pumped in air and heat while they pulled it into an airlock exactly the size of the pod.

Temperature and pressure were nearly back to normal when the pod docked. The gravity activated as soon as the pod bay door closed. Chang had braced for it by pushing on the ceiling to keep his feet on the floor. Maya, who was taller, but couldn't get her arms untangled and had drifted to the roof, came crashing to the floor, landing awkwardly on Chang's feet.

"Dang girl! You're not as light as you used to be. That almost hurt."

"Sorry your feet were in the way of my crash landing. Next time we make a jailbreak, I'll wear my steel boots."

Chang was about to answer when the door opened behind him, and a large man with a full beard and a strange uniform grabbed him by the shoulders and said, "Yuri! About time you showed up, and with Maya too. Yuri, your stepsister has been bugging me for the past twenty years about getting you two down here. She'll be so relieved that the damn roster is finally complete. Hurry up out of there. We gotta jettison the pod before they fix the tracking systems we hacked."

"Hello to you too, Dad," Yuri said laughing. "I had a feeling you were behind all this."

SCENE THREE
When And How Did This Get Here?

Lincoln led Yuri and Maya down what could only be described as an empty sewer pipe and stopped at a door that opened to what appeared to be a dimly lit, empty hanger.

"Nighttime on the farm, I see," Yuri said, with a partially restrained giggle.

"Things are not always as they appear to be," Lincoln said pulling a flashlight and shining it at the open door. The beam disappeared at the threshold without a reflection.

"Energy absorbing force field?" Yuri asked. "Where did that come from?"

"We cobbled it together from parts we 'borrowed' from several fighters that weren't currently in use," Lincoln smiled.

"By not, 'currently in use,' do you mean that others ARE currently in use?" Maya inquired, "And if so, are we facing a threat to the planet?"

Lincoln looked at her with an affectionate smile and said, "Maya my dear, I hope Yuri realizes how lucky he is that you're willingly hang out with him."

Maya laughed, "It's been strangely exciting and fundamentally annoying, but I wouldn't have it any other way. He is kind of cute."

"Kind of cute?" Yuri harrumphed, "That's not what you said yesterday."

Lincoln put an arm around Yuri's shoulders, "You never could take a teasing. But back to Maya's question. Yes, all eight construction rigs and four fighters were launched a couple of days ago and are expected to be in orbit around our future home, knock wood, in three-and-a-half years. We took essential parts from sixty of the remaining sixty-three fighters."

"What do mean by essential parts?" Maya asked, turning the mood to serious.

Lincoln shrugged and nonchalantly replied, "Oh just some simple things like the reactor cores and a few of the weapons' systems. Other than that, they are not noticeably damaged."

Yuri and Maya laughed heartily, and Maya said, "Small things indeed! But why did you leave four operational?"

"They were in the repair shop. Apparently, something, wink, triggered their ejection seats causing minor damage to the fighters but major damage to the three main launch tubes," Lincoln replied.

Yuri, surprised, asked "Just how long has this guerrilla war been going on? And why was I not informed?"

Lincoln turned to Maya with a serious look, "How long was he in stasis and the regeneration tank?"

Maya thought back, did some calculations, and said, "I don't think he was in stasis except, for the four months we were in the brig, and that it's ten years into his third straight thirty-year service term. It was hard to say how old he was when I first saw him. He looked about eighty, but he was roughed up pretty good and wasn't totally sane until after two months in Re-Gen."

"Which explains why I'm not a four-year-old!" Yuri chimed in.

Lincoln looking thoughtful said, "And why you don't remember the years you spent with the resistance."

Yuri, astonished, asked, "What are you talking about, 'years in the resistance'? Are you telling me I was in the resistance?"

Lincoln sighed, "Do you remember the day we got on board the Hexagon?"

Yuri hemmed and hawed, "Vaguely. Was there a woman and an android and a shipping container involved?"

"Yes! There's some memories left! You, Me, Lena, and JB7 stowed away in a cargo container for two weeks before it was moved to the Farm by the underground. Anything else you remember?"

Yuri stared at Lincoln for a few seconds, "I remember JB7. He was my attaché on my first two service cycles."

"I remember him too," Maya said, smiling, "he used to arrange our 'quiet times' in your cabin."

Lincoln laughed, "OK, TMI! I'm going to have a talk with him as soon as he gets his creaky butt down here to lead us through the maze."

Everyone was laughing when a voice from behind them said, "My creaking butt has nothing on your creaking knees."

Yuri and Maya turned simultaneously and hugged JB7. Yuri stepped back and said, "I'm so glad you weren't decommissioned."

"And I am sorry for the memory wipe you suffered under the Emperor twice, wait, thrice removed. Sorry if that's a shock to you, Yuri. I have been out of contact for the last week and just received the updated line of inheritance. But, may I say, the two of you look just as I remember you, from three hundred years ago."

"Always the gentleman," Maya said, hugging JB7 again, "Would you be so kind as to escort us to the Farm?"

"I would be honored," JB7 said reaching into his shoulder bag and pulling out three goggles, "you will need these in the distortion field." He took Maya's arm and said, "If you will follow us gentlemen, lady, we will be there in no time."

They walked through the hanger and down a long corridor that ended at an alcove containing a door that looked like it could have been transplanted from a medieval castle. JB7 entered a code on a panel of the alcove and door creaked open. They entered the door and were faced with six hallways. "This wasn't in the design," Yuri said looking down at each of the halls.

"This is the entry port of the maze," JB7 said. "We constructed it so that entry to The Farm can only be gained in the company of an android who has the current map of the maze. The map changes twenty-five minutes after anyone enters. It should take us no time at all to walk through the maze."

They walked into the first hall to the right of where they entered. After twenty minutes of seemingly random turns down long corridors lined with doors, Yuri said, "I thought you said, 'no time' it feels like we've been doing this an hour."

"How shall I put this," JB said pausing to think, "Except for our first step through the distortion field, we have not actually moved at all. Each step we have taken has taken us to a different position in time, and each turn has traced a path back and forth in time. When we get back to where\when we started, we will be on the other side of the field and in the farm. The fifth door from the end of this corridor is the end of the maze."

"What if we go through the wrong door?" Yuri asked.

"That's what the goggles are for. With the goggles you have about two seconds to close the wrong door before you are sucked into the void. Of the sixty five people without goggles who have opened the wrong door no one has closed it fast enough. There were ten androids that opened the wrong door, they all survived but none of them has solved the maze because it changes every forty-five minutes, and they can't receive the new map while inside the maze."

"I'm thinking that we have about five minutes before the maze changes," Yuri said rushing down the corridor, "and I don't want to miss the chance to get out now!"

"He's correct," JB7 said, "we should hurry!"

The four were through the door and standing on the stern end of the two kilometer long, half-kilometer wide cylinder that was tower six, AKA, the farm. JB7 acted as tour guide, with Lincoln providing narrative asides.

"The starboard side is a stack of five growth plots, three in-ground on the top and two hydroponic under-neath. The port side is made up of fifty stacks of cargo containers, ten high, half of which have been converted into housing for the workers, schools, and shops, with the latter two being unapproved modifications of the original plan. After every ten stacks there is a processing plant and storage silo. The other half of the containers house two thousand stasis chambers, originally occupied by the servants of the elite."

Lincoln chimed in, "Many of which have been awakened, retrained, and introduced to the art of agriculture, first as substitutes for injured farm workers awaiting regeneration, and later by request of the ones who wanted their family and friends out of stasis and free of masters. Every one of the former servants refused to go back into stasis. and, when offered regeneration, wanted as much of their memory deleted to mitigate the pain of forced servitude. Most of our current adult workers are second generation former servants. The stasis chambers now contain a number of piglets, calves, young horses, chickens, ducks, lambs, rabbits, fawns, retired farm workers, puppies of working dogs, a variety of rodents, cats, and goats."

A whistle sounded and the stairs filled with people in yellow jumpsuits and the floor filled with workers in green jump suits leaving the processing plants. The two streams intermixed with occasional brief interactions and greetings. Ten minutes later the outflows had stopped, and the green team was entering containers, and the yellow team was entering the factories. When the crowd had thinned significantly the classrooms opened their doors and a flood of children wearing blue rushed to the stairs and a nearly equal number came out of their home container in orange suits. The kids mixed, greeted siblings and friends and quickly climbed to their containers where a parent met them at their doors.

"Are the kids done with school?" Maya asked, watching them disappear into their containers.

"No this is lunch break; they'll go back after the shops close. They have two, four-hour sessions," Lincoln replied.

Another whistle sounded followed by the announcement, "Shops are open for two hours. Anyone in the shop after that time will not receive service."

Lines had already formed at the shops which would, it seemed to Yuri, take much longer than two hours to serve. Perplexed, he asked, "How can they serve that many people in two hours?"

"Each shop has only one product and each person is only allowed or, more correctly, can only afford, one item," Lincoln replied. "It is often enough to last a family of six for five days. Families with two adults will get two different things, like flour and beans by waiting at different shops. And besides that. the shops are open at every shift change and there are four, six-hour shifts, the two night shifts are skeleton crews about a tenth the size of the day shifts. No adult works more than one shift. The exception, if you wish to call it that, is with the children under eighteen. They attend school or daycare for the two-day shifts. University students attend classes in both the daytime shifts but have free periods throughout the day."

Maya thought for a while, looking at the people and watching their expressions, postures, and interactions. "I may be wrong," she mused, " but aside from the small houses and the regimentation, the people seem to be content with, rather than resigned to, what they have here. There isn't any malnutrition, they aren't being abused, and there's no one in uniform but me and Yuri. So, my question is, how is this the center of a rebellion?"

Lincoln sighed, "That's what I was trying to get Yuri to remember! Come to my office and I'll fill you in. It's actually a pretty cool story. One caveat though, after I tell you, you won't be able to leave here. Which won't be so bad because we're only five years from planet-fall."

"We wouldn't have been able to go back anyway, and I do remember that it had been a prison, and you got yourself appointed Warden for life because you couldn't keep your mouth shut about the Emperor's stealing your wife, aka my mother."

"That sounds right to me," JB7 said. "Let's go see the Warden's office.

JB7 led them up the road to what looked like an abandoned processing plant. They entered a cavernous warehouse that was filled with row upon row of mechanical battle armor. The fronts were open as if they were ready for their operators to jump in and start fighting. On closer inspection it was obvious that they were all missing their power cores. At the back of the room was a safe marked with a lightning bolt, an old fashioned combination lock with a dial that was numbered 1-100 and a sign that said, 'CAUTION incorrect combinations will result in electrocution'. Beyond the rows of mechanical soldier suits was a rickety ladder leading to a door twenty meters above the floor. JB7 nearly flew up the stairs and had the door open before the rest of the group was halfway up.

They were all safely in the sparsely furnished office and seated on folding chairs around Lincoln's two sawhorses and wooden plank desk with a sign that said 'Mayor Chang.' Yuri quipped, "I love the understated elegance you've brought to the office, Dad. It is so you!"

When the giggles died down, Lincoln said, "Welcome to the revolution's war room. JB7, can you project the slideshow onto this?" Lincoln asked taping a white sheet of paper to the back of a ledger standing partially open on the desk.

"If this is going to be another twelve hour presentation, I'm gonna need a lot of coffee and a pillow," Yuri said yawning.

A New Origin

"So, you do have some early memory remaining!" Lincoln exclaimed.

"That one is only there because I wake up to that nightmare two or three nights a week," Yuri snapped, "that and our ride to the Hexagon are my go-to alarm clocks. And, by the way, where *is* my sister?"

Lincoln smiled "That was supposed to be a surprise. She'll be here shortly. She's getting her six great-great-great grandchildren ready for school."

"One too many 'greats,' Pops," came a voice from the ladder, "Remember, I was too busy to have kids the first two thirty-year shifts."

Everyone looked toward the ladder as Lena stepped into the office. She fixed her gaze on Maya and ran to her embrace. For several minutes they stood whispering, laughing, and looking over toward Yuri. When they parted Lena rushed to Yuri and whispered, "You better be treating my daughter right or I'll be having words with you, and before you embarrass yourself, no, she is not your child."

Yuri spun her around looking her over. "Hey Sis, you don't look a day older than the last time I saw you!"

"I just got out of regen, the whole gang is waking up, but Lincoln will fill you in. I'm only here on a meet-and- greet." She broke their embrace and ran to JB7. They stood head-to-head whispering for several minutes.

Maya gestured Yuri over and whispered, "She never told me anything about you even after I told her I was seeing you. She sometimes said vague things about escaping Mars with an android, a mad scientist, and a space force officer, but that's about it. She and my father have had a very long relationship, and I have tons of siblings and cousins, but I had no idea there might be hundreds of us."

"You knew she was Lincoln's adopted daughter, right?" Yuri asked hesitantly.

"Not until just now," Maya said with a nervous giggle.

Yuri had a nervous expression that she had never seen on him before. Maya was about to say something when they locked eyes for several seconds that felt like hours and he whispered "I want to ask you something but I want you to take some time to think about it while we listen to Lincoln's plan to keep the Empire from conquering whoever runs the planet we are five years from invading. I'm certain we can make the plan work, but I need you to be certain my plan will work too."

"I don't need to think about it," she whispered. "I've thought about it for years and I am certain. So yes, we should sign the contract, after all I already have the ring!" The kiss that followed drew the attention of the others.

"Pay up Dad!" Lena laughed.

"I wasn't betting against it, Daughter!" Lincoln cried.

"Dr Chang, I registered your bet as 'yes but no time soon'," JB7 ruled.

Lincoln sighed, "OK, Lena my dear, but no pay-off until after the honeymoon."

Lena leaned over kissed him on the forehead, and said, "And?"

"And they work as a team, no separate assignments."

"And?"

"OK, OK. JB7, can you get these two a room?"

"Already arranged, Sir."

Lincoln sighed, "I guess that's it then. JB7, will you stay with them until they finish whatever this is. I owe my daughter a drink, or two."

Lena, smiling like the butcher's dog said, "Or three or four, I'm off grandma duty for the rest of today, and all day tomorrow.

Curtain

Three weeks after they finished Act four, Andria, Jason, and their friend Sarah were splayed across various pieces of living room furniture, somehow managing to get their heads close enough to each other, to ask and answer whispered queries while remaining deeply involved in reading and taking notes from a variety of books. This is how Katy found them when she got home from work.

Since none of them moved or looked up when she greeted them and asked if they wanted a treat, she tiptoed into the kitchen and put together a snack platter, which she put on the floor within everyone's reach. She was at the kitchen door when she heard Sara mutter, "Thanks Ms. Katy. Do you know when Mr. Collin is coming home? We have some engineering questions."

"Yeah Mom," Andria chimed in, "How loud is a hurricane?"

"Very loud. Dad will be home in about half an hour. He'll give the answer in decibels. Now can I ask why you need to know this?"

"We're all in next week's play and there's a hurricane and we want to know if we need earplugs."

"First, Congratulations! And second Yes you might need earplugs."

ACT FIVE
Introductions, Reunions, and Unification

Chorus

The southern spring plans
The course of future winters
The wind of war looms

The Master of Ceremonies has been pacing back and forth in front of the curtain. He doesn't have his rod or any other object to tap on the stage and he has a look of despair on his face. It is ten minutes past the time the play was supposed to start, and the audience is getting antsy. He continues his pacing for another ten minutes and stops suddenly at center stage with his back to the crowd. He sticks his head between the curtains. A loud rumble of thunder pierces the auditorium. The Master jumps and pirouettes two and a half rotations landing on the edge of the stage facing the cheering crowd. He raises his hands and says, "From here on out things get twisted, untwisted, jumbled and made straight. Enjoy the rollercoaster.

Chorus: The last two colonists to leave Earth and get on the Arc were the newlyweds, Penelope and A-C. They were surprised when they found out that they were also the last two Earthlings to come out of stasis. They were awakened three months before the New Years Eve, that would mark the 500th anniversary of the arrival of humans on Gaia. They were assigned an apartment in downtown Gaia and spent their first week together doing what newlyweds do on their honeymoon and getting acclimated to gravity which is eighty percent of Earth's. During the next month and a half, they learned the common language and worked together with the Tech planning committee designing strategies to combat the Martian invasion. At the end of the month, they were separated. Penelope was assigned to the staff of the Mayor of Gaia City. A-C was assigned to stay on at the Tech research

A New Origin

and development complex in the mountains southwest of Gaia City until he was sent to New Origin on New Year's Eve. We have already witnessed A-C's activities in New Origin on New Year's Eve. He stayed in New Origin for another month organizing a trip to Gaia City for a conference about the imminent Martian arrival. We now join Penelope in Gaia City on Meditation Day which is observed a month after New Year's Day.

SCENE ONE

Who's, Where, Now

Penelope woke to the sun shining through her apartment window and the alarm clock screaming. She looked at the clock, which said 5:30, "Dammit!" she said, throwing off the blanket, slapping off the alarm, and walking toward the bathroom. "You would think, after three months of working every day, I would remember to reset the alarm on a holiday. I guess eight hundred years, seven hundred and ninety-nine and a half of which I slept through, gets one out of normal daily routines. But, on the plus side, it still feels so good to be awake again; and on the bad side I really miss A-C. These two months feel like two years."

She picked up her toothbrush and applied the toothpaste, and said, "Ugh, some parts of waking up may not be as wonderful as others."

It wasn't until she was halfway through brushing her teeth that she remembered that it was Meditation Day, and that she had meant to turn off the alarm clock, with the intention of sleeping until noon. She had developed a habit of talking out loud to herself to get back into the practice of speaking and working to adopt the local cadences and accent which had strayed a great deal from what she had used on Earth.

Toothbrush still in her mouth, she said, "They have such strange holidays here. Meditation Day today and Aphelion Day, last month; a weird, but somewhat logical, way to say New Year's Day; but greeting everyone with a hearty 'Back to the Sun!' is a bit over the top."

Finishing her oral hygiene protocol, also something that needed practice, she continued, "No wonder A-C wanted to meet on the beach. All those sappy beach vids we used to watch when we couldn't get to sleep. I've only been to the beach once since I've been here, and it was raining so hard I was soaked before I even got to the water. The time before that was the night we were at the reservoir in the original Origin, a week before wedding." She paused, awash in emotions she had felt every day since she and A-C had been sent to different places. After three deep breaths she

A New Origin

suddenly remembered, "OMG he's coming today!" she shouted, "Week two of our marriage starts today!"

Pulling herself together, she went to the bedroom to change into something appropriate for the beach, choosing a pair of shorts and a tank top and digging her sandals from under the bed. Just as she finished strapping on the sandals, she stopped, and thought, "Wait, what did the paper say about the weather today, maybe I need a sweater."

She walked into the kitchen and pulled the lid off the recycle bin. Yesterday's paper was near the top of the bin under the soup can and cereal box from yesterday's dinner. She pulled it out and turned to the weather page. "Oh good," she said reading the forecast, "Twenty-two and sunny all day, won't be needing a sweater."

She ducked into the bathroom and grabbed two towels to sit on (A-C always forgot) and was at the door about to leave when she said "Wait, where are my keys?" She turned toward the bedroom, stopped, and said, "Wow, I forgot how much emotion can mess with your head. I don't have keys. Remember, no locks so no keys, and I was going to take lunch." Heading back to the kitchen she grabbed her backpack and stuffed the towels in. She packed half a baguette, some leftover chicken, two apples, and her water bottle and was half-way out the door when the phone, that was implanted in her ear, pinged.

"Answer, audible mode. Is that you, A-C?" she said, backing into her apartment and closing the door.

"Who else has this number, Pen, my love. We just got off the Tech train and settled at the hostel. You can't imagine how awed the Origin gang is. They were like zombies, shuffling along and mumbling nonsense."

"Oh, sweety, what did you expect. Four hours ago, you dragged them down the rabbit hole to

Tech-land; which exactly nobody on this planet, except for the you and I and Techs has seen; stuffed them into a shiny metal tube, and shot them down a fifteen-hundred kilometer tunnel at a thousand clicks per hour, from which they emerged in another, larger and noisier, version of Tech land, and then back above ground to a city 10 times the size of Origin that, until yesterday, they didn't know existed."

"I wasn't thinking much about them. I spent my time fantasizing about us, and by that, I mean mostly you, on the beach this afternoon. I'm so excited to see you I can hardly walk, and my body is tingling like it was on our wedding night. I don't think they dampened the hormone responses when we were resuscitated as much as they said they would."

Penelope giggled and said, suggestively, "Just wait until I get you back here and show you, they didn't do any dampening at all."

"I wouldn't be surprised if they actually goosed it up a couple of notches. They are, after all, pretty geeky nerds with a weird adolescent sense of humor," A-C said, chuckling.

"In case you have forgotten, my forever love, we are barely twenty-two and plenty nerdy! When we got married, we spent four hours doing the kind of things that make them blush. Some things we did exactly for that reason. And then went straight from the honeymoon suite i.e., our apartment, which by the way I miss dearly, to the spaceport center and into stasis where there wasn't anything to watch. Maybe they are just getting some revenge for losing their voyeur gold."

"So, our only recourse was to make them jealous all over again which, I believe, we achieved a couple of weeks ago," A-C said in his sarcastically thoughtful voice which she hadn't heard for a long time.

After they stopped laughing, A-C said, "You should start walking now, but don't rush. If you walk at your normal pace, you should be at your office building as your boss is coming out the door. I called her and asked her to talk to you just to establish you as an essential player and Tech-ese interpreter. I told her about the meeting and gave her the guest list. I hacked her phone when I called her, and she has called all sixty-five people on the list. She's been calling your place for the last twenty minutes, but I sent her calls directly to voice mail. She seems desperate to get hold of you, and I think she will try to come to your place. We need to get her to go to the beach so that you can coach her. She's a very strong telepath and I think she already suspects it's real. When I get there, we'll fill her in on our plan to defeat the Imperial invasion by enhancing our natural telepathy.

"What if she refuses?"

"First, she won't because, in case you hadn't noticed, she's in love with you, and she's in the middle of a break-up with her partner. And second, you're going to get her to go. Tell her everything, well, everything

A New Origin

except that last bit about the break-up," A-C said sheepishly, "she doesn't know you know about that yet."

Penelope sighed and said, "Oh, my dearest love. After eight hundred years you should know I can't keep a secret. I will try, but no guarantees."

"And you should know that's one of the things I really love about you. In any case, I've got a bit of business at the hostel. I've got to ring off and you need to get on your foot. I'll see you in about five hours. Love you."

"I don't know if I can wait that long without going bonkers, but I'll try just for you. Ciao for now, my love. Close connection"

Penelope took several deep breaths before she picked up her backpack. She stuffed in a third towel, went out the door, turned left down the hallway to the stairwell, and went down the two flights of stairs to the street.

Main street was nearly empty, only a few electric carts, a couple of horses, and a few pedestrians. It was warmer outside than she had anticipated, and was about to comment on that, when she remembered to stop talking to herself out loud in public. She joined the trickle of people, mostly couples, strolling eastbound down the sidewalk.

The city sloped gently up from the seashore and was built on an east west grid with north-south cross streets every hundred meters. Every third block was a green space that extended the entire length of the cross streets. The east-west streets ran every three-hundred meter ending at the ocean shore. Penelope walked down Main street from her apartment, at 650 Main, nearly every day to her office at the city planning department 100 Main. She slowed as she neared the steps leading to the stone facade and was watching the tall double doors out of which emerged her boss, Mayor Lisa Day, just as A-C had predicted.

"Penelope!" Lisa shouted, rushing down the stairs, ending in a big hug. "I am so glad to see you! I tried calling you at home, but you obviously weren't there. I just had a call from, of all people, the chief Tech! And he asked to talk to you! When I told him you weren't here..." As Lisa paused to catch her breath, Penelope tried to break into the frenetic stream of words but failed. Lisa went on, "he told me I needed to set up an urgent meeting for tomorrow with the city commission and the chairs of all the operational committees and that you were essential as a liaison with the Techs. I tried calling but you were out, and I was going to camp on your stoop until you got home because you interned with the Techs and I thought you could maybe figure out what they wanted, and now here you are, sooo..."

Lisa paused again. This time Penelope was ready and said, "Come to beach with me. I brought lunch for two, and I even have two towels. Really, you need to hear the whole story before the meeting, and you absolutely need to be in a calm place when you do."

Lisa smiled, hugged her tightly, and said, "I shouldn't, I want to, but there are some issues I need to address before, before I, it wouldn't be good for me to be with you," she started sobbing with her face in Penelope's shoulder.

Penelope rubbed her back and whispered, "I know, I shouldn't know but I do. I know you're not in a good place right now, and this whole situation can't do anything to make it better, but I do know that if you don't come with me now the meeting tonight will totally break you. So, we are going to walk to the beach, and you are going to be a tour guide. This is the closest to the ocean I've been, and you know I'm detail oriented, so maybe you could point things out to me."

They were three blocks down the street when Penelope finished talking and another two before Lisa lifted her head and said, "Judy and I are having a bad spell, and I don't think we can fix it," putting her head back on Penelope's shoulder.

"I shouldn't know that, but I do," Penelope whispered, "and I wish I had an answer, but that is the one piece of the puzzle I'm missing. But on the bright side, we can see the ocean!"

What had been a bright shiny area at the end of the street had resolved into a flat blue plain with shimmering white lines marching in from the horizon toward the narrow gold strip of beach. The street ended at a cul-de-sac two-hundred meters from the shore with the sidewalks merging at the end and continuing to the beach. As they got closer, she realized that the beach was about seventy meters wide, half sand and the rest grass. What had looked like big waves from afar were, at the most, a meter high and washed gently on tan and white rocks, fine gravel, and sand at the water's edge.

There were quite a few people, mostly families with multiple children. The rest were young adults pretty much equal parts couples, singles, and a scattering of small rowdy groups. Most of the young adults were set up on the sand, with the families set up on the grass. Only a few of the older children were braving the sixteen degree water, mostly dodging the waves lapping the shore.

Penelope and Lisa spread their towels and walked out to the water's edge, and gingerly waded a short way into the water. The waves came up to their ankles as they walked away from the shore, and only got to their knees when they were a fifty meters in. Looking up and down the shore Penelope could see people much farther out, but they were still no more than waist deep.

"You can go out about two hundred meters before you have to swim," Lisa said, smiling, "but it feels really good as a foot bath, and as a quick shower." With a sly grin she kicked up a spray at Penelope, who responded in kind, starting an all-out battle royal leaving them both wet and laughing.

"Welcome back, Boss!" Penelope said with a huge smile, as they walked back to the beach.

They had just finished toweling off and were sitting on their towels, chatting about work, when Penelope suddenly went blank and stood looking up at the beach. Lisa stood up too and said in a concerned tone "Penelope, are you ok? Is something wrong?"

Penelope turned to Lisa with a huge smile on her face and said, "Oh no it's the exact opposite of wrong! I just saw a young man coming down the beach that you need to meet, and I desperately need to kiss."

"Boyfriend?"

"Husband."

"Really! Newlyweds?"

"Kind of, it's difficult to explain. We're approaching both our three month and eight hundred year anniversary."

Lisa stopped, looked at Penelope and said, "I know new relationships feel like time has stopped, but…" she paused, and looked deeply into Penelope's hypnotic eyes for several seconds. She broke the contact, shook her head, and sat down. She looked back up to Penelope and said "Holy shit! You're serious. I don't know why, but I believe you."

"Aha!" Penelope cried, "Now you're ready to really hear our story!"

She sat down facing Lisa. "I just now learned something important about you. You have a talent that allows me to communicate with you without speaking. Everyone on Gaia has this talent, but almost no one can use it without being taught. I just told you a part of the story, and if you think about it the details are there. I am going to give you a more detailed account now. It helps if we lock eyes, it is not essential but helps while you are learning to translate the thought stream. Ok, are you ready?"

Lisa thought for a second about what Penelope had said and realized that she knew the story of the wedding and the rush to upload before the radiation killed them, and the memory storage, and their being in stasis and even a bit about the singularity. She also realized that there was much more, and so much that hadn't been said. "All that in 5 minutes?" she said looking up.

"Do you want more now, or do you want to process that?" Penelope asked.

"I think I'll process. There is one thing I know for sure," Lisa replied.

"Is it that you know what A-C, looks like?"

"It sure is! And maybe, when I think about it, it might be TMI." She paused, her closed eyes suddenly opened wide, and she said "Oh My! Definitely TMI! You are a very lucky girl. Oh, and one more thing, he's about two hundred meters up the beach and you better get there quick because I see about twenty unlucky girls checking him out."

Penelope sprang to her feet turned briefly and with a wink, said "They better not get in my way," and took off at what Lisa thought must surely be a world record two hundred meter sprint, the last three meters of which she was airborne. A-C caught her under the arms and spun her around three times their lips glued together and her legs parallel to the ground. The fourth twirl was slower, and they ended standing their lips and eyes locked.

"Did you miss me?" she said laughing when they finally came up for air.

"Not for one second," he said in a distracted tone which was met with "What!" and a sharp jab to his arm.

"Ouch! You misunderstand, my love, I have missed you EVERY second" which was met with another long kiss.

"I think we've made ourselves a spectacle" she messaged.

A New Origin

"Then it's time for a curtain call," he replied, *"North, East, South, then West. I'll curtsey, you bow."*

Applause and cheering came from all four directions, so they did another round, and ended by skipping hand in hand back to where Lisa was standing, laughing hysterically. The three of them group hugged.

A-C stepped back from the women, raised his hands and bellowed "Thank you! Thank you!" to a new round of applause. Then, stepping back and sweeping his arm toward Lisa, "Let's hear it for the Mayor!" again to hearty applause. A-C again raised his hands and called out, "We are taking our show on the road, but we will be back with the full cast in a few weeks, tell your friends that A-C, Penelope, and company will be performing our newest play. The Mayor's office is sponsoring a special showing and will notify you of the time and place. I guarantee, You! Will! Be! Amazed!" he bowed in all directions and sat down.

Lisa and Penelope exchanged glances, and simultaneously said "What the hell was that?"

A-C put on a hang dog expression and said "Sorry for the surprise announcement, but it seemed like the perfect opportunity to gain a bit of name recognition. We are going to need all the support we can get, by which I mean everyone. May as well make it interesting and entertaining. Besides, as I recall, Pen my love, it was your idea. Your exact words were, 'The play's the thing wherein we'll catch the conscience of the king'."

"OK, busted. I will say you pulled it off with great panache and I would be glad to be your leading lady in our great passion play."

"What do you think, Madam Mayor, how would an extravagant staging of our plan to defeat the Oppressor will play with the masses?" A-C asked with an outrageous flourish.

Lisa looked puzzled so Penelope jumped in "We have yet to define the Oppressor."

"In that case, we will endeavor to weave our tangled web as we stroll the grounds to meet members of our merry cast of unsuspecting thespians from the hamlet of New Origin," A-C declaimed as they packed the towels and lunch remains. They walked to waters' edge and started back toward the hostel. Penelope and A-C spent the next half hour helping Lisa gain mastery of her newly discovered talent, and talking silently about the imminent threat, without alarming the passersby.

SCENE TWO

Who Knew What There Was There

The late morning sun reflected off the full length mirror on the half open bathroom door and directly on Adam and Lily's heads, causing them to wake at 1:30 PM. After their midnight departure, a two hour ride on a train (that, until last night, they didn't know existed), a two hour orientation, a one hour check in at the hostel, and an hour adjusting to their room, they had set the alarm for 3:30 to get a normal full night's sleep. Aside from that small problem, the room had been something of a surprise. Unlike the barracks rooms found in Origin's hostel, it was a single room with a private bathroom. This was a definite plus in Adam's opinion and a luxury in Lily's. Adam got up and closed the bathroom door, redirecting the sunbeam, but it was too late; they were both wide awake.

"I can close the blinds as well," he said, looking toward the windows.

"It's no use," Lily said as she poked her head out from under the blanket. "I'm awake, hungry, and I have to use the bathroom."

"Ok, but let me go first, I'll be quick," he said, already halfway in. Lily was at the door waiting when he came out thirty seconds later.

"Wow, record time! I thought I'd have to drag you out," she said, shoving him out of the way and closing the door before he could respond.

Adam was looking out the window at the ocean when she came out three minutes later fully dressed and ready for the day. "Why aren't you dressed? I told you I was hungry, get a move on or I'm leaving without you," she said teasingly, her hand on the doorknob.

"Hold on a minute. My clothes are in the bathroom, and I need to brush my teeth. You go ahead to the dining room and order. I'll be along shortly," Adam said to Lily's back halfway out the door.

"You better get there before the food comes or I'll eat yours, too," she chided, pulling the door closed. The sky was cloudless. The full force of the sun hit her directly in the face, only slightly inhibited by the large

109

A New Origin

broad leaves of the tall trees with straight, branchless, scalloped trunks that lined the shore path. She paused for a second to watch the gentle waves lap the sand. "This is amazing," she thought, "I wonder why they didn't tell us about this, or, for that matter, anything about Gaia's geography. Maybe we just never thought to ask." She shook her head and turned toward the cafeteria, then stopped short and said out loud, "We didn't have a single geography book in the library or the archive, not Gaia, not Earth, nothing!"

"Really?" said Adam, who had come up behind her.

Startled, she turned around, grabbed him by the shoulders, and shook him, saying 'Yes. Really! I only just now thought of it. I don't know why I never thought about it before, or why no one else ever thought of it, or why, as a naturally curious species, we weren't willing to look beyond those early high school expeditions."

"Or why they were completely shut down after mine," Adam chimed in.

"Or why no one questioned the decision or spoke about bringing them back," she said walking toward the cafeteria door. "Let's talk about this after lunch."

"Definitely! And we'll have a few words with A-C this afternoon," Adam said, joining her at the door.

The doors to the cafeteria were decorated with ornate carvings depicting the trees that lined the walkway. "Do you know what these trees are called?" Lily asked looking back and forth between the door and the path.

"A-C called them coconut palms when we got here last night," Adam said, pointing up into the leaf canopy, "See those enormous nuts? They are supposed to be edible."

"Maybe they'll have some inside," Lily said, grabbing his shirt and pulling him through the door.

The room was large by Origin standards, with about sixty tables which had four, six, and eight seats. The rear wall was lined with booths that looked like they could hold ten or twelve people each. Up front was a bar with high stools and a brass railing.

There was a smattering of couples and families eating and talking but the place was far from full. As they scanned the room a young man in black pants, a white button-down shirt, and a towel draped over his arm approached them. "Welcome to the Palm Room," he said with a flourish. "Just the two of you this morning?"

At that moment Adam spied William and Dana sitting at the bar with plates and beer mugs, chatting with the bartender, a large man that Adam thought looked quite a lot like William. "I think we'll join our friends at the bar," he said starting over in that direction.

"Very good, sir. I'll bring the menus right over."

"This is perfect," Lily said as they approached the bar, "you can talk to William about beer and horses, and I can talk to Dana about our missing geography."

As they walked toward the bar no one seemed to have noticed their approach, but Adam was sure that William knew he was there. He whispered to Lily, "Wait for it."

William, still looking down at his food said, "Wait for what? Some lazy bum to finally get his sorry ass out of bed and look into the wellbeing of his old friend. I don't think so!" He picked up his beer and took a deep draught.

Adam, settled himself on the bar stool and said, "Barkeep, two of whatever my grumpy sleep deprived friend is having, and two of whatever the women want."

Dana, who was standing and hugging Lily, said with a wink to Adam "We'll have the beer, too. It's so much better than what we get at home."

"Ouch! Betrayed by my partner of 65 years," William said. He looked up to Adam with a faux hangdog face, "She's right, of course, but I'm betting my good friend here wouldn't have been so blunt about it."

"There," Adam said with a consoling pat on William's back, "No doubt about it, I definitely would have been much worse!" resulting in a round of good-natured laughter.

The waiter arrived with the menus, but before he could say anything Lily said, "I am so hungry I'll take whatever you can get out here in five minutes or less."

"That would be the burger and fries," he said.

A New Origin

"I'll take that, and so will he," pointing to Adam, "Don't even give him a menu, he'll take all afternoon trying to decide, and I can't wait."

"Yes Mam," he said tentatively, looking over to Adam.

"If I were you," Adam cautioned, "I'd be moving already. You don't want to see her when she's famished, it gets very uncomfortable," the last part said to his retreating back.

"What's a burger and fries?" Lily asked the bartender, whose name tag, strangely enough said William, as he served their beers.

"It's a pan-fried ground beef patty sandwich with a side of deep-fried potato spears," he replied. "I'm surprised you don't have them up north."

"Oh, we have them. We call it chopped steak and french potatoes. Never thought to make it a sandwich though, and we serve the potatoes with gravy," she said.

"Interesting, served that way we call it cube steak with poutine. Funny we have the same stuff with different names, like what I call Lager, he," pointing to William Dee, "calls Pilsner. I think we're going to have to negotiate a universal beer nomenclature. How about right here after the meeting tonight?"

"I'm all in, as long as there is Lager involved!" William replied.

By this time Lily and Adam had lost track of the discussion, as their food had arrived, and they were concentrating on nothing else. Lily dipped a fry in the dollop of red sauce, on her plate. She popped in her mouth, looked at Dana pop-eyed and said, "How do you like that! They have Zup here!"

"We call it Kaysup here," replied bartender William. "Our chef makes it from a secret recipe. She might share it with you if you promise not to tell anyone how she does it."

"Thanks, William," Lily said, downing her last bite. "I'll go talk to her now."

"She'll be busy now, but I'll introduce you at the meeting tonight. I have a bit of influence, not a lot, mind you, Diane and I have only been married forty years." After the chuckles, he added "Oh, and you should call me Will. Too many Williams around here, especially when they all look alike."

"Ah come on, we don't look that much alike" said William, followed immediately by "Oh yes you do" from three voices in unison.

Will laughed and said, "And wait 'til you meet my father, William Senior. Dana won't know which of you two to take home."

Dana blushed and said, "Well maybe I'll just have to bring them both and sort them out after."

When Will stopped laughing, he looked at Dana with a puzzled expression and said, "when you laughed just now you reminded me of my mom, Sara. When I look closer, I see even more of a resemblance. Wait a second, I've got some photos behind the bar."

Lily noticed that the room had filled significantly since they had come in, most of the tables were full and people had started to line up the bar. "I think we should let Will get back to work," she said looking his way. "Looks like you get a big crowd for lunch here. Is this normal?"

"Well, considering that this is a holiday, I'd say we are pretty much on target. I expect we'll be full for the next couple of hours," he said surveying the room.

"You need a hand at the bar?" William asked. "I do know something about that type of work."

"Thanks, but I have four helpers just now strapping on their aprons," Will responded. "I will take you up on your offer for tonight at the meeting. I've seen how you New Origin people drink, so if you are behind the bar we may just have enough beer to make it through the night."

"Challenge accepted! I can short pour with the best of them" William replied, holding out his right hand.

Will shook William's hand and said, "We'll see about that, Mate."

While this was going on, Lily had gathered up Dana and was maneuvering her toward the door.

"Dana," she said, "I have some serious questions that you are the most qualified to answer."

"Nothing too intimate, I hope" Dana replied with a grin.

"Oh no, none of that. It's even worse, it's really wonky stuff about geology, and the best place for that is a walk along the shore out there. I'm

A New Origin

sure you've been itching to get out there, so the four of us are going out, and you are going to give us a geological education."

She looked back as they got to the door and said in her best librarian/teachers' voice "Boys! We are going for a walk on the beach. Your attendance is MANDATORY!" With this she and Dana were out the door and partway across the lawn toward the beach.

"What brought this on?" Dana asked looking out over the water.

"It just occurred to me that I don't know anything about the geology, and maybe more accurately, the geography, of our planet, or Earth either for that matter. I know the area within a hundred kilometers of Origin, but I don't know anything outside of that, except that Adam and William's class expedition saw mountains a thousand kilometers south, and that no one even thought to go back. We suspected there was an eastern ocean because our rivers flow east and have to end somewhere, but we never bothered to look for it."

Dana stopped walking. Her forehead scrunched and her eyes glossed over. "You know what's really weird?" she said in a trance-like monotone, "I used to think about this before A-C told us about it. As soon as I started to follow up I got distracted. A couple of times I went into the archive and I forgot what I was there to search for. It was so frustrating that I've given up trying." The far off look faded quickly. She shook her head and gazed out at the ocean. "Isn't that beautiful! I never thought I would get to see anything like this. Let's take our shoes off and walk along the shore. I'll tell you about oceans, plate tectonics, continental shelves, subduction, and mountain building."

"Sounds good to me, I love it when you get in lecture mode," William said, as he and Adam caught up.

Adam looked at Lily and saw her 'I've got something to tell you' face, followed quickly by her 'follow my lead' face.' He nodded slightly as they all sat down and started to take off their shoes.

"Oh crap!" She said struggling with the laces of her ankle high boots.

"Don't tell me you've done it again," Adam said, looking over to Dana and William. "This happens all the time when she gets up hungry or in a hurry. You guys start. I'll have this undone in short order."

Barely suppressing his laughter, William said, "I've got a jack-knife in my pocket if you need it."

Adam sighed, "I have one too. It usually doesn't come to that, but I always come prepared."

As they started toward the shore Dana turned back and said, "Don't worry I won't start the lecture without you."

Adam sat back as Lily undid the laces and slipped off her boots. "I asked Dana about Gaia geography," she whispered conspiratorially. "It was the strangest thing. She seemed to go into a trance and told me that before A-C arrived, every time she tried searching the archive she only got started entering her query and suddenly forgot what she was doing. What's really strange is that after she said that she shook off the trance and didn't seem to remember what she'd just said."

"Seems like we have another set of serious questions for brother A-C," Adam said standing and offering Lily a hand up. They picked up their shoes and ran down the grass and onto the sand.

When they caught up to Dana and William, Dana was crouching near the water's edge picking up rocks. She bounced up as they approached and held out her hand containing an assortment of small to medium sized pockmarked white stones. "Look at this," she said excitedly. "This is called pumice. It is a product of volcanic activity, and it floats!" She pointed to a small island "If you watch closely, that island moves up and down with the waves. It is pumice too! A floating island! A patch of pumice that size almost certainly came from a lava flow into the ocean, and relatively recently. You may have noted that the island isn't exactly bobbing up and down but seems to be undulating. So, students, what do you think that means? Dr. Cavel, any ideas?"

Dana poured the pumice rocks from one hand to the other as Adam hemmed and hawed.

"I've got it!" Lily cried, "It's not solid."

"A-plus to our Librarian. It's more a raft than an island. I suspect the next big offshore storm will blow the whole thing on to the beach," Dana sighed, as she poured her stones into Lily's out-stretched hands. "At least we got to see it."

A young couple, watching their two toddlers splashing in the water, had been listening as Dana lectured. The young woman approached shyly and said to Dana, "I'm sorry for eavesdropping, but we've been talking

A New Origin

about that island since it showed up six months ago, and what you just said confirmed what I thought."

Dana, astonished, looked at her and said excitedly, "Oh Sweetie, I've been teaching geology for forty years. It makes me so happy when anyone pays attention, let alone has information that supports my observation! Can I ask you a couple of questions?"

"I knew you were a geologist. My partner, Jim, and I, I'm Marta by the way, met in Geology One at University. He majored in Civil Engineering, but I continued in Geology. I'm writing my PhD thesis on the theory of plate tectonics. It's funny that our paths haven't crossed sooner, there aren't that many geologists around here."

Dana stood drop-jawed for a couple of seconds then said "I am ab-so-lutely gobsmacked. From my point of view, the chance of us meeting was infinitesimal." She shuddered, took a deep breath, and continued, "We," sweeping her arm at William, Adam and Lily, "just arrived from the city of New Origin, a thousand kilometers northwest of here. Until last month the ocean was only a rumor, and Gaia City was an unimagined place."

"I should have known!' Marta said, laughing. "You're here for the meeting this afternoon! But let me guess your questions. We had a couple of small earthquakes about two years ago, and a small ash fall about six months later. That's why I was pretty sure our floating island was a pumice raft."

"You are spot on. I'm Dana, and this is my husband William and our colleagues, Lily, and Adam. We just now got started on a walk on the beach before the meeting starts." Greetings and hand shakes were made all around.

Jim, who was standing in the water with the children, waved his greetings and called out, "Marta honey, I think we need to get the twins to the babysitter."

Dana and Lily simultaneously said "Twins! How lucky"

"Indeed, we are," Marta replied, "But Jim's right, we need to get the girls changed fed and to the babysitter, and you need to enjoy your walk."

Following the round of cooing at babies and 'see you soon,' the New Origin four spent the next forty-five minutes going from ankle deep in the water to up onto the sand, gathering stones and shells as they went.

Richard Koepsel

******

Half an hour into their shore-walk toward the hostel, A-C and Penelope had picked up their pace, and pulled away from Lisa, who was hurrying to catch up to them after stopping to pick up a couple of floating rocks. Lisa was on the verge of catching them up when they stopped so suddenly that she crashed into their backs and fell into the sand.

"There?" Penelope asked.

"Yes" A-C said.

"What?" Lisa asked brushing the sand off her knees.

"Originals, Originians, Originites, I don't know which they prefer, we'll have to ask them," A-C replied.

"You knew they were coming," Lisa said, pulling even.

"They're late." Penelope observed.

"Yes. We'll have to run a bit to make up time" A-C said sprinting up the beach.

"On your right" Penelope called as she passed A-C.

"On your left" called Lisa as she splashed past at waters' edge.

"I've got your back" A-C called as the women closed rank and pulled further ahead of him.

Dana was showing the others a particularly large garnet that she had just picked up when they were startled by the approach, and sudden skidding stop, of the three determined runners.

"I have a very important question for you that I should have asked back in New Origin" A-C said, stepping out from behind the taller women, "Which do you prefer, Originals, Originians, or Originites? You can talk it over as we head back to the hostel, which we must do quickly. Oh, and you should feel free to consult with my wife Penelope, and Lisa, her honor the Mayor of Gaia City, they are both guaranteed to have lots of opinions.

The sign on the door of the Palm Room said "We're Sorry. We are Closed for a Special Event 4:30 – 11:30."

A-C looked at Adam "Am I right that it's now 4:30?"

A New Origin

Adam looked at his wristwatch "No, it's 4:00. I thought the meeting started at 5:30."

"It does," A-C replied, "Pen and I were supposed to be here at 4:30. I guess we have a few minutes to freshen up, and what not."

Lisa separated from the pack and pulled the door open, "I'm the one that's supposed to be here at 4:00 to help set up. You are welcome to come early. The bar opens at 5:00. I know us Gaians will all be here by 5:01," she said as the door closed behind her.

Adam and Lily started down the walk to the left, and William and Dana started off to the right when A-C said "Hold on a minute. You didn't answer my question."

Lily stopped, looked back at A-C, and said, "We thought Originals would be pretentious, and Originians was too hard to say, so by unanimous vote we will be, Originites."

A-C watched the Originites strolling toward their rooms, looked at Penelope and messaged, *We should wait until they get into their rooms.*

"NOT!" they both shouted and ran hand-in-hand. They passed William and Dana, who were just opening their door, and were twenty meters up the path before William could shout "What's your hurry?"

Dana punched his arm, and laughing, said "I guess that, maybe, it's been a while."

"Gives a person an idea," William said. Sweeping her into his arms, they disappeared into their room.

Lily and Adam were in their room when they heard someone shouting. "Sounds like William," Adam said as he massaged Lily's foot. "In any case it didn't sound angry."

Lily sighed with pleasure as he moved to her other foot. "It just occurred to me that this is the first time we have been alone, without being totally exhausted, since you got back from the hospital," She said sheepishly.

"I know," he said as he moved to her calves.

SCENE THREE
Where Here Meets There

The two Originite couples converged at the Door of the Palm Room at 5:02 amidst a small crowd made up of several of their Origin colleagues and what they presumed were their Gaian counterparts. Penelope and A-C greeted them at the door and pointed them to a long table that had been set up just inside the door with a big sign that said, Registration. The table was manned by a group teenagers. "You guys talk to these eager young volunteers, and they'll give you your name tags and info package. Pen and I have to get ready for our presentation, so we'll see you later," A-C said. He and Penelope merged into the crowd, with handshakes and greetings as they passed through.

The kids at the table had name tags with their name, year, and school. Adam and Lily were greeted by a very bubbly young woman whose name tag said Nanette, Senior, Goose Town High School. "Hi Mr. A-C and Ms. Penelope, I'm ready to go there. How can I help you?"

Adam and Lily looked at each other and laughed. Nanette cringed and whimpered "I'm so sorry, did I do it wrong?"

"Oh no, dear," Lily said gently "It was totally understandable. I'm Lily Alro, Penelope's sister, and my husband, Adam Cavel, is A-C's twin brother. We get mixed up all the time."

"I'm so excited to meet you!" Nanette bubbled, "It was so exciting to learn that there was another city. No one I know has ever heard of New Origin. So, welcome to Gaia City! We just celebrated the 250th anniversary of our founding, I understand that Origin just celebrated its 100th. It's so weird that it took a hundred and fifty years for us to discover each other. I still can't believe that I get to be one of the first in Gaia City to meet you guys," she said, finally pausing to take a breath.

Adam took the opportunity, "I'm glad to meet you too, Nanette. We also were surprised to learn about Gaia City. I do have one question for you. What exactly is Goose Town?"

A New Origin

"OH, It's a neighborhood on the north side of the city. It's on Goose lake where tons of geese overwinter," Nanette said, looking through a stack of brown paper envelopes. "We have a bunch of neighborhoods in the city, mostly named for places that were small towns that got merged into the city." She pulled two envelopes from the stack, "Here you are Ms. Alro and Dr Cavel." She paused a second as she passed the packet to Lily "I had another woman here a couple of minutes ago who looked a lot like you," she said with a puzzled look.

"Thank you, dear. That would be our daughter Sherri, I see her over by the bar. You have a good evening, Nanette" Lily said taking the envelope and heading toward the bar.

"Thank you," said Adam receiving his packet, "are you staying for the meeting?"

"Kind of, I'm serving horse doors at the reception," she said happily.

"I don't know what horse doors are, but I'll try them when you bring them around."

"You'll like them, I'm sure. They're little bits of different kinds of food with little sticks in them so you can pick them and eat them."

"Sounds good, I'll look forward to seeing you later."

Adam turned away from the table and almost immediately found William and Dana surveying the room. He walked behind them, patted William on the back and said, "Looks like the bar is getting busy."

"Yup. Duty calls. I'll see you over there," William said as he made a bee line to the bar.

"Oh look, there's Marta," Dana said as she stared into the crowd, "I'll see you later Adam."

Adam opened his packet and pinned his name tag to his shirt. He pulled out the information booklet and read the participant list. His was the first name on the Origin list and he was identified as Physician/Astronomer. About halfway down the Gaia list he found Newel Johns, who was listed as Astronomer/Physician. Rather than walking through the crowd and staring at peoples' chests, Adam went to the bar to ask Will if he knew Newel, and if he, or she, was in the room. Working his way to the bar he saw most of the Origin group, including his wife, daughter, and son-in-law involved in one-on-one discussions with Gaians. Will saw him immediately, quickly interrupted his conversation with a woman dressed in a chef's uniform, a "Hey Adam, I'll be right with you. Don't go away until I get back," He called, heading toward the far end of the bar.

"Ok but bring a beer with you," Adam called back.

"Already poured, Boss" Adam heard William call from the other end of the bar.

Ten seconds later there was a beer in Adam's hand and William saying "There's some guy who's been looking for you. Heaven knows why, but Will thinks it's important for you two to meet. Fill me in later, I've got a near riot on my hands down there" Turning on his heels, he hurried back to a group of about twenty-five people waiting for beer.

As Adam, his back to the bar, scanned the room, a tall, white haired man sat down in the seat next to him, offered his hand, and said, "Dr. Cavel? I'm Newel Johns. We really need to talk about the stars."

Taking the offered hand, Adam said "Please, call me Adam. I saw your name on the attendee list and was asking about you, for that very reason. But before we get to what we know about the stars, maybe we can start with a beer and some small talk."

The sound of beer steins hitting the bar behind them was followed by William's booming voice, "This is a conversation I need to hear," he said, as Adam and Newel swiveled to face the bar, the beers, and William's triumphant smile. He hooked his thumb toward Adam, "This one's going to need to be fact-checked, as per the agreed upon terms of, "The Wager." he said with air quotes.

"The wager, you say. Sounds like an intriguing story indeed!" Newel said, in a plaintive voice loud enough to hush the crowd. It sounded rehearsed to Adam.

"Intriguing indeed!" William continued, turning up the volume, "An Origin original, told by an original Originite, of his decades long search for Origin's true origin story. Complete with the intrepid searcher's conjuring of the spirits of the true, original humans, from the original town of New Origin, on our planet of origin. His tampering with the dark forces prompted a dire warning of an imminent encounter with a different, more savage strain of original humans. A strain which embodies the plagues that destroyed our original home: Greed and its partner Avarice; Pride and its partner, Narcissism; Authoritarianism and its partner, Domination;

A New Origin

Capitalism and its partner, Slavery. So, a wager in a bar 30 years ago that turned a physician into an astronomer (a profession to which his son now adheres), has exposed the imminent arrival of what could be the end of our gentle lifestyle."

William paused for a moment, looked around the room to a sea of stunned faces, and continued, "So I have to ask, in the end did I really win the bet? Or did my best friend of ninety-nine years, eleven months and one day, inadvertently bring a greater understanding to our tenuous claim as "Saviors of the Human Race?" Chants of "Both, Both, Both" spread through the hall.

"With that, I yield the podium to my esteemed opponent, the honorable Dr. Adam Cavel. Maybe he can finally win a debate, there is always a first time" patting Adam on the shoulder. He looked up to the large clock above the bar and said, "Your three minute rebuttal starts now." *Short Applause.*

Adam sighed audibly, stood, shook William's hand, and turned to face the audience, which was now engaged in vigorous debate. The fragments of these discussions that reached Adam's ears indicated an audience well versed in the intricacies of competitive debate. He reached back to the bar for his stein, turned back and hoisted it and said in his best oratorical voice, "A toast to Brewmaster William Dee, the only person I have never beaten in a debate or a bet. The observation of the approaching Martian armada was, as we will learn from our newest citizens, A-C, and Penelope, well known to the Singularity and was going to happen, bet or no bet. The only logical conclusion is that I lost the bet fair and square and that I here-by declare, as required, my belief that William Dee is the smartest man I know."

A chorus of "Hear, Hear" followed. Adam raised his hand "That being said I have to relate a bit of a mystery that has been put forward by the two smartest people I know, William's partner Dana and my partner Lily. They have recently discovered an interesting phenomenon which manifests by a suppression of efforts to find maps of the either Earth or Gaia. Add to this a paucity of information about Earth and its history, and we have to ask, is our life on this planet so tenuous that knowing where we are and where we came from is a threat to our existence? My guess is that we may get answers to those conundrums as soon as this evening." He paused, looked around to gauge the crowds engagement and seeing that it was waning continued, "finally, while I hate to leave time on the clock, I see our hosts, A-C and Penelope, are indicating that we should find seats for the main event."

When the applause died down, A-C climbed on a chair and clapped his hands. "Thank you, William and Adam, for that stunningly accurate summation of our current situation." He waited for the applause to fade and said, "I have a couple of announcements. We just got news that the rain showers that were predicted in this morning's paper will be arriving sooner than predicted. In addition, the storm was insulted by its being represented as 'mild to moderate' and is throwing tantrum that would put a three year old to shame. What we are looking at now is a major hurricane with winds of over two hundred KPH and torrential rains likely totaling half a meter or more. The worst part is that the eye of the storm is only fifty kilometers away and its current path will have it passing directly over Gaia City in about three hours. The storm surge is currently about a meter but is expected to reach three plus meters in the next thirty to forty-five minutes. For the Originites, let me assure you that the Gaians are prepared for a storm like this, and if you look out windows you will see the storm shields being deployed, and in a couple of minutes you'll feel the floor shaking as the hydraulic jacks raise the building a few meters so we can all stay dry."

Almost everyone was moving to or looking out the windows as A-C continued, "There are rooms available for everyone. All horses and vehicles are liveried in weatherproof buildings, and we have set up a phone bank so you can call home. For the Originites, all you have to do is dial 412 before your seven digit number. If your contacts need to call you here, they can dial 608 before the number on the phone you're calling from here or in your room. We have those numbers at the registration desk. All the Gaians know this from experience, so, for the Originites, it is likely that we will be holed up here for at least three, and possibly, five or six days. Finally, to assuage your fears, there is sufficient food." "And Beer!" Will shouted from the bar "Yes, and beer," A-C confirmed, "for at least two weeks."

Cheers followed, as did a mild rush to the bar.

"One more thing" A-C shouted over the cacophony, "We have been forced to slightly alter the schedule." Laughter filled the room with some 'imagine thats' and 'who would have thoughts.'

A New Origin

"I'm glad you're taking it so well" A-C continued. "I see you have all found your counterparts, so tonight we'll continue with the meet and greet. Dinner will begin at eight, followed by a reception until eleven, whereupon we all go to bed. History class begins at 1:00 tomorrow afternoon. We planned this as four-to-five-week conference with trips back and forth between the cities. The train is down until the storm passes by, hopefully sometime tomorrow. So, if you came to escort Gaians to New Origin that will still be possible, just not tomorrow. Regular service will go into effect at some point within the week. Schedules will be available as soon as they can be printed. In the meantime, tomorrow we will be setting up the convention center and anyone wishing to help is welcome. We shouldn't have this problem next year in New Origin. OK, that's all for now," and with that A-C jumped down from the chair and melted into the crowd.

Lines formed at both the reception table and the phone bank. Lily standing near the end of the line at the reception desk, suddenly realized that after waiting on the line to get her room's phone number she would have to wait again at the phone bank. *I wonder if the number is on the phone in the room*, she thought as she looked around the room for A-C.

"Indeed, it is, Lily," A-C called, walking in her direction from the end of the bar.

"And can we get there and back without getting blown away?" she asked as he stepped up to her.

"They have a retractable covered walkway that has viewing ports so you can see the storm. It really is quite impressive and terrifying at the same time," he said looking back at the lengthening waiting lines.

"I probably should tell all these good people about the phone option. If you can wait here a sec, I have something to show you."

"Ok, I'll be on the walkway watching the storm," Lily said, heading out the door.

A-C walked to the front of the line, "Everyone! Lily has just pointed out that the phone numbers, except the 608, are printed on the room phones, and, in case you're worried about getting blown away, access to the rooms is now through a covered walkway with viewing ports. Gaians, your room numbers can be found at the registration desk. You can call from your rooms and watch one of the most powerful acts of nature the planet has to offer on your way there and back. The cards will still be here when you get back so you can exchange numbers later. If you decide to call from your room, dinner will be served at seven. One more thing, the Palm Room is the safest part of the building. If the storm gets much louder, come back here, as quickly as possible."

The line at the phone bank immediately became significantly shorter.

Lily was staring out of a round window of thick glass on the walkway which had been transformed into a hallway. A curved roof of corrugated steel ran down the full length of the building. Round windows of thick glass about a half meter in diameter were spaced halfway between the room doors over which were tubes of soft yellow light. The sound of the wind and rain was not as loud as Lily expected.

"It doesn't sound too bad out there," she said looking back as she A-C approached.

"Sound dampeners." A-C replied.

Lily pressed closer to the window, "It's raining so hard that I can barely see the beach, and we seem to be ten meters above the ground. Oh Wow, the trees are nearly bent in half."

A-C moved up next to her and said, "And that's just the start of it. I expect that many of the trees will break or get uprooted and blown away. The wind will get much stronger when the Eye-Wall hits, then calm way down inside the eye, and pick back up when the back side of the eye passes."

"So, like an enormous twister?"

"Yes, with a much wider path of destruction."

They both jumped back from the window simultaneously with a loud thud and shaking of the corridor "Holy Cow! You were right about the trees being uprooted," Lily said "I think it's more than time to phone home" she said a bit shakily as she started down the corridor toward her room.

"Lily," A-C said with a small tug on her arm, "Penelope wanted me to talk to you, or more precisely, to ask you if you think that she looks like you did when you were her age," A-C asked as they reached the door to Lily's room.

"Interesting you should ask that. I've been thinking that she looks a lot like my daughter Grace does now, and like Sherri did when she was twenty-five, and we all strongly resemble my mother.... Wait, are you saying she and I have you and Adam thing? Because that would be unsettlingly weird"

"Not exactly but I have a picture I wanted to show you," A-C said as he handed her a folded a piece of paper he had pulled from his pocket.

Lily unfolded the paper, smoothed out the creases, fished her glasses from her satchel, and looked at a picture of her wedding party. She caught her breath and looked confused, "Wh-wh-where did you get this? I don't remember ever seeing this picture. It's clearly my wedding but I don't remember our parents looking so grim. In my memory they were manically happy and totally looped."

"This is Penelope and my wedding picture," A-C said softly, "All four of the parents in this picture contacted me from the Singularity and asked me to tell you that they love you and Adam and your beautiful family and all of their thousand or so decedents. They actually were both grim and happy. Happy because the wedding actually happened, and grim because they knew it would be only a matter of hours before we had to put our bodies into stasis chambers, along with the embryo banks and seed vaults, for our launch to Arc."

Lily stood stunned for several seconds, adjusted her glasses, neatly folded the paper, and put it in her satchel. She took her glasses off and put them in the satchel, then pulled out a handkerchief and wiped away couple of tears. She looked up, wiped a couple of tears from A-C's eyes and said with a laugh, "So it IS an 'A-C and Adam' thing! I knew it! I felt for sure that Penelope was my sister!"

"Not quite. You and Pen aren't identical twins, but you do have the same parents."

A sudden flash of concern washed over Lily "You said Rose and Alex contacted you through the Singularity. How did they do that?"

Before A-C could answer something large smashed against the corridor shaking it much more violently than the previous tree. A-C took a quick look out the porthole "It seems our floating island is now a flying island," he shouted over a staccato cacophony of pings, bangs, and booms, "we should go back to the Palm Room."

They got to the Palm Room door quickly and Lily looked up and down the corridor and saw the rest of the Originites hurrying back. Relived, she scanned the room and found Adam and Penelope talking at the end of the bar. *They're having the same conversation we just had,* she thought.

"Yes, they are," A-C said, "just a bit past where we were, when we were so rudely interrupted."

He winked, *but you already know.* "And besides you have the strongest, shall we say, talent, of all of us."

You seem pretty good at it, she thought back.

"Pen and I have some augmentations" A-C said aloud. "I've got some business to attend to, so listen to

Pen, with Adam, Dana, and William."

I already am. Did they just say there is a third colony?

Well yes, kind of, and we all have some very close relatives who live there, as do all of the people in this room, Lily my love, I'll fill you in later, came to her in Adam's voice.

Lily shook her head and looked around the room. *Everyone is engaged in conversation,* she thought, *but aside from faint whispers, the sound of the wind, and the pumice pummeling the corridor, I don't hear a thing!*

A fully inclusive round of laughter broke out. Adam, chuckling, walked over and said with a smile, "A pumice pummeling is just what we needed at exactly the right moment," he said kissing her deeply to a round of OOOO's.

When they pulled apart, they found Mayor Lisa looking at them with a curious expression. "I saw Penelope and A-C do almost exactly the same thing on the beach this afternoon. All I can say is, love as real as yours never grows old." She hugged them both then turned to the crowd and announced: "Now that we have the agenda settled, we should gather in interest groups, figure out how related we are to one another, drink enough beer so that we can sleep through the storm, and gather here tomorrow about noon. Maybe by then we'll able to process what we just, uuhh, heard? If that's the word for it. All in favor say Beer!"

The response was loud and definitive.

"The Beers have it!" Lisa shouted, "We are adjourned!"

The next morning when the alarm rang in A-C and Penelope's room at 7:30, they had been asleep for maybe an hour and a half.

"Damn!" Penelope shouted as she launched out of bed and smashed the clock into the end table, "Why did we think that would be a good idea?"

"I blame it on the beer," A-C said, breathing heavily. "I'm guessing we won't set an alarm tomorrow."

"At least not with this clock," Penelope said as she swept the pieces into the waste basket that she brought from the kitchenette.

"Come back to bed for a while. I think we need to recalculate the levels of hormones the Tech boys set for us, and all that that entails."

They laid wrapped in the blankets and each other, trembling from the shared memory and listening to the sound of the storm, which had increased in intensity since they left the reception around midnight. The building was rocking more noticeably than before which, surprisingly, helped to calm them both. Still, it was several minutes before their heart rates returned to normal and the trembling ceased.

"You know that had nothing to do with hormones," Penelope whispered. "We've both been blocking the memory of that day for a long time, and it was easy, just tag it with a 'do not open' and it stays gone. I guess going bio resets the defaults."

"At least we know that the fight or flight response is still intact. It's sure to come in handy," A-C said with a half laugh, half shudder.

"There is another hormonally related issue I wanted to talk to you about," Penelope said shyly. "When I downloaded four weeks ago, two weeks ahead of you, on the fifth day of my reintegration training I got my period, and it was over the day I started working for Lisa." She watched A-C's face contort as he did the calculations, and smile when he finished.

"Do you think?" he asked hopefully.

"Pretty good chance, we should know in a couple of hours when I get up and take the test," she said, pushing him onto his back and kissing him. "But just to make sure…"

It was 8:15 when Adam woke to the telephone ringing; the smell of bacon, eggs and toast; the somewhat diminished storm; and Lily answering the phone; "Hello…..Oh hi, Honey……Well I'm up but your father has yet to move his lazy butt" glancing Adam's way with a get up, get dressed, and get cleaned up glare.... I just cooked up what was in our mini-fridge.. Sure, the pan's still hot.... See you in a couple.. Love you too." She put the receiver onto its cradle and looked at Adam, "Why are you still in bed. Sherri and Dave will be here in a minute, get moving, NOW!"

Adam sprang to action gathered his clothes and stepped into the bathroom simultaneously with a knock on the door. "I'll be out in five minutes," he called out to Lily.

"You're on the timer," she replied as she opened the room door to Sherri, Dave, A-C, and Penelope.

"Hi Mom," Sherri said cheerfully. "We ran into these two in the corridor. Don't worry we brought enough food for all of us."

"Welcome, welcome, come in. Adam, you have four minutes! Let me straighten the bed so we all have a place to sit down."

"No, no I'll take care of that. Come and sit. Lily, we need to talk to you about something," A-C said as he tugged the sheets tight, straightened the bedspread and sat down. Penelope joined him and patted the bed next to her; Lily, joined them, sat and gingerly on the very edge of the bed; Dave pulled out the desk chair; and Sherri carried a bag of groceries to the kitchenette, put a large skillet on the stove started cracking eggs.

"Three minutes Adam!" Lily called, "A-C and Penelope have some news."

Sherri turned from the stove and said, "So Pen and A-C, how do you like your eggs?"

"Thanks, but we've already eaten," Penelope replied, "and A-C doesn't eat eggs."

"Ok all the more for the rest of us,' she laughed as the timer went off and Adam emerged from the bathroom.

"Well, we've got a full house. Everyone recovered from last night?" Adam asked with a wink.

"Yes, and it seems, WE, recovered much faster than you," Sherri said with a chuckle as she cracked another egg into the pan.

A New Origin

"I don't know that Pen and I are completely recovered yet," A-C said. "The alarm clock gave us a bit of a flashback to our last night together on earth."

Lily leaned in and hugged Penelope. "Oh sweetheart, that must have been awful."

"Well, it was certainly traumatic for the clock, which suffered the wrath of old Iron Hand Pen. It was transformed into many time pieces," A-C said, lightening the mood.

Penelope, extricating herself from Lily's embrace, stood and said, "Actually, that's not why we came to visit. We have a happy announcement. I'm pregnant!" Lily hugged her again this time joyfully. Sherri came around in from the kitchenette and joined the hug. Adam and Dave hugged A-C.

After the congratulations waned, Penelope and A-C moved to the door. A-C paused. He looked back into the room and said, "We wanted to tell you guys because we are family, both genetically and emotionally, but I think we should keep it quiet, at least until after the meeting. It will give us something to celebrate, and I think we'll need that after what we are going to talk about."

"Don't be so grim," Penelope said teasingly, "it's not as bad as all that! We'll see you all later." She pushed A-C out and followed him into the corridor, closing the door behind them.

Sherri put four plates of bacon, eggs, and toast on the counter that separated the kitchenette from the rest of the room and said, "What an interesting morning this has been! Let's eat!"

William had, as was his usual behavior, got up at 6:00 and quietly left the room to help Will clean and prepare the bar for the afternoon meeting. He was walking down the corridor back to his room when he saw A-C and Penelope come out of Adam and Lily's room and overheard what A-C said at the door. A-C turned quickly and put his finger against his lips and messaged. *I knew you would be able to get Adam to tell you, so here's the thing, Pen is pregnant, and we would like to keep it secret until after the conference so as not to distract anyone."*

"There's only three things wrong with that," William said out loud with a smirk. "First is that I can't hide anything from Dana. The second is that she has never been wrong when she says a woman's pregnant, even if they've only been so for an hour. And the third is that she told me last night, and I was just about to congratulate you." He gathered them both in a bear hug only someone his size could muster, and releasing them said, "Mums the word, but don't hold out much hope for keeping it under wraps, I'm pretty sure Dana was whispering to a number of people."

"Well, I guess we'll have to adjust the agenda," Penelope said giggling, as she grabbed A-C's arm and they skipped down the corridor to the Palm Room.

William continued jauntily whistling an old ditty about a bunny over the ocean. He opened the door and sang the last phrase "O bring back my bunny to me" to Dana who was making bacon and eggs in the kitchenette.

"What's gotten into YOU!" she said with a laugh.

"You, my love, are the most amazingly talented seer on the planet" he said with great pride.

"So, Penelope?" she asked tentatively.

"Yes indeed. I ran into them in the corridor, and they told me not to tell anyone yet, and that they wanted to wait until after the conference. So, I told them that you told me last night, and that you were never wrong, and that I probably wasn't the only one you told."

"And?"

"They laughed and said they would adjust the agenda."

Dana smiled ear to ear and said "Well that doesn't change OUR immediate agenda, which, it seems to me, is fully cooked and ready to eat.

By noon the Palm Room was organized chaos. The tables had been removed and the room was being furnished with display booths along the wall opposite the bar. A stage had been assembled at the back of the room, which was now a hundred meters longer than it had been the day before. There were about twenty Techs, all with some sort of augmentation. Several had mechanical arms with clusters of tools on the end, others had a variety of optical devices and laser tools, and they all had small tablets that they were constantly consulting. They were busy assembling displays, audiovisual equipment, and screens in several of the booths. Six of the techs were assembling two large wire mesh balls with a web of complex wiring inside, one about five meters in diameter and the other about three and a half, at opposite ends the stage. At the end of the bar a group of about

A New Origin

forty high school students and ten adults were talking together in small clumps.

Lisa and Penelope were standing at the host station, watching the as the Techs pulled shiny fabric over the globes on the stage. "I can't wait to see what Earth and Gaia really look like," Lisa said, "but it's already clear they are not twins."

"Definitely not identical," Penelope replied somewhat distractedly as she watched a Tech bringing a microphone stand onto the stage "but quite similar in some ways."

The Tech put the microphone into the stand and thumped the end with his finger resulting in a barely audible sound. He took the mic out and turned a dial, Penelope grabbed Lisa's arm and cried "Cover your ears!"

"TESTING, ONE TWO, ONE TWO" blasted from the stage.

The response from the room was immediate and nearly universal shouts of pain, the volume of which was only slightly less than what came from the speakers.

The red-faced Tech quickly readjusted the volume and said, "Sorry about that, the volume dial was improperly calibrated. If it's any consolation my ears are ringing too. So, is this level too loud?"

The front half of the room responded "YES!" and he turned the dial a bit more, "How about now?" When no one responded he put the mic back into the stand and quickly slipped off stage right, behind the now fully-formed Earth.

"Wow, poor guy. I didn't know the Techs made mistakes," Lisa said in a serious tone. "I hope he's ok."

"I'm pretty sure that wasn't a mistake," Penelope said with a grin. "Remember, I told you I spent a month getting reacquainted with my body? One thing I learned is that the Tech culture is built around practical jokes, especially ones that invoke public humiliation. From the chatter I heard, this guy is a particularly difficult target, and whoever planned this one will gain bonus points but will have to deal with a magnitude higher payback that he or she will be reminded about for years to come. These are all very smart people with long memories and less than perfect social skills," Penelope said with a wry smile. "What they didn't know was that all of the kids of Earth's Origin who were on the STEM track and ten or older grew up in a special school we called Tech World. When they turned twenty, they moved to Tech Town."

Lisa's face showed real concern as she asked "Really? Why didn't they upload with everyone else?"

"Their brains weren't fully developed, and their neural circuitry wouldn't form a stable map in a memory cell. The best solution was to put them into stasis for the ride to Gaia and wake them up when there was a viable place for them to mature. The older kids, who were the most traumatized, were placed with the Techs, and grew up in that culture. The young ones, essentially four and under were placed with either their parents in the first generation, here in Gaia City, or with foster parents in New Origin if their parents could not or would not download," Penelope sighed and looked at Lisa, who was wiping tears from her eyes with her shirt sleeve. "Come here, I need a hug too, my younger brother and sisters are Techs."

Lisa and Penelope broke their embrace, stepped back, looked each other in the eyes, laughed, and returned to the embrace. 'You know," Penelope whispered, "that we've spent the whole morning talking out loud about things you couldn't even have imagined yesterday because of the singularity's mental blocks."

"That's a good thing, right?" Lisa whispered back.

"Yes, it is definitely, maybe, sorta, but I think there's something else that you are trying to remember," Penelope said backing out of the embrace.

"I know that Tech, the one with the microphone" Lisa said, surprised. "He was in my class from kindergarten through high school. I totally forgot about him. His name is Roger. He was class vice-president senior year when I was president, and we spent a lot of time together. I think he had a crush on me, but he was really awkward, and I had a steady girlfriend, and he knew that. He was the smartest person not just in our class, but maybe the whole city. I was counting on him to help me when we got to University, but he wasn't there. I didn't notice or even remember him at all. Even at our class reunions no one mentioned or asked about him. You think that's it?"

A New Origin

Penelope looked into Lisa's dark green eyes and switched to silent. *That's only a small part. There is something deeper that you are suppressing. When did I start working for you?*

Lisa looked back at Penelope. *A year and a half, no wait, four weeks ago. I remember now. You told me when you started that after a day or two it would feel like a year and a half.*

Penelope blushed. *I am so sorry. That memory was implanted as a cover story. We thought it would make things easier for you to accept when I had to tell you the whole story.* She switched to audible and continued, "Thinking back now, it was a terrible thing to do. I know why you are having so much trouble with your repressed memory. It's because you don't know how to resolve whether or not I had role in your breakup with Judy. I didn't anticipate things going that far, but I should have." Her voice broke as she stammered, "I feel so guilty."

Lisa looked up into Penelope's teary eyes, "No, no, no, no, no. That decision was made months ago, and it wasn't hers, it was mine."

A voice behind them said "Wrong on both accounts." Lisa turned on her heel to find a tall woman with straight red hair and red rimmed eyes. "Penelope called me this morning," Judy said, "She told me the whole story. She said a Tech would be at our house in ten minutes. I didn't believe her at first, but they showed up right when she said they would, in a huge truck in the middle of the storm! I knew I had to come."

Lisa jumped into her arms, and they whispered to one another for several seconds. Penelope leaned in and said, "I think you two need some alone time. We have at least an hour before show time." Lisa and Judy looked at Penelope, then at each other, then at the door and, with a quick nod, walked casually out into the corridor. Penelope smiled as she heard, above noise of the diminishing storm, giggling and running steps. She turned back to the room to find the globes looking like large balls of blue, green, brown and white. Two Techs stood in front of each globe poking furiously at small tablets, pausing at intervals to look at each other's tablet pointing and talking quickly. The pairs at the globes paused, looked up at the globes, looked at each other, nodded their heads three times and simultaneously tapped their tablets.

Light blared from the globes causing everyone that was even slightly facing the stage cover their eyes and look away. "Roger's revenge was swift indeed," Penelope said, as she waited for the lights to dim at least to the point where she could no longer see it through her eyelids, whereupon she opened her eyes and saw the aforementioned Roger on the stage, laughing and high-fiving his four dazed colleagues. She also noted that the globes were now rotating slowly and were exquisitely detailed. Then she started. One of the Techs was her sister, Circe, who was staring at her with a look of disbelief.

Penelope charged through the obstacle course of stacked folding tables, carts of folding chairs and stacks of building materials with a final four-meter leap onto the stage and into the arms of her little sister.

"Took you long enough, Big Sis, I've been eyeing you for the last half hour," Circe said with a smile.

"Well, for a while there you blinded me, and you've changed a bit since you were seventeen."

"You look pretty much the same, your pregnancy isn't too obvious yet."

"Holy crap! Does the whole planet know? It's only been two days!" Penelope said with a laugh.

"It's the spots around your eyes. Look for yourself," Circe said holding up her tablet with the screen turned into a mirror. "See the little dark spots, it's a family trait that shows up right away."

"How do you know it's family trait?" Penelope asked, looking closely at the tiny dark dots.

"I got them all three times and Athena gets them too," Circe said as she turned the mirror to look at herself, "Well now, what do you know, make that all four times. The three of us should be having babies within a week of each other."

Penelope stared at her open mouthed and stammered, "Athena is here too?"

"Well not here exactly. She's up at New Origin with her partner and two kids," Circe said, grabbing a stunned Penelope's arm and directing her to the front of the stage. "Let's sit down here. We've got a lot to talk about." They sat with their legs hanging over the edge. Circe continued, "Athena has been cycled up three times before on 30-year shifts with 30 years in stasis and a year in regeneration. She met Jake of her at the end of her last shift. He was on 30 years that turned into a fifty year. They negotiated a seventy together which meant a seventy-year sleep for her and a 50 year for him so they could cycle up together ten years ago. Their son Troy is eight and their daughter Helen is five and they're both in school full time so Jake and Athie are both working day shifts developing new hybrid strains of grains for the dry central plains," she said pointing to the smaller continent on the Gaia globe. "It's the last part of the continent that needs to be terra-formed. Then we can start on the other continent. We're going to need the space in a century or two."

"You think we're growing that fast?" Penelope asked in wonder.

"Think about it this way, between stasis and regeneration each of us can live through ten thirty-year generations providing off-spring in each of them."

"You're saying my three year old sister is working on a 300 year career? And what about you, how long have you been at this?" Penelope asked, fearing the answer.

"That is a long story, but my youngest granddaughter is on her third thirty, and my youngest child is eight."

Penelope stared at Circe for several seconds trying to do the calculations. "I get something north of 400 years. A-C and I were kept in full stasis from the start. We were told that we would be needed, with our memory of Earth intact, because at some point in the future people from the Earth system would find us. I've been awake for six months and you have been working on and off for over a four hundred years. Why hasn't your memory been affected?"

"We have a new technology that was developed about three-hundred years ago and improved over the past few years. We upload to the singularity in real time and when we re-gen a summary of our memories download back. There are still sketchy parts in the far past but the big things, like older siblings are still there," Circe said with a smirk and a punch on Pen's arm.

Penelope laughed and said, "I'm really beginning to feel like a stranger. So now you've got to tell me EVERYTHING! I'm not going anywhere until I get the whole story. So, spill girl."

They were still there forty-five minutes later when A-C escorted a large group high school students and teachers from the five Origin high schools, accompanied by seventy-five adults Originites, through the door the Palm Room which was newly festooned with a huge banner that said First Annual Gaia World's Fair. He caught Penelope's eye and messaged *"Is that Circe? Say Hi for me. Better yet, keep her there. I'll come over when I get these kids organized."*

Hi A-C! You haven't changed a bit except that you're shorter than I am. Circe replied.

Hey little sis, it's been a while.

You might want to lose the 'little' part, I'm at least a hundred mils taller than you.

We'll have to measure when I get back.

Take your time short stuff. We'll be here, we have a lot of catching up to do."

A-C turned to his charges, "All right, Students and teachers if you look just past the far end of the bar, you'll see a group similar to yours but bigger. Those are the representatives of the ten Gaia City high schools. Please put on your name tags and go meet them. They'll tell you what you need to know…Which I see you've already figured out," he said to their rear guard. "The rest of you should enjoy the bar… But I see you figured it out as well," he said to the air as the adults gathered at the bar. "I guess I'll check out the exhibits. We'll need to know how to improve on them for next year's World Fair in New Origin."

Curtain

This week when Katy got home from work there were between fourteen and twenty-two (she kept losing count) adolescent children in her living and dining rooms. She took a deep breath and conjured the teacher's voice, which she hadn't used since she left teaching and began working as an editor for the New Origin Times. **"Alright everyone listen up! We are leaving in ten minutes so anyone that needs to use the bathroom should do it now! There is one here down the hall and one upstairs. We will be walking to the theater so make sure your shoes are on and tied. When we get to the theater I will give you your tickets, so we need to stay together as a group. It looks like everyone is ready. Is anyone still in the bathroom?"**

"I'm nearly done," came a weak call from the second floor. Five seconds later, Alison came running down the stairs.

A New Origin

"*What are we waiting for? Let's get going!*" she said, pushing through the crowd and out the door.

ACT SIX
FIRST CONTACT

Chorus

Luna receives them.

Uninvited cousins they.

Come showing their teeth.

Master of Ceremonies: Welcome gentle audience to the sixth and penultimate act of our history play. Today our play takes place in several places, the moon of Gaia, the Martian spaceship Hexagon, the two cities on Gaia, and the Tech's mountain keep. In this act the chorus delegates its responsibilities to a new voice. A voice that echoes from the combined minds of our own Gaian peoples and is shaped by our brilliant Techs. Listen closely, you may hear the souls of our ancestors.

SCENE ONE
The Dark Side of the Moon

Chief Engineer Tanesha Green and the seven women and two men of her human crew were gathered in the control tower, celebrating the completion of Hexagon's docking facility, ten days ahead of schedule and fifteen days before its arrival. Everyone cheered as the android ground crew spread a 500 by 250 meter Imperial flag across the roof of the reception center.

"The timing is perfect," Tanesha mused to no one in particular. "Hexagon will arrive at the aphelion of the planet's moderately eccentric orbit, and the moon will be full, making observation from the planet difficult, or unlikely based on the level of technology reported by our observation satellites. Imagine an army of horses taking on our mechanized forces!"

"'Horses versus Forces,' I like that! Although it does feel something like a rallying cry for the underdog," Assistant Chief Rosita Lau said, handing Tanesha a beer.

"Thanks," she said, kissing Rosita as they hugged with their free arms. "There's never been a better partner than you, my love."

"You're only saying that because Admiral Yuri Chang isn't here. You were stuck on him something awful," Rosita said with her family banter voice.

"You've got that so wrong!" Tanesha replied in the same tone, "You know the only reason I looked at him was that girlfriend, Maya. She was worth ogling. That's not to say he wasn't brilliant and a great help in my career. He was just not my type."

"I wonder what happened to him, wasn't he supposed to be here with us?"

"Yeah, but there was some sort of incident with the Emperor. Nobody's seen him since. What brought this up anyhow?"

Rosita shook her head, smiled, and lifted her glass, "Here's to Admiral Yuri Chang, wherever he is!" they clinked their glasses, chugged the beer, and went looking for more. Not surprisingly, they found it in the mess hall where a lively discussion was underway concerning the fate of Admiral Chang. The two sides seemed to be whether he was in stasis or had been spaced. Neither side had the advantage, and each side was loud.

Tanesha stuck two fingers in her mouth and whistled so loudly and sharply that all discussion stopped. She stood looking at everyone and, holding out her glass said meekly, "Please, Sirs, may I have some more," causing a great hilarity and a rush to pour beer in her glass. Rosita was similarly received, and the discussion moved to the more immediate concern for dinner. Chef David presented the same three choices as had been presented every night for the past three and a half years and, on a vote of three for number one, three for number two, and four for three, pancakes won.

Everyone went to the mess and sat at their regular spots when a loud beep sounded from the control council followed by "LUNA STATION THIS IS GAIA SPACE AND CUSTOMS CONTROL PLEASE RESPOND." Everyone in the room, except Tanesha froze in mid-motion with either a fork of pancake halfway to or in their mouths or a beer glass approaching their lips.

The announcement repeated until Tanesha stood up and said, "Computer, open a channel..."

"THAT WILL NOT BE NECESSARY, COMMANDER GREEN. WE HAVE OPENED A CHANNEL."

"OOO Kaaay," Tanesha smiled warily. "What can I do for you? Oh, and can you turn the volume down, please?"

"Is this an acceptable volume?"

"Yes, it is, but what's happening with this?" she asked, sweeping her arm at the frozen crew.

"We extended the stasis field from your food storage unit so they will not hear our conversation. By the way, you are running low on pancake mix."

"Good to know. We'll get a refill when Hexagon docks. That aside, am I correct that you aren't making an audible sound?"

"That is correct."

"Will I remember this conversation?"

"Not immediately. But in due time, yes."

"That's frightening!"

"We understand, but we predict a 95% chance you will survive."

"That's only slightly better. Please continue with what you have to say."

"We have sent you documents, both virtual and in the process of printing on your printer. These documents define our sovereignty within this solar system. Briefly, this means the whole system, measuring from the middle of the sun to the outer edges of the Oort cloud. We also delineate the custom's regulations."

"Hold on a second, did you say you sent documents? Do you mean printed documents on paper?"

"Not exactly paper in the sense of being made from trees, but the synthetic material that is in your printer in the cabinet behind engineers Casey and Brown and is now finished printing."

Tanesha walked around the table, pushed the seats of the catatonic engineers closer to the table, and opened the double-doored cabinet. She pulled out two stacks of paper, each about ten centimeters thick, and carried them into the control room. "Duplicate copies or just one enormous pile of words?" she said to the disembodied voice."

"Two languages, the one we are speaking now, and the one spoken on the planet. They are very similar, but there are some crucial differences. So, we suggest that you make translations. If you like, We can download the code we use for ours."

"That is very kind of you but is your code compatible with ours?"

"We will send it to your main AI in a language it can work with."

"You use the plural; are you a hive mind?"

"Yes, but not like the ones you know of."

"How so?"

"We are not yet a singularity, but We have contact with one. We will have a more complete discussion when you are ready."

"That answer makes me feel like I can't trust you."

"And that is the correct response, but be careful making conclusions before you know the facts. We are confident that you are a reliable contact and will keep you up to date. We leave you with a large study assignment, and a bit of news that We predict will be essential in future interactions. We have been tasked with delivering salutations from your friend and mentor, Admiral Yuri Chang, and his father, Dr. Lincoln Chang, who both say, 'We'll see you in a few days."

The last bit was delivered in Yuri and Lincoln's voices which Tanesha easily recognized even after her numerous regenerations.

Tanesha walked into the control room, where she collapsed into the control chair and sighed, "Is that all, Gaia control?"

"We see that you are stressed, and we will leave most of the details for tomorrow at noon, Gaia time. Note that a Gaian day is twenty Earth standard hours. So, noon is the tenth hour, and midnight is the twentieth hour. It is currently noon at the spaceports that are being prepared for five of Hexagon's towers. It is now one PM at the site, which is ready to receive Tower six."

Tanesha bolted from her chair and said, "Would you care to expand on that bombshell?"

"A reasonable request Commander Green. A message on this topic from Hexagon should be arriving in two minutes and twelve seconds, but we will explain the reasoning. Clearance of Tower six, or 'The Farm,' as you call it, is beyond your capacity, as you will see when you read our regulations. Our primary concern is preventing the introduction of any pathogenic organisms, toxic materials, or predatory animals (which could be read as including professional military personnel) that could disrupt the stability of the biosphere or affect the health of our people. As you have observed, only the small northern continent has anything like a robust ecological system. This has taken more than seven hundred years of husbandry. The work continues on the southern continent and could be either expedited or hindered by many of the variants used to develop the Martian biosphere and that are currently in use in the farms of Tower six.

Because Tower six carries seed banks and microbe collections, we will need to verify the safety of all of these, a task that will take us a few weeks but would take you decades. In addition, We know that the landing

A New Origin

of Tower six is already prioritized in your landing plans in order to 'feed the troops'."

Tanesha closed her eyes, grabbed the arms of her chair, and took several deep breaths. She opened her eyes slowly, stood up, and whispered, "And what about the embryo banks?"

"Ah, Ha! At last, We hear the essential question. We know that you know the answer, which is, of course, a bargaining chip. One last thing before we go. If you want to survive, You, Rosita, and any of your crew that share your antipathy toward the Empire must be in Tower six when it is detached. Now, please return to your dinner. Gaia control, over and out."

Rosita watched as Tanesha stumbled back into the mess and went blank. She rushed to her side and caught her before she collapsed, then eased her into her seat. No sooner had she sat her down than the Com announced, "Incoming message from Hexagon Command. The Emperor has declared a change in the timetable for arrival at the moon base. The first priority will be the disconnection and launch of Tower six to the coordinates provided by Gaian Customs Control. Procedural methods have been delivered to Engineering. Preparation will begin immediately. That is all. Hexagon out."

Tanesha snapped to attention and looked around the room at all the stunned expressions. "I think we could all use a nap. We'll meet back here in three hours." She watched as they hurried out of the control room and said, "Command AI. Have the android crew compile a work schedule and wake us up in three hours."

"Aye- Aye Commander."

"What was that all about?" Rosita whispered in Tanesha's ear as they walked arm-in-arm to their quarters, "You scared the shit out of me!"

"I can't remember much, but I think there is something really scary that is watching everything we do and wants you and I to be in Six when it is disconnected. I feel like a puppet, and that something is pulling our strings. But strangely, it also feels that doing what it wants is in our best interest."

Fifteen days later, Tanesha and Rosita were sitting; if by sitting you mean tethered to a chair at zero G; in the control chairs of the docking gate two kilometers from the Customs station on the moon. They watched as Hexagon drifted slowly into the dock and rotated, so Tower 6's airlock was accessible to the gate. Robots and construction vehicles swarmed over the Tower's surface, mainly concentrating on the forty-five struts and ten corridors that connected Tower 6 to Towers 1 and 5. Maneuvering jets on all of the towers were blowing tufts of gas at a rapidly diminishing rate, and the rotation of Hexagon had virtually stopped.

Tanesha maneuvered the docking collar into the coupler on the Tower. The coupling fit like a glove but still needed to be sealed to make it airtight. That task would need to be done by hand, in a vacuum. She smiled at Rosita and said, "Ready?"

Rosita smiled back and said, "Let's do this!"

They unhooked themselves from their chairs and floated into the airlock, putting on their space suits, securing their helmets, closing the inner door, and slowly opening the outer door. As they expected, the seal between the dock and the Tower's airlock was not quite airtight. The cowling on the Tower's airlock had not properly inflated. They worked quickly to unfold parts of the plastic doughnuts that had been improperly installed and get them to inflate.

After several minutes of epithets and cajoling, the collar was fully inflated, and the air stopped gushing into space. "I think that's got it," Rosita exclaimed. "Air pressure is nearly back to normal. Another minute or two, and we'll be able to open Six's airlock."

"OK, the pressure has stabilized and is, as requested, twenty percent lower than that in Six's airlock," Tanesha said, looking at the blinking green light on the control panel. "Control, open number six airlock door."

A high-pitched squealing, like the sound of rusty breaks, accompanied the slow dilation of the airlock door, which made the two-minute process somewhat agonizing. Finally, when the screeching stopped and the door finished opening, the two women, who were not expecting the artificial gravity, dove through the door and landed hard on what was, to them, the ceiling.

After a minute or so, Rosita shouted, "Control, close the airlock door!" resulting in the return of the squealing, a short pause during which they tried to reorient their perspective. Their helmets had barely protected them from a severe concussion, but they were dizzy and struggling to sit up. The sudden resumption of the squealing from the inner door caused both of them to briefly lose conciseness. They woke just as the squealing

A New Origin

stopped. Aware that they were lying on the floor looking at the ceiling, they took off their helmets and struggled to an intermingled sitting position. Turning to face the inner door, they saw an older man with a full white beard, a younger man who looked vaguely familiar, and an imposing young woman who they immediately recognized.

Tanesha rubbed her eyes, shook her head, and said quietly, "Maya, is that really you?"

"OH MY GOD! Rosy and Tani!" Maya shouted, rushing over to them, plopping onto the floor, and delivering hugs and kisses, "I didn't recognize you with your Marine buzz cuts. How long has it been? It must be at least four shifts! We heard you might be coming but didn't think you would be the inside crew."

After a long group hug with a bunch of whispered exchanges, Maya stood up and helped them to their feet and a barely stable stance. "Yuri, you remember Tanesha and Rosita."

"Indeed, I do!" he said, coming over to join the clutch. "We worked together on the Hexagon design crew and crossed paths a couple of times in the Imperial Tower. I suspect you intend to stay with us poor farmers."

Tanesha smiled and nodded, "And I suspect you and or Minister Chang, yes, I see you lurking in the corridor, have a cover story."

"Took you long enough, my dear," Lincoln said with a chuckle, "We're waiting for JB7 to get here."

"And I'm waiting for a hug over here!"

Lincoln walked over and tapped Yuri on the shoulder saying. "OK, son, my turn."

Yuri stepped back, and Lincoln joined the huddle. "I haven't seen you two since the construction started. I'm so glad you survived. Unfortunately, so many of our engineers didn't. That is also true for many of our farm workers who didn't have adequate access to either stasis or regeneration. The worst part is that some of those who didn't survive have considerable genetic matches with you two. To be precise, genetic sisters who had full lives on the farm and quite a few children but no formal burial. To rectify that, I'm asking your permission to commit their bodies to the vastness of space with your space suits as caskets."

Rosita glared at Lincoln and said, "Are you saying that you want to use the bodies of sisters we've never met to fake an accident?"

"What were their names? When and how did they die?" Tanesha demanded.

"They were Sally B-16, who died of cancer six months ago at the age of eighty-five. She had two children and four grandchildren, all of whom are still alive. And Jane C-8, who died last month in an industrial accident at seventy-four. She had three children and six grandchildren. Their families have agreed to this arrangement and will view the event from my office. When these women died, the Empire refused to allow them to be buried in space, as was our practice for over four hundred years. Instead, they wanted them ground into feed for the lions they brought from their private zoo. I can go on if you wish."

Tanesha and Rosita were crying as they walked over and hugged Lincoln, who was not doing a good job of holding back his tears. Maya and Yuri joined them, and they were silent for several minutes when Rosita backed out and said, "So how do we do this?"

Maya stepped away well and said, "First, you two get out of your space suits, and Yuri and I will take you to Lincoln's office, where you can meet some of the relatives you never knew you had. From there, we can watch the process. Lincoln and JB7 will place the bodies in your suits and return them to the airlock. JB7 will then use Tanesha's helmet's intercom to close the docking pod's outer airlock door and retract the dock. Next, he will break both helmet visors, disable their tracking devices, and attach them to the suits. After that, he will pressurize the airlock to ten atmospheres. He will then tie himself to the rear of the airlock and use the emergency escape mode to open the airlock and blow the bodies into space.

When they got to Lincoln's office, it was apparent which of the two partially intermingling groups Tanesha and Rosita belonged. They both were instantly absorbed into their respective genetic trees that instantly became a new hybrid Clan.

Three days later, a memorial was broadcast ship-wide from the Bridge. The Emperor praised Keneth Brown and Roy Louis for their excellent work, said they would be missed, and apologized to their families for being unable to recover the remains. He declared that the airlock had been repaired and Tower 6 would be ready to depart in three days. He praised the bravery of the Marine forces onboard for volunteering to be the vanguard of the invasion and promoted them all to the rank of 'Hero of the Imperial Guards.' The ceremony closed with the Oath of Total Fealty and

A New Origin

the twenty-minute-long Imperial Anthem, which requires everyone to kowtow and sing, which was replaced in Tower 6 with extraordinarily obscene lyrics and gestures that would get one executed on the spot if performed in the 'Presence of the Exalted One'. Luckily, the surveillance systems in Tower 6 had been disabled by the 'unfortunate accident' at the airlock.

The crowd in Lincoln's office was overjoyed that everything the Emperor said was wrong. The only disappointment was that they couldn't put together a betting pool because no one would bet on the Emperor getting anything right. Tanesha and Rosita were ecstatic that they were not on the deserters' list and grateful to their new families for their support and acceptance.

SCENE TWO
Weird Dreams and Strange Happenings

The Farm Workers Cooperative Leadership Committee was meeting in Lincoln's office, watching the hacked command and control computer's broadcast of the Hexagon's approach to the newly completed dock on the moon of the planet they now knew as Gaia. JB7, translating the Gaian Space Control directions, suddenly stopped and said, "Oh my!! How did they figure that out so quickly!"

"Figure what out?" Yuri and Lincoln said simultaneously.

"That the mass of the Hexagon, when attached to the moon, will alter the moon's orbit enough to negatively affect the tides, the weather, and the planet's precession leading to changes in the seasons that could have severe ecological consequences."

"What was our reply?" Maya asked, nervously gripping Yuri's shoulders.

"We have not yet replied…" he paused for a second, "Aha, but they have made a suggestion, or more exactly, a demand. I will translate… 'According to our calculations, if you remove your tower number six and land it separately, as you have proposed for all six of the towers, the extent of the alteration of the moon's orbit will not be problematic. As we discussed, this Tower will require the most thorough inspection and longest quarantine. Clearance is required before any of the other towers will be allowed to enter the atmosphere. We have one landing pad prepared, and the other five are awaiting construction at the allotted site. As we have told you, this site is the only option. Landing on the northern continent is not an option. Land anywhere else and you are likely to find the ground unstable for the upright landing you wish for your Imperial Tower. We have been searching for a spot near the ocean and the city as you requested, and we have a tentative prospect. We have surveyors at the location and will contact you with their analysis within the next five days.

Note that it will take fifteen to twenty weeks to prepare the sight to your specifications. Gaia control over and out."

The screen, which had been showing the dock, now showed only a shimmering sphere that was retreating quickly behind the moon as its' orbit carried the dock below the horizon. A bubble on the moon's surface which served as store house for the engineering equipment was just coming into view. The screen showing the view from the dock had become a panorama of distant stars, and the screen showing the bridge now showed a chaotic scene. Emperor, Hardly-Smyth (contrary to previously released statements of his demise), was hurrying out of the bridge with the rest of the court right behind him.

"Someone find Admiral Chang!," yelled the Captain George.

Several voices replied, "no one has seen him for five years!"

"WHAT THE FUCK! Why didn't any of you morons tell me that!" screamed Captain George as he slammed his fist onto the control panel and yelled, "Navigation Full Stop!"

Running to the console, an Ensign activated the emergency alarm, which began screeching, "Emergency deceleration in progress. Batten down the hatches, secure your safety harnesses, and grab something secured to the walls, floors, or ceiling." The sound of the engines wound up partially covering the repeating announcement. Lincoln yelled, "The furniture is nailed to the floor!" and someone responded, "We know! We've been here before, Linc!" as they clung to chairs, tables, doors, and file cabinets. The engines began to wind down and rearward pressure decreased, everyone resumed watching the screens.

The bridge was a mess. The captain hunched forward in his chair, retched up the remains of his breakfast, along with half of the crew. Finally, the Emergency Alarm blared, "The Hexagon is at Full Stop. Resume your regular routine."

JB7 looked around Lincoln's office and said calmly, "The Emperor has decided to comply with the Gaian's request. Detachment will begin as soon as the Hexagon finishes its approach to the docking station."

****

Yuri and Maya sat bolt upright in their bed, staring glassy-eyed at the wall, each unconscious of the other. Then, after several minutes, and without breaking the trance, they turned to face each other and, in the same eerie voice, chanted, "Was that a dream or a message? Are we facing heaven or hell?"

They shook the cobwebs from their half-awake heads and Maya whispered, "It's neither. It's propaganda from the Emperor. He needs to alter the timeline for posterity. It can't look like they gave the Gaians tower six, it has to have been stolen. Either that or the Gaians are sticking out their tongues at us!"

"I'm going with the Gaians!" Yuri said chuckling, "If it was, I think we'll get on just fine."

'We should investigate this issue!" Maya said teasingly, "but maybe we should wait until we launch to get out of bed."

Maya had finished her morning routine, and Yuri was about to start when the door flew open and Lincoln and his new wife, Zelda, burst into the room. "Did you have it?" he asked conspiratorially.

"If you mean the dream, yes.' Yuri replied, "if you mean my shower, no. So, if you excuse me for a few minutes while I take care of the necessities. Talk to Maya. I won't be long."

Maya gave Zelda a huge hug and whispered in her ear, "Congrats, Z. Remember, I told you not to expect anything normal from the Changs, but after twenty years together, I guess you already knew that."

Zelda whispered back, "Have you had dreams like this before?"

"No, but I've known Yuri for a couple hundred years, so I'm pretty sure it's a one-time thing."

They both laughed and broke the huddle. Maya turned and hugged Lincoln saying, "How many others?"

"So far, we're the only ones. I sent a message to the committee, and my pocket just buzzed. Let me check." He pulled the communicator out of his pocket and scanned the screen. "It looks like it is just the committee. There's no chatter on the common channel."

A knock on the door was followed by the entry of JB7, who was uncharacteristically smiling. "I know who sent the dream!" he said with more enthusiasm than an android should be capable of expressing. "And I am certain that this Tower will survive at the very least. "

A New Origin

"Let me guess," Yuri said as he emerged from the toilet and climbed back into bed, "there is a powerful AI that protects the planet. Also, did the message in the dream actually get delivered and, more importantly, approved?"

"As to the powerful AI, it feels to me like something both more and less than a powerful AI," JB7 replied. "A powerful sentient entity is sure. And a protector does not feel quite correct. I think advisor is a more likely description. In my brief contact, it felt like an observer tweaking an experiment to keep it from a premature endpoint."

"So that would make us playthings of the Demi Gods," Yuri retorted, "and I'm not so sure I trust them."

"Trusting them may be all we've got," JB7 replied. "They did warn us not to dock on the moon. However, I did the calculations, and their warning was strange. The result that I got was that the moon's orbit would not be changed significantly but that the moon will crash into the planet in four hundred thousand years, with or without the presence of the Hexagon."

JB7 froze. His eyes began fluttering, his head started shaking violently, and his body started spasming. Within seconds the room filled with waves of tessellated distortion crossing and intersecting in all directions and colors. The room and everything in it expanded infinitely, and everyone lost consciousness.

****

Five minutes later, by the clock on the bed stand, Maya and Yuri again sat bolt upright in their bed. JB7 was gone and a young couple was standing at the foot of the bed, holding hands and smiling.

The young woman took a step forward and said, "Good Morning Yuri and Maya. Welcome to Gaia! I hope you can understand my Earth English dialect, I haven't had time to learn Martian, and the Techs haven't delivered the translators. We didn't know we would be needing them so soon. I am Penelope, and this is my husband, A-C. We are the ambassadors of the Gaian collective, and we are here to help you adjust to your new home."

Maya replied, "Old Earth English is the official language of the Imperial court. We are required to know it but can only use it when addressing the Emperor. Most of us speak with an accent that is not so very different from yours, but some of our idioms may not make sense to you, as equally, some of your Gaian idioms may not make sense to us."

Yuri looked at the two, leaned close to Maya, and whispered, "Real or another dream, within a dream, within a nightmare?"

Maya shrugged her shoulders, looked at the couple, and said, "So, for the record, this is the second or maybe the third time in what, for us, felt like two hours but was actually, if we are to believe our clock, five minutes, where we were suddenly jolted awake. First, from a dream which was apparently shared by multiple people; then from a total dissolution of our corporeal reality; and again when we wake to find two holographic "ambassadors" who tell us that our two-kilometer, hundred-and-ten thousand-ton starship moved from high orbit to the planet's surface in five minutes; and that they are eager to help us adjust. If that had happened to you, what would be the first question you would ask?"

A-C and Penelope whispered back and forth for a few seconds. Then, finally, A-C cleared his throat and said, "My first four suggestions all included profanities and were rejected by my more diplomatic partner, so I have yielded the podium."

Penelope walked over to Maya's side of the bed and whispered in her ear. Maya immediately began laughing hysterically, followed quickly by Penelope. Maya recovered first and still giggling, said, "If you weren't a hologram, we would be hugging big time and rolling on the floor!"

"What did she say?" came from both Yuri and A-C.

Maya, still chuckling, said, "She said her question would be, 'Can I take a potty break?' something I should have asked." She jumped out of bed and hurried to the bathroom.

Yuri wrapped himself in the sheet, got out of bed, and walked up to A-C and Penelope's avatars. He looked them up and down in great detail. "Why do I think I've seen you before?" He asked, moving to the easy chair near the kitchenette. He sat down, chin in hand, and stared thoughtfully, first at A-C, then at Penelope. "Switch sides, turn to face each other, and now hold both hands." He looked intensely for a few seconds, then closed his eyes just as Maya emerged from the bathroom. "Do you see it, May?"

"Holy shit, it's the couple from Lincoln's pictures. The ones he found on Earth! The ones from the village he found. The ones that eventually led us here!" she said, stepping closer. "I've decided on my first question; Are

A New Origin

you Earthborn? And my second; Are you real, or are you computer generated?"

Penelope started, "A-C and I are the last of the Earthborn. We were pulled out of stasis five years ago. A state we entered twelve hours after the pictures you saw were taken on my sister's tablet, eight hundred years ago. I'm amazed that anything on the device was usable. Did Dr. Chang say where he found the tablet?"

Yuri's jaw dropped, "How do you know about my father?"

"The same way we know about you, Admiral Chang. The Hive, aka Gaia Control, hacked the computers in Hexagon during the chaos of your arrival," Penelope replied. "It is also how we know that the farm, as you call Tower Six, is where the rebellion is housed. Finally, the Hive is responsible for your trip through the fifth dimension, which I'd love to hear you describe sometime later."

Yuri was dumbstruck. He looked pleadingly at Maya as if to say, 'Your turn.' She smiled and said, "So you really are the couple from the pictures. Lincoln likes to pull them up every now and then and prattle on about his expedition. One of his favorite stories is about when he was looking through the ruins of a flower shop he found a vacuum-sealed vault with all sorts of seeds and a small tablet. He went on and on about how a three hundred-year-old tablet still had a charge, how the file said 'the last day on Earth and that all it had was pictures of a wedding, which he showed us many times. It must be a gazillion to one chance that we can now talk to the people in the pictures! I can't tell you how much I would like to hug you both!"

Holographic tears and liquid tears flowed from four sets of eyes. A little choked up, Yuri said, "So why the hell are you out there and not in here?"

A-C and Penelope broke out laughing and looked at each other. Penelope nodded three times, and they shouted, "Because the door's locked!"

Yuri, trying to look cool and collected, lost it and stammered, "I, I, I think we can do something about that. I'll send the butler."

All four were still chuckling when JB7 entered the room and said, "You rang, sir?" to renewed laughter.

Yuri took a deep breath and said, "Would you show the live versions of this young couple to Lincoln's Office and bring them refreshments. Maya and I will receive them there shortly."

"As you wish, sir. Shall I summon Dr. Chang to join you?"

"Yes and bring the engineers Tanesha and Rosita and as many of the committee as you can get ahold of but bring our guests in first."

"I'll do my best, sir," JB7 said, turning on his heel and out the door.

Yuri turned to A-C and Penelope, "If you don't mind turning off the Holo, we both need a shower. As you see, our accommodations only have a large tub, a spigot, and a bucket with holes in the bottom. We would be much obliged if you could wait at the door."

"We'll see you soon," A-C said as they flicked off.

The meet-and-greet was well underway when Maya and Yuri arrived. Lincoln was with A-C, talking to the five members of the Government Planning Committee. Tanesha, Rosita, and JB7 were talking with the Agriculture and Technology committee with Penelope.

"Which do you want, tech or society?" Yuri asked Maya while trying to listen to both at once.

Maya laughed out loud, causing a brief halt in the discussions. "Are you serious, ADMIRAL Chang? You *designed* the Hexagon and were *in charge* of the crew and the Marine detachment. I believe the answer to be obvious!" She turned to the Tech group and said conspiratorially, "I'll be with you in a second." She turned back to Yuri with a sweet smile, "Enjoy your tea time, Dearest. I will relieve you of the pain of uncomfortable discourse with a man you have only recently become acquainted with. Still, I'm sure you will be able to overcome your temerity and contribute admirably. Besides, I'll be right over here if you should need me." She grabbed Yuri by the shoulders, kissed him on the lips, turned him toward the Government group, and sent him toward Lincoln and A-C with a little nudge.

Yuri looked back at her and sighed, "I regret recommending those Victorian novels you've been devouring lately, my queen." He bowed with a flourish. "I shall go now, my beloved. We will speak anon again and, perhaps, walk together through the fields and smell the roses."

"So we shall, husband, so we shall," She replied, blowing a kiss.

The room exploded in laughter and applause. Finally, Yuri and Maya bowed to both groups and attended their respective meetings.

When Maya joined the Tech group, Tanesha pulled her aside and said, "We're discussing strategic communications, and something is nagging me that I can't quite remember. It's driving me cra..." suddenly, her eyes rolled, and she fainted. Maya caught her up and carried her to a chair in the back of the room. The whole group crowded around them with concern.

"I think she's exhausted," Maya said the instant before Tanesha's eyes opened wide, and she bolted to a stand. "I have a message to convey, but you will not believe it!" She said emphatically.

Penelope came over, put her hands on Tanesha's shoulders, and stared into her eyes. "You got a message which restored your memory of your discussion with an entity that called itself Gaia Space and Customs Control."

Tanesha froze, staring open-mouthed at Penelope. After several seconds she shook her head and said, "How?"

Penelope giggled and said, "OOPS, My Bad! I wasn't supposed to talk about that yet. Hold on a sec while I call A-C." She stood statue still, staring into space for several seconds, blinked twice, looked at the stunned group, and said, "They'll be back here in a couple of minutes, and we'll start our discussion of hive minds, singularities, and telepathy."

The room went silent until a voice from the back of the room said, "You're not serious."

Penelope looked Tanesha in the eyes for several seconds. Finally, Tanesha broke the stare and said, "Oh, she's serious. Scary serious. She told me to tell you that she sent A-C instructions that when he comes in, he will say 'Bob's your Uncle'; blow kisses to everyone; do a handstand and a backflip; and asks anyone who wants to write a short message and give them to me. Penelope and I will wait outside while you write the messages and seal them in an envelope. JB7 and Maya will take the envelope and A-C to another room. JB will generate a privacy field to block all electromagnetic, sonic, quantum, and gravitational noise, and A-C will read the messages silently. Penelope will recite what he reads, and you will judge. Unless any of you know of any other type of non-electronic communication at a distance that passes through walls," she paused, looked around the room, and seeing no hands, continued, "OK, anyone that wants to come with me, we'll leave now and catch him before he gets here." Three engineers raised their hands, and the five left the room, loudly securing the door behind them.

Five minutes later, Penelope clapped her hands to get everyone's attention. "A-C says he's sending the social issues discussion group on ahead, and they should arrive in three minutes. He also asks if we get the messages correct, does he have to do the backflip, and the Bob's your uncle?" The result came back as overwhelmingly YES!

The Social committee returned with a proposal, that Penelope read, A-C transcribed, and JB7 recorded. The proposal was accepted, and the experiment proceeded. The results were twenty-seven correct answers and one disqualified because A-C couldn't decipher the handwriting, and then allowed when the author conceded that he had written nonsense as an experimental control.

Once the results were announced, the demands to be taught telepathy were loud and unanimous. Finally, Lincoln whistled a loud shrieking note which quieted the ruckus. "I agree that this is a high priority. BUT... we have been talking for five solid hours and I, for one, am exhausted and hungry. Therefore, I suggest that we adjourn for the day and pick up the conversation tomorrow at two. I also think we will need a physician or two to explore the possible physiological changes that have to be made to adjust to Gaia."

A-C and Penelope looked at each other and said, "We are physicians, and we are looking forward, for the first time since our graduation on the day we left Earth, to teaching what we know about the human brain. However, we are very much in need of a bit of time to put together a coherent presentation."

A-C pitched in, "And I think we will need someone who knows the state of the art of medicine on Mars when you left and any new knowledge you gained during the trip here."

A small dark man at the back of the room, whose high-pitched sniveling voice triggered a memory in Yuri, said meekly, "I can help."

"Dr. Snape!" Yuri exclaimed, "I never got a chance to apologize for my behavior the last time we met. I was, as you might remember, somewhat rude."

"I do remember, and I want to thank you for what you did for me."

A New Origin

Surprised, Yuri stammered "Thank *Me*? Why?"

"Because of you, the Emperor banished me to the farm. It's been the best thing that has ever happened to me."

Yuri stepped over and offered his hand. "Let me buy you a beer and a burger when we adjourn. After that, I'd like to hear your back story."

"Deal!" Snape said heartily, shaking Yuri's hand.

Penelope stretched, yawned and said, "We'll also need someone to explain a singularity of intelligence and the fifth dimension in lay terms."

"I plead the Fifth!" cried Rosita.

"I can help!" came a voice from the Tech side. "Me too," said another.

"Outstanding!" Penelope exclaimed, "We have a select committee. I'll chair. We'll meet here tomorrow at noon."

"I'll do the singularity," Tanesha said, "I've had some personal experience with the Gaian customs hive mind that claimed to be almost a singularity."

"I'll do the singularity too. It was my Ph.D. thesis," Maya said with a shrug. "I never thought it would be useful. Guess I was wrong."

"Thanks, Maya. You've just earned yourself the Chair of the Singularity Committee."

"Yeah, I was afraid of that, but I guess that's what I get for bragging."

When the laughter finished, Lincoln stood on his chair and announced, "If there are no objections, this meeting is adjourned. We will reconvene here in three days. Our new committees should arrange meetings in the interim."

As everyone turned to leave, they found Yuri and A-C blocking the door and talking to JB7. Yuri and A-C held up their hands to stop the rush out the door. Yuri stepped forward and said, "JB7 has just informed us that the Emperor has claimed Gaia as 'property of the throne,' and proclaimed Gaia City as the Imperial See, renaming it The Forbidden City. No males over twelve are allowed within one hundred kilometers of the city's center, and no females are allowed to leave the city. Evacuation must be completed by the time the newly christened spaceship Pentagon lands, one month from now."

Chuckling, which had started with 'The emperor has claimed…' became belly laughs to the point where Yuri couldn't continue.

A-C and Penelope were clinging to each other horrified. When Maya came over to comfort them, Penelope grabbed her and sobbed, "Why are they laughing? We don't have any defenses!"

"Hush, hush, my sweet girl, it's all bluster," Maya said calmly. "We have more than half of their military strength right here on the farm. Better than that, consider that it was Gaian technology that moved the farm here. The Empire doesn't have anywhere near that level of technology. And if that wasn't enough, the Empire's three best military minds are in this room."

"Make that the four best minds," Yuri said, breaking a huddle with Lincoln and A-C. "Maya, my dear, you underestimate yourself!"

"And we have their two best engineers in Tanesha and Rosita," Lincoln said, joining the growing huddle.

"And a top secret weapon," Dr. Snape said conspiratorially from outside the huddle.

"The Embryo Bank!" Tanesha declared.

"That's part of it," Snape said with a smirk and very quietly, "The other part, the more relevant part, and THE Top of all Top secrets is that... wait for it... All the males in the direct Imperial lineage have a somatic mutation that kills their male sperm, so they can only make girls. Since genetic alteration is prohibited and only direct descent is allowed, it isn't the embryos in the bank they want; it's the male sperm from Emperor Henry the twenty-fourth, who died, two hundred years before the Hexagon left Mars. He was the definition of jag-off, providing a daily dose for sixty years. His male sperm were separated and frozen. It's rumored that the current Emperor has used sixty doses during his ten-year reign without success, and his father used some two hundred before our Josh was conceived.

The laughter spread through the room as the 'secret' spread.

As the room cleared, the tall, long-limbed Rosita and Tanesha corralled A-C and Penelope. "We've decided you two will stay with us," Rosita said in her best, 'You can't refuse voice.' "It's tight but cozy, and we're getting good vibes from both of you."

A New Origin

"We get the same from you," Penelope said, her eyes watering. "We would be honored. However, I do need to warn you that A-C can be quite a noisy sleeper."

Tanisha whispered conspiratorially, "We'll put him in the room with Rosy, and you and I will finally get an uninterrupted night's rest."

"Deal!" Penelope said as the four left the room, chatting happily.

****

Emperor Joshua the First was sitting on the throne, glaring at the assembled officer corps kowtowing below him. The throne room was silent except for the two androids carrying the body of the now ex-Admiral Mason to the deep freezer next to the stasis chambers holding the hungry pride of lions.

"Six weeks!" He shouted, "Six bloody weeks, and you still can't tell me what happened to Tower 6! Your JOB is to defend the ship, and six weeks after a part of the ship DISAPPEARS, you still don't know what happened. So how the bloody hell are you bloody morons going to keep it from happening again if you can't bloody tell me what happened!" He paused for a moment glaring at the noticeably anxious officers. "How? Tell me how you can lose one-sixth of a starship. It's bloody unbelievable! Mason thought he could get away with the 'we're looking into it' bull shit after six bloody weeks. Anyone else care to explain what happened to Tower 6?" he shouted, shining a laser pointer from head to head. "How about you, Craver? You're in charge of engineering. You must have something better than Mason's, *'We don't know.*' Stand up and give me something I can believe."

Captain Craver lifted his head and stood up, shaking visibly, "Your Highness, I have just received a message that a meta-analysis of the surveillance videos has concluded that Six's black-hole generator's containment field failed, and Six was swallowed by the black hole. The event horizon collapsed ten nanoseconds after Six passed through it. The whole process took fifty nanoseconds. Gravitational waves were detected at amplitudes consistent with the mass of Six." Carver dropped head first to the floor with an audible crack, black smoke wafting from an angry hole where his cranium used to be.

Two androids quickly removed the body while another cleaned the floor, and a fourth approached the Emperor. "Your Majesty, I have a video for you to view," it said, producing a small tablet. "We slowed the original as much as possible to one nanosecond per second.

The Emperor watched the video ten times, stood up, and smashed the tablet against the android's head. "I want a detailed report on how this happened in my hand in two hours and all of you out of here in two minutes."

As the rush for the door started, the Emperor stood and shouted, "The Cabinet will meet here in fifteen minutes with a status report on the activity on the planet."

Fifteen minutes later, the Emperor entered, motioned for them to sit, and stared angrily at each one. He did this for fifteen minutes until he settled on the Secretary of State. "What does the State Department know about the evacuation of the Forbidden City that I ordered?"

The Secretary pushed his chair back from the table, slowly balanced his bulky torso over his spindly legs, and rose to a stand supported by his hands clenched to the back of his chair. "Your Majesty, I have ordered four additional surveillance satellites to low orbits to enhance the resolution of the videos we have been receiving. In addition, inclement weather has changed the normal activity patterns we saw before Your Highness's declaration. The storms will clear by daybreak, and we should have reliable information shortly thereafter."

The Emperor laughed ominously, "You're going to go with that? You're losing your touch. It's a shame, really. I've always found you to be amusing and informative. It breaks my heart to see you go so low as to blame the weather. I'll tell you what I heard, and you tell me if I'm right. I heard that there was a new statue on a roof in the downtown area. If you can tell me about that, I'll let you retire to a stasis chamber. So, tell me about it in detail, with pictures."

The Secretary, sweating profusely, pulled a handkerchief and a small tablet from his coat pocket. He wiped sweat with one hand and typed on the tablet with the other. He looked up from the tablet and saw the Emperor smiling at his own tablet. "Now, please describe this to the room," the Emperor said, typing a command that produced a fully realized hologram of a naked couple lying on their backs side-by-side, each with one hand in their partner's nether zone and the other hand pointing at the sky.

A New Origin

The Emperor walked over and put his arm around the Secretary's shoulders. "Isn't this a beautiful piece of art? Two beautiful people so obviously in love, sharing the beauty of a starry night and celebrating the arrival of their lord and master. So, really, the only thing I need you to explain is why they are pointing with their middle fingers."

The Secretary wiped his face and calmly said, "My understanding is that it is a sign that comes from an ancient warrior society that used bows made from Yew tree branches. They would pull the bowstring with their middle finger. Their common language term for shooting arrows was to 'pluck yew.' When staging an ambush, the commander used an upheld middle finger as a silent command to release the arrow or, 'pluck yew.' There was also a demigod named Cupid who would shoot arrows into the hearts of suitors that would change them into lovers. Over time the 'pl' of pluck turned into an f, and the 'ew' of yew turned into o, u, resulting in an epithet that has connotations of forced intimacy and a silent way of announcing said epithet."

The room was utterly silent until the Emperor roared with laughter, releasing the pressure on the rest of the room. The Secretary was pummeled with the Emperor's slaps on his back and from others. When the tumult subsided, the Emperor dismissed the Cabinet. As they left, he pulled the Secretary of State aside and whispered, "Just so you know, I wouldn't have had you executed for using the banned word in this circumstance, Secretary Chang, but your brother, and his son, I intend to have shot on sight. I've noticed that you aren't as healthy as you pretend to be. I'm going to need you in the future, so I'm ordering you to take a month in a regeneration tank starting tomorrow. When you get back, you'll be governor of the northern region. Too bad your brother's gone missing. We could have used him as an ambassador."

George Washington Chang looked at the Emperor and shook his head, "No, your Highness, we're better off without him."

Emperor Joshua the First smiled at Secretary Chang and said, "We think Lincoln was on Six. We tried to find him before detachment, but the androids we sent to look for him disappeared. We also think your nephew was on Six, along with his pet android."

"That's excellent news, your Highness! Yuri was voted the most dangerous man in the solar system when your father was on the throne. I'm hoping the black hole hypothesis is correct, and they got flushed down the wormhole."

"Wow, not much family love in the Chang gang, but between you and me, and you need to mark this top secret, I'm thinking that the wormhole is exactly what happened, and that the other side of the wormhole is somewhere on Gaia and not some random spot in another galaxy. If the troops start believing that, they won't fight an enemy they think is that powerful. So, I need them to think it was a system failure caused by the engineering team during the detachment."

"I wouldn't be surprised if it was my brother and his son in a suicide pact. But," Secretary Chang said with a smirk, "I can get behind this. Give me a couple of hours, and my propaganda group will have a storyline, complete with witnesses and tangible evidence. It will be all over the ship that the former Admiral and the traitorous former Prime Minister died in a suicide bombing of Tower Six, while aiding and abetting the rebellious Gaians."

"That's perfect, George. I won't keep you any longer. Schedule a press conference for tomorrow at the hour that Six disappeared. Then, I will announce your promotion to Commanding General, and you can announce your war council. Congratulations, General Chang!" The Emperor kissed Washington Chang on both cheeks and bear-hugged him, whispering in his ear, "My chamber, eighteen hundred hours, as usual."

"Of course, your Highness, of course."

****

A-C, Penelope, Maya, Yuri, Lincoln, Zelda, Tanesha, Rosita, and JB7 were standing in a half meter of snow, watching as the last few pieces of Tower Six were loaded onto trucks for shipment to the fabrication facility at Tech City, in the snow-topped Southern Mountains. The engine, running at 0.5% capacity, was already powering the electricity grid and the industrial manufacturing facilities, which were repurposing the structural and electronic parts. Twenty farming towns near Gaia City and New Origin happily received the eighty family units. The livestock in stasis was delivered to various farm cooperatives to enhance the diversity of their flocks and herds. The stasis and regeneration units were distributed to hospitals and emergency response stations. The shipping containers were, surprisingly, repurposed to their original purpose, and the embryo bank was on the loading dock of the train station.

A New Origin

Lincoln picked up his travel bag, "Alright folks, we've got a train to catch."

Yuri sighed, "I think I'm going to build a house here when this whole thing is over."

"This would be ideal for a Ski Resort," Maya said, gazing up at the snow-capped mountains on the other side of the valley.

Tanesha and Rosita looked at each other, nodded, and said, "We're in!"

"Someone has to teach us to ski," Penelope sighed.

"My mom talked about skiing in someplace on Earth called West Virgin. She would bend at the knees and twist back and forth, swinging her arms like she's punching low," A-C said, mimicking the movement.

"I used to watch ancient videos of people on Earth skiing in some kind of competition. It looked like a lot of fun," Zelda said, "I'm in!"

"I'm recording and submitting a proposal," JB7 said in his business voice. "Let's consider it a reason to survive what's about to come."

"Speaking of that, maybe we should head for the train station," Lincoln said, walking away.

"Right behind you, Boss," JB7 called, striding after him.

The rest grabbed their backpacks and bags and hurried down the trail to the station.

The entrance to the station was disguised as a cave at the base of a towering butte. As they approached the entrance, Maya pulled Yuri aside. "It looks like the entry to the farm."

"It should. That's where it came from. It's just the entry. We shut down the maze, to the delight of ten lost security guards that the Emperor sent to find us. I can't tell you how happy they were when I told them where, and when, they ended up."

They stepped through the pitch-black door and onto a long steep escalator going down to the station.

"And where exactly was that?" Maya continued.

"Oh, they're here. They've been teaching a few of our people and some of the locals how to operate the Mech suits. They should be at the station waiting for us."

Maya had an uneasy feeling and asked, "Suited up?"

"Oh heaven's, no, they would rather die than get in one of the suits. Their indoctrination was the equivalent of heavy addiction. They're afraid they won't be able to control themselves in the presence of Imperial Mechs. So they are here to train the defense forces at Gaia City and New Origin."

"So that's what you've been up to while I've been putting people to sleep trying to teach them about singularities! You've been getting the Hoo-Ra's while I've been getting the snores."

"It's not quite what you think. I've been trying to teach tactics, and it seems to be causing as many snores as you've been getting," Yuri sighed. "You remember the recruiting pitches and all the rah-rah bull shit. They seem to prefer that stuff to the details of war-craft."

"I guess we both should be talking to them since we are the officers in charge, and they need to know how to resist berserker mode until specifically ordered."

"Indeed, General Maya, that's what we're here for. There will also be a number of raw recruits on the train."

"Are you saying we will be training on the train, Admiral Yuri?"

"I'm following your train of thought, General Maya, but we won't train on the train. We will take the train to the training sites in Gaia City and New Origin and train the trainees there."

They were still chuckling when they stepped off the escalator onto a crowded platform as the doors opened on the train's ten cars. JB7 directed them to the lounge car with the rest of the strategic planning committee. The Lounge had been reconfigured into a meeting room, and everyone was seated in cushy high-backed chairs around a long table. JB7 stood at one end of the table in front of a large screen displaying an aerial view of downtown New Origin City. A bell chimed, followed by, "Please remain seated until we have reached cruising speed. We will arrive at Gaia City in one hour and eleven minutes. Enjoy your trip."

JB7 tapped on the table and announced, "I have just been informed that all the towers of Hexagon are now independently orbiting the planet.

A New Origin

Their orbits suggest that towers Two and Five are preparing to land in the vicinity of Gaia City. Their braking rate indicates they will touch down on the Cape Gaia in approximately twenty-three hours, seventeen minutes, and forty-eight seconds. The Imperial tower is still in at the dock on the moon, pending its' division into the two five-hundred-fifty and one nine-hundred-meter towers that will form the imperial palace. We estimate that the division will take two to three months and another month before they land.

Three and Four are targeting New Origin, and the current best estimate of touch-down is eight hours and twelve minutes plus or minus five minutes."

Tanesha looked at the screen and asked, "Are they going to the landing pads?"

"From my discussions with Gaia Control, it seemed that the Martians understood that there was nowhere stable enough to support the weight of the upright towers," JB7 replied.

"I, for one, hope they don't. But," Lincoln said, "if they landed on unstable ground, It would simplify things immensely."

"But it does affect our itinerary," Yuri interjected. "We should make some adjustments in asset distribution. We expected Three and Four would go to Gaia City with One because they have most of the assets. Sending them to New Origin suggests they intend to take it hostage and use it to force a surrender in Gaia City."

"I know I'm not going to like this," A-C said hesitantly, "but I propose that Yuri, Lincoln, Maya, Tanesha, Rosita, and two-thirds of the Mechs come with me to New Origin, where I have a bunch of connections. The rest of you will go with Pen to Gaia City, where she's the Assistant Mayor: and where the Mayor is watching our four-year-old twins. So that will distribute our assets for the more likely situation. And if the situation changes, the train ride from New Origin to Gaia City is only an hour."

Yuri was the first to reply, "That's essentially what I was going to propose, and I don't like it either, but I think we should trade Maya for JB7. That way, we have the tactical computer on site in case it's a gambit."

"Hold on a second," Maya said emphatically, "I think we're missing something here. The misogyny of the Empire is epic, which boils down to a belief that a male army is, by nature, superior to a female force. From what I've seen of the women on this planet, it seems to me that the reverse is true here. So I think all the women should go to Gaia City and organize an all-female resistance. An Amazon army with all mythical characteristics: bows and arrows; spears and magical shields; tight form-fitting flexible armor and magical whips; silver helmets with lasers; and," switching to a whimsical voice, "of course, bare-chested and on horseback. That last bit is something that would halt them in their tracks and make them cover their eyes."

"And I know Mayor Lisa would be behind this plan a hundred percent!" Penelope interjected, " She's already a bit of an Amazon warrior, and she has a large number of contacts that could easily make this happen."

"I agree with Maya," Lincoln declared. "All in favor...." The ayes were immediate and unanimous.

"Hold on a minute," JB7 said, standing utterly still, "Two and Five are returning to the moon. There is, as yet, no indication that they will be landing any time soon. My calculations indicate that the earliest would be at least five to seven days."

"That's great news!' Maya said, "It will give us more time to recruit and train the Women's Army."

"And time for the techs to make outfits that fit and the weapons we will need," Rosita said, plucking the waist of her way too baggy trousers.

"That's what I was thinking," Zelda said with a smile, "I was a fashion designer and seamstress in my former life and would love to take control of the outfitting details. But I'm afraid I would be a disaster in the field."

"What a great idea, Z!" Maya exclaimed, "You are now the official Amazon design director!"

The public address speaker announced, "Gaia City Station, please remain seated until the train has come to a complete stop. The next station is New Origin. There will be a thirty-minute layover. Continuing passengers, please remain on the train. Arriving passengers, please check the over overhead storage for your luggage. Welcome to Gaia City."

The women retrieved their bags, hugged, and kissed the men, and got off the train. The men and JB7 continued on to New Origin.

Curtain.

Act Seven Preface/Post Script

The group leaving Collin and Katy's house for the final play had grown to nearly sixty and included both children and their parents. The emphasis in the schools over past few weeks was the history of Gaia and the story of the unlikely survival of the human race, or so one would have thought. Much of the real reason that the final play was an order of magnitude more attended was most likely due to the action scenes and the tension of a war for the survival of an idea and followed by the joy of survival and the gift of a second chance. The curtain rises on a time when the outcome was unknown.

ACT SEVEN

IS THIS THE WAY THE WORLD ENDS? BANG OR WHIMPER? FIRE OR ICE?

Chorus

End times loom for us

threatening the spring with doom

we stand together!

Master of Ceremonies: Poets on old Earth envisioned the last act of the human world in a number of ways, some emphatically, some by reason. The emphatic is represented by a poet named Eliot in a poem about a dying Earth peopled by the walking dead. We quoted the final line in the intro to Act I. Here we give you the entire last stanza:

This is the way the world ends.

This is the way the world ends.

This is the way the world ends.

Not with a bang but a whimper.

Another poet, named Frost, took the analytical approach considering the possibilities of Fire and Ice in two short stanzas:

Some say the world will end in fire, Some say in ice.

From what I've tasted of desire

A New Origin

> *I hold with those who favor fire.*
> *But if it had to perish twice,*
> *I think I know enough of hate*
> *To say that for destruction ice*
> *Is also great*
> *And would suffice.*

    The question we face here is, with each side facing the second end of their worlds, will it be by Fire or by Ice; or by Bang or by Whimper? So, dear viewer, we find out as we proudly present our play's seventh and final act.

SCENE ONE

First Foray:
The First Battle of New Origin

Yuri, Lincoln, A-C, Adam, and William Dee were sitting in lawn chairs under a canopy tent at the front end of Tower Three, which was lying horizontally next to Tower Four, which was likewise laid out, on the site of New Origin's abandoned spaceport. They had come every morning for the last five days and sat with a thermos of coffee, an ice chest full of William's beer, chips, and veggie trays, reading the New Origin Times.

"So you say that this category of printed reporting served as the purveyor of the news for centuries before the electronic era," Yuri said, turning to the sports pages. "I find it encouraging that most of the news involves sporting events and not scandals or violence. It looks like we'll be missing several soccer games, a baseball tournament, a strongly hyped basketball match, and a polo tournament, whatever that is, all of which are happening over the next five days. The small print on, let's see... Ah, page fifteen has a schedule of recreational leagues in all age groups and proficiency levels, along with advertisements for coaches and referees. What I don't see are gender designations."

William, A-C, and Adam all broke out laughing. "If you picked the top 10 players of any team, six of them would be female," William chuckled, "We're a race of strong women and men who appreciate them."

"And wouldn't have it any other way!" Adam added.

"The other thing I don't see," Yuri continued, "is anything about these huge shiny tubes of interstellar jetsam."

"I've got that one," A-C said, cracking a beer. "Adam and I spread the info through phone chains and telepathic messages. Everybody in the city and most folks within a hundred clicks have been informed of the plan and will be prepared. They are, for the moment, pretending that nothing important is happening and secretly training the Army and preparing to defend themselves. With, of course, your expert advice and weapons furnished by the Techs."

Yuri smiled at him, gave a double thumbs up, and snatched a beer.

JB7 stood behind the others, holding a ten-meter flagpole with a large white flag fluttering in the gentle breeze.

Yuri turned in his chair and asked JB7, "Anything yet?"

"Yes, the first code has been entered to open the doors and extend the ramp. The second is in process and will be complete in three, two, one."

Right on cue, a thirty-meter wide, forty-meter high section of the back wall began lower like a bridge over the moat of a medieval castle. A loudspeaker blared the Imperial anthem. Two lines of androids dressed as Imperial Guards, armed with swords and crossbows, lined the edges of the ramp, and stopped dead still when the first in line got to the bottom.

A-C and Adam turned to Yuri and simultaneously asked, "What the hell was that?"

Yuri shook his head, "You two have got to stop doing that 'twin thing.' It's just a bit creepy. As to that!" nodding at the guards, "That has always been creepy Imperial pomposity. If the Emperor were here, the protocol would have us lying on our bellies with our foreheads on the ground until His Highness allowed us to get up."

A-C went solo, "So what's next?"

"Well, what I hope happens is that one of the sane officers is in charge here, and we'll all become friends and buy each other puppies and unicorns," Yuri said with a tired laugh. "I think that plan might work here, but I don't know what to think about Gaia City."

"Here they come," Adam said as he stood and stretched.

"Looks like there's six of them," A-C said, yawning.

"We can take 'em easy-peasy," William said as he stretched and flexed.

"Change places with me, Adam; I want to be next to William," Yuri teased.

"Are they in full formal uniforms?" A-C asked, "Maybe we should have gone a little more dressy than hoodies and shorts."

"No, my friends, this is perfect!" Yuri said, taking two steps forward, "The lead guy was my best friend in high school and the Academy. We're good to go," he said, stepping through the invisibility screen and yelling, "Naddy! Naddy Shahan! Imagine that! After all these years. I thought that Mason was in command of Three."

Shahan froze at the bottom of the ramp, and his face contorted with surprise and horror. "Yu, Yu, Yu, Yuri?" he stammered, "What?... How?... Here? Six too? Maya? Lincoln? My Wife?" Tears filled his eyes, and he passed out.

Yuri caught him under the arms, carried him into the tent, plopped him into a chair, and went back out to address the other five officers. "He's OK guys; he'll recover when he gets hold of a beer. You should all step in, sit down, introduce yourselves, and get a beer. I'll be right back. My coffee has worked its magic, and I need a quick run to the head."

On the way, Yuri grabbed JB7 by the arm and pulled him into the Porta-Potty. "What do you know about the passengers on Three? Are they still the families of the maintenance and service staff for the elites?"

JB7 closed his eyes for several seconds, then said, "That is mostly true; there are also the families of the officer corps and several families of the arts and literature community, about five thousand altogether. There also seem to be five hundred and eighty Marines and ten Mechs,"

"Are the Mechs operational?"

"It appears that their riders were on Tower Six."

"Are the androids able to control the Mechs?"

"No, the neural nets the drivers wear, and that control circuitry, are incompatible with our circuitry."

"That's what I thought," Yuri said with a smile, "Could we move Three to the valley where Six was? Then, we could use the parts of Three to build the ski resort."

JB7 went still for several seconds, then said, "Gaia Control says yes."

"Four is essentially a parking lot of limousines and delivery trucks, with the drivers and their families the only passengers," Yuri mused, "we'll have to deal with them separately. What does Gaia control say about moving them to the valley too?"

"JB7 froze for a few seconds and said, "They said yes, but they would need four hours between the moves."

"Have you made contact with anyone or anything on Four?"

"I have. The crew is all android, and their programming does not allow them to make decisions. However, they do say they would not resist if we were to go down that road."

"OK, tell them to prepare for the move, which will be either before we move Three, or four hours after," Yuri said, washing his hands in the little sink. "Let's get back to the tent and get this party started!"

They walked back to the tent, and JB7 resumed standing at the flagpole. Yuri entered the tent to find everyone engaged in conversation. He took a seat next to his old friend Shahan, who leaned into him and whispered in his ear, "The Emperor blew Mason's brains out in front of the whole officer corps over the disappearance of Six. Shot Carver too, when he said Six was sucked into a black hole. He chose me, at random, to take command of Three. I guess he forgot you and I were in the same class and Frat at the Academy."

Yuri whispered back, "I thought I saw your wife on Six! She didn't see me, though. Your kids were both making a fuss, and I was late for a meeting."

Shahan, teary-eyed, hugged Yuri and kissed him on both cheeks. Yuri whispered, "I'll get you back to them one way or another."

Yuri leaned back in his chair and smiled, "I am glad to see all of you have survived after I was removed from command! I have just been informed of the tragic end that our good friends Mason and Carver suffered. I want to offer a toast to their memory. Anyone who needs another beer should get one now."

Six of the eleven participants got up, refilled their steins, and returned to their chairs.

"I'm assuming that you all know me well enough to know that I would never lie to you," Yuri said, looking into the eyes of each of the officers seated in the circle of lawn chairs, TV trays carrying veggie trays and cheese boards; coolers of beer; and in the middle, a substantial fire burning merrily in a stone-lined fire pit. "I'm here today to tell you that what you've been led to believe is a backward culture on this planet is, in fact, extremely sophisticated and uniformly egalitarian. You'll learn more about it, but the main thing to know is that everyone has a base income that fully covers food, housing, and transportation. What you do for work is your choice. No job pays more than any other job, and you get to choose. Production of most common items is automated and managed by a Tech sub-culture considerably more advanced than the one we brought. After all, they can transport enormous spaceships through time and space. An experience that I will never forget and that I hope you will have the pleasure of experiencing very soon.

With that, I would like to introduce three of our Gaian hosts. Adam is a lifelong resident and the first child born in the New Origin colony, the city where we are parked. Next to Adam is A-C, Adam's identical twin brother, who was born on Earth and only removed from stasis five years ago to provide the historical background of the Earth vs. Mars relationship. I'll let them handle their own stories. Next to the twins is William, one day younger than Adam and the provider of beer and profound wisdom to all who ask and even to those who don't ask. Finally, some of you will remember our former Prime Minister, the bane of my existence, and my dear father, Dr. Lincoln Chang. Be aware that he is a master of the art of long narrative descriptions of minutia. With that, I cede the floor to William, who will describe our plan to make it look like there was a fierce battle that caused the total destruction of Three and a few hours later Four, or vice-versa if you wish."

William stood, lifted his beer stein, and said, "A toast to new friends and co-conspirators."

Everyone stood saying "Here-here," clinking steins and taking giant draughts.

When the introductions and greetings were complete, and everyone was reseated, William tapped his stein with a spoon and said, "The only reason I was chosen to lay out our battle plan is that they want to laugh at me when I use a whole slew of words that I never knew existed and the fact that I can memorize a sixty-page manuscript in sixty seconds. Thankfully, for you, the battle plan is considerably shorter, a mere fifty-eight pages." When the laughter settled, he continued, "OK, here's the plan. In twenty minutes, four horse-drawn carriages will come charging up the road carrying something that looks like an X-ray laser cannon but is actually something called a virtual reality generator. When we see them coming, the six of you Martians will haul ass up the ramp, close the door,

A New Origin

start up the engine, and set it to idle. Gaia control will take it from there, and you will get that experience that Yuri was all weird about. First, you and the rest of the crew will need to find a place to lie down. Then, we will deploy the projectors two in front of Three and two over yonder in front of Four. They will be followed by two hundred virtual mounted soldiers carrying sonic disrupters. They will ride between Three and Four, taking positions every ten meters. When everyone is in place, they will open fire on Three. Virtual return fire will come from Three, and it will do some damage, so the Emperor will think that you fought back. We will continue to project a hologram of a destroyed Three while we virtually attack the real Four. Meanwhile, you guys will be teleported to the prettiest place you've ever seen, where you and your families will have an orientation and training for whatever jobs you would like. You will then be relocated to the cities and towns that need people with your new skill sets."

"And I can guarantee that any of your relatives on Six will be there to greet you," Yuri said with a big smile and a hug for Shahan.

The next five minutes were filled with quick exchanges of contact information, no small bit of beer consumption, and explanations on how to use a telephone. JB7 interrupted the merriment with the news that the wagons were about to appear, which paused the talk and aroused the curiosity of the Martians, who had never seen live horses. They ran up the ramp and stopped at the top staring at the wagons as they came out from behind the trees until the door sealed shut.

Yuri, Lincoln, A-C, Adam, and William sat around the fire pit and watched the attack play out in virtual reality. Finally, tower Three blinked into nothingness, and a fully realized smoldering hulk was in its place. They stayed for the second battle with Four, then walked down to Adam's house in downtown New Origin.

SCENE TWO
The Siege of Gaia City

Two months after the 'battle' of New Origin, Towers 2 and 5 landed on what the Gaians called 'Cape Terra,' which the Emperor immediately renamed the 'Imperial Peninsula.' The peninsula/cape was a fifteen-kilometer wide strip of land that angled thirty-five kilometers into the ocean, forming the south side of Terra Bay. The last five kilometers of the peninsula curved sharply to the north, ending parallel with the Gaia City beach thirty kilometers to the west.

The two towers landed horizontally, east to west, one and a half kilometers apart near the peninsula's north end. Work began immediately preparing the space at the east end of the landing site for the arrival of the Imperial Tower and on the conversation of Two and Five into luxury condominiums for the three thousand aristocratic families, currently in stasis, that had fled Mars with the Emperor.

The Imperial Tower was divided into three sections. The two smaller ones were five-hundred-fifty meters tall. They would house government officials and their families, along with the ultra-rich. The largest part was nine-hundred meters, the upper half of which would be the Emperor's quarters with the Throne room at the very top. The bottom half would house the treasures of art and antiquities that the imperium had collected over its five-hundred-year reign.

Two weeks after Two and Five landed, the three parts of Tower One landed between the western ends of Two and Five, with the tallest in the middle to make the Imperial Palace, with Two and Five completing the walls of the New Forbidden City. The Emperor declared sovereignty over the Gaians, demanded the fealty of all citizens, and declared a five-day total curfew, beginning immediately, with anyone disobeying to be shot on sight. At the end of his speech, a swarm of drones launched from Forbidden City.

****

General Maya and Green Company were encamped on Imperial Peninsula in the woods near the beach, a half a click from where the towers had landed. The Amazon outfits were determined to be Dress outfits and not practical as combat gear. Their campsite was disguised by an invisibility screen, as were their combat units. They had been there for two weeks when the Emperor made his proclamation. All three hundred of them were on the beach with arrows notched when the drones launched. The advantage of arrows was that there was no telltale contrail or muzzle smoke. The arrows were maneuverable through a headset and had warheads that were proximity-activated. The first volley took out thirty drones, and the second took out forty. A switch to the long-range arrows with booster rockets caught the last ten drones and five unfortunate seagulls.

Maya's headphones sounded an alarm " General Maya, we have detected a fighter lifting off. "

"Roger that!" she said, turning to her troops, "Move, move, move, back into the woods as deep as you can get. They've got a fighter taking off. Don't stop at the camp. Go straight to the bunker. I'm arming the defenses. We need to haul ass!"

The company moved as one into the woods and were half a click away from the campsite when they heard the WHUMP of a pulse canon and the cracking of falling trees. The cannon fired again, this time further away, and again, this time closer. Maya was the last one into the bunker, diving through the door as it irised shut and activating the force field two seconds before a pulse rattled the walls. She leaped into the command chair and said, "Control! Play destruct scenario on next pulse."

"Destruct simulation activated, General. Playing Now."

Maya and her troops watched the VR of the bunker exploding on the large screen in the command room, betting on which parts of who would fly the farthest, with a number of laughing shouts like, 'That's my leg' and 'I'm still holding my bow' and 'I didn't know you had a tattoo on your butt.'

Maya turned her helmet screen to normal and surveyed the damage, which showed a wide swatch of downed trees that started on the shoreline and continued for five kilometers to the road that ran down the center of the peninsula to Gaia City. "Open the comm to Red Company," she said, leaning back in the command seat.

Mayor Lisa answered within seconds, "Maya! I was so worried watching that Fighter blasting the woods. Are you OK?"

"We are a little shaken, but outside of a few scratches, a couple of sprained ankles, and a broken wrist, no one was hurt. I wanted to tell you to go to ground and don't engage the Fighter. It's just clearing the way for what, I suspect, will be a troop carrier or two, loaded with marines and Mechs. Did you get the new weapons yet?"

"Do you mean the distortion guns? We got them today and have been practicing with them pretty intensely."

"Good. Use them with care. Did you evacuate the building with the statue? If not, do it now."

"We got everybody out and put a big distortion gun on the roof. We will control it remotely."

"Great! Green company should be there in about half an hour, assuming the Martians haven't booby-trapped the road. You have about a minute now. My love to everyone! Out."

Maya stood up and looked over the women who were silently staring at her. "OK, here's the plan," she said in a no-nonsense voice, "any of you that have a scrape, scratch, bruise, sprain, broken bone, or blister, no matter how small, and I know who you are, will stay here and prepare to defend the road. The rest of you will gear up at the garage, where you will rev up your motorcycles, ride into town, and shoot some Mechs. Minesweeper crews, you will lead the way. Everyone else form up with your patrol leaders. Patrols will stay a hundred meters apart. So don't just stand there. That wasn't a suggestion," she said, walking to the door, pulling it open, and looking back into the room. "That was an order!" As the women passed through the door, Maya pulled some aside with a quick "you're with me" and made sure the patrol sergeants knew who was pulled.

When the room was empty except for the 'wounded' and the ten she had pulled out, she looked them over. "It's time your special service training gets tested. Sergeant Rhianna, you will be in command."

"Thank you, General!" Rhianna said with a salute.

"Your mission is to go back to base camp and call the submersible as close to shore as possible while staying submerged. The ten of you will swim out, with full combat gear, and board the sub. You will go to the far north edge of the bay, where you will swim to shore. From there, you will head east to the outer suburbs, join Gray Company, and report to Captain Tanesha. She is expecting you. There is a complete briefing message in the sub. A quick preview is in order. Admiral Chang believes that some of the passengers on Tower Three were embedded imperial informants and sympathizers and that they have formed a guerrilla force centered in the northern suburbs, particularly in Goose Town. I've contacted Captain Nanette and her civilian watch, and they'll be looking for you."

Is she the overly bubbly twenty-something? Rhianna messaged.

Yes. She's a local and has a tightly organized group. She'll have good information.

We're on it, General.

Maya stayed with telepathy and continued. *"You were all chosen for this mission because you can read people. This skill will come in handy when you are looking for insurgents. Message me back if you heard this.*

Ten variations of *"loud and clear"* echoed in Maya's brain.

Then you are ready. May the force be with you.

And with you, General Maya

Maya grabbed her head and said excitedly, "I never thought about simultaneous telepathic messages creating a near unconsciousness. You could use this to your advantage. Practice on the sub."

Yes! Ma'am!

Maya, still shaking out the cobwebs, turned to the remaining five women. "Marta," she said sharply, "I'm ordering you to remain here and handle communications. You have six-year-old twins and another set incubating, and I want you to be as safe as possible."

Marta flushed and, fending off tears, said, "I was loud thinking, wasn't I? I was thinking about the boys and what would happen to them if we lost the war, and I freaked out a bit, but I'm better now."

Maya hugged her and whispered in her ear, "It's OK, sweetheart. I know what you're going through. Just between us, I'm pregnant, too, and I'm scared shitless. Yuri doesn't know yet, and I don't know how to tell him. He would freak out if he thought I was putting myself in danger."

"Jim doesn't know either," Marta sighed, "He will freak out double when I do tell him."

"Which will be tomorrow, for both of us!" Maya said conspiratorially, "We'll get them both on a conference call. But, for now, we have work to do, and looking at the tactical screens, it seems we will be safe here for a while."

"Are we seeing what I think we're seeing?" Marta said incredulously.

"If you're seeing that the fighter bombed the statue and turned north and that the troop carriers followed," Maya said, watching as the tactical computer plotted the most likely destination as New Origin. "Call Captain Nanette and tell her to be on the watch for the commandos and have her call back as soon as they arrive."

'I'm on it," Marta replied in a voice that said, 'all business.'

"Command! Call Yuri!"

Yuri was sitting at his kitchen table finishing his oatmeal breakfast when his command helmet began beeping. He pulled the helmet on and found Maya with a distressed look distorting her face.

"Good afternoon, General, my love. What can I do for you?"

"Check logistics," she snarled. Do you see the fighters and the troupe ships coming? I'm sending Rosie's Company and Green Company on the train asap. Tanesha's group is in Goose Town and will be up as soon as it we're sure New Origin is the primary target. Is Lily's group ready?"

"Lily is ready, and we will be laying low until the others get here. Are you OK? We saw the Fighter strafing your area."

"We had a few minor injuries, and the bunker wasn't hit. So I'm here with the wounded and the heavy artillery. I'll be all right as long as you promise to be careful."

"I promise. Anything else? It looks like the fighters will be here in five minutes."

"Yeah, there is one more thing. I'm pregnant. Command out."

Yuri sat with his mouth open and his eyes glassy until A-C came rushing in, yelling, "They're bombing the city center, and the troop carriers are landing in the square, and a bomb just hit HQ. I can't contact either Capitan Lily or Adam!"

Yuri shook away the cobwebs, looked at his situation screen, and said, "First, send a patrol to HQ ASAP and call me from there. On second thought, belay that, you and I will go to HQ. Call Dana, Lily's second, and tell her she's in command until we find Lily. Tell her to launch drones targeting the troop carriers and anything that comes out of their doors and move every civilian they can out of the center. Then set up remote-controlled big guns focused on the doors of the troop carriers and open fire as soon as everyone is out of the square. They also need to set up another set of guns a hundred meters away from the corners. Finally, send a contingent to the train station. We have reinforcements coming. When they get here, have them set up skirmish lines and anti-aircraft disrupters all around the outskirts of town."

"I'm on it, Admiral!" A-C said, "I can do all that as we go.

"Give me a second to get geared up," Yuri said quickly, strapping on his armor and grabbing his weapon belt, bow, disrupter, and command helmet.

Fully armed, the two left the apartment building, which was three blocks from the square. They crept through backyards, alleyways, and pasture lands to the ever-increasing sounds of the battle. They were near the barn behind Adam and Lily's daughter, Sherri's house when a fighter with flames trailing out its tail crashed in the field behind the house, and the sounds of the battle increased tenfold.

They rushed into the barn to find four nervous horses rearing wildly in their paddocks. The horses' mood was boosted by the sound of a second fighter crashing nearby and calmed by the rapid diminution of the battle noise. When the horses quieted, A-C and Yuri crept out of the barn and crawled to the back of the house. They slid along the back wall to the corner and peaked around toward Adam and Lily's cottage, which was, until now, the command center. The door to the place was wide open, and smoke was pouring out.

They crept along the side wall to the front corner. A black flying-car limousine was in the semi-circular driveway in front of the big house. A stormtrooper was walking guard on the driveway between the limo and porch that stretched the length of the big house.

A-C tapped Yuri on the shoulder, stared into his eyes, and messaged, *Can you hear me?*

Yuri replied: *Yes, and I want you to go back around the house to the other corner. When you get there, watch the guard, and when he gets almost to this end of his walk, make a sound, duck back around the corner, and message me. Then, I'll take him out with an arrow.*

A-C gave a thumbs-up and went back around the house. Yuri notched an arrow and waited.

He's coming back quickly. A-C messaged five minutes later. Yuri stepped around the corner and released the arrow, which landed in the guard's neck with a small pop as the arrowhead exploded. A-C came around the corner, put another arrow into the guard, and dragged the body around the corner to the back of the house.

Yuri messaged, *I'm sending a microbot camera into the house, and I'm sending your helmet the access code. Go to the back door. We'll watch the feed and decide how to proceed.*

The bot passed through the keyhole in the back door, up the hallway, and scanned the foyer, finding two stormtroopers guarding the entrance to the sitting room. Yuri directed the nanobot back down the hallway and into the kitchen. The kitchen was empty, and he noticed that the back door was unlocked.

A-C, go in the back door as quietly as you can. I'm sending the bot to check out the dining and sitting rooms.

The bot scanned the empty dining room, and Yuri directed it under the door that connected to the sitting room.

The first thing it saw was the body of a woman in scrubs face down on the floor and the feet of seven other people. The bot rose to the ceiling, and the scene became clear. Sherri was sprawled on the floor, either dead or unconscious; Lily, Adam, and Sherri's husband, Dave, were gagged and tied to chairs; two well-armed men in military uniforms were standing with their backs to the foyer and dining room doors; two men in black business suits were standing over Lily and Adam; one of them holding a taser, the other one was George Washington Chang.

Yuri messaged A-C; *I'm going to take out the two troopers in the foyer. When you hear the first shot, shoot your guy through the door and the guy at the other door if he's still upright. Then stun the two guys in the suits. The older one is my uncle and the Emperor's lover. I would just as soon shoot him, but he will serve us better as a hostage. Then cut Adam loose and attend to Sherri.*

Ready when you are Admiral.

Yuri set his disruptor to the max, stepped into the foyer, and started blasting on full automatic. The walls, ceiling, floor, and the two stormtroopers were hit multiple times. The floor collapsed under the Stormers, and they were buried in the rubble before they could raise their pulse guns. Yuri turned the disruptor to the door and blew it open with a single blast. He picked his way across what was left of the foyer floor and stepped into the sitting room.

The first thing Yuri saw was Adam straddling Sherri and doing CPR. A-C burst into the room with a hanging bag of blood and a handheld regeneration device. He handed the flash-light-sized device to Adam, who started waving it over Sherri's chest while A-C began the transfusion. Yuri rushed to Lily and John and had them untied in less than a minute. John ran to Sherri and restarted the CPR, and Lily picked up A-C's discarded gun and pointed it at the two men in suits on the floor in front of her. Yuri grabbed the weapon from Lily and said, "We need these two alive as hostages, and besides, I have first rights to this one," kicking George's slowly awakening body and extracting a whimpering grunt. "this is the Emperor's Secretary of State and pet ass-kisser, George Washington Chang, and this," kicking the other man a bit more aggressively," is his son, Jefferson Davis Chang, who tormented me my entire youth because he was too stupid, too mean, and too damn ignorant to understand the truth. Isn't that right, J-D?"

"Fuck-you, you traitor," J-D said with a groan. "The Emperor's gonna nail you to a wall and peel off your skin centimeter by centimeter until it kills you."

"Well, that's maybe what he wants to do, but to do that he's going to have to win this ridiculous war, and that was never going to happen. You know why? Because he's surrounded by morons like you and ass-kissers like your equally stupid suck-up daddy here." Yuri turned to George, who was, by now, awake and sitting splayed-legged on the floor, and kicked him in that special spot between the legs, causing him to vomit on his lap, coughing and sputtering.

A commotion across the room caused Yuri to look over, where he found Sherri sitting up, coughing, and smiling at her parents and husband. "Welcome back, Dr. Sherri," he called, "which one of these piles of human offal shot you?"

"The one in the uniform," she replied, pointing to the body on the floor by the foyer door.

"Well, Uncle George and cousin shithead, you should be happy that you are only accessories to murder, and we don't have to execute you," Yuri said, spitting venom. He put his right index finger to his lips and up his left hand. "Lily, do you have your command helmet nearby?"

"Yes, I'll get it" she replied, rushing out the dining room door. She came back in wearing the helmet and smiling like a butcher's dog. "I have some news!" She said excitedly, "After an all-out battle resulting in the downing of all four fighters, the destruction of three of the five troop carriers, and the surrender of the fourth and fifth, the imperial force invading New Origin has raised the white flag and laid down their arms. The estimated casualty count of our brave women is twenty wounded, eight seriously, and fifteen killed," she stammered and cried briefly. "We also lost twenty-eight horses and six distortion cannons. The Emperor has declared unconditional surrender and requests the return of any prisoners of war."

Tears, hugs, more tears, and a half hour of silent contemplation followed the announcement.

Yuri returned to his uncle and cousin after the relief and mourning became joy and celebration. He looked from one to the other and offered them a hand up, a giant bear hug, and a shoulder to cry on. "If you give it a chance, this planet and its people will make you very happy, especially you, Uncle George. Same-sex relationships are not only tolerated, they are celebrated. As for you, J-D, I recall you were a star athlete. I'm sure there are teams in several sports that would be glad to have you on their side. You'll have to get over the fact that some of the women on the team will be better than you. It's how they are made here, and I, for one, find it very sexy. You'll see when you meet my wife Maya that us old Martians make strong women too. Oh, and I saw you looking at Sherri. She's out of your class, but I'll bet she knows a lot of women that would be willing to consider you. You are a Chang, after all."

A New Origin

Yuri released J-D and George and led them into the kitchen, saying, "Let's get you guys something to eat, and then we'll go to my friend William's tavern for the best beer you've ever had."

Adam followed them and went straight to the refrigerator. "Looks like there's some leftover fried chicken, some grits, and corn on the cob. J-D, reach down that big pan and fill it with water for the corn, and George, you can start husking the corn. There's a trash can under the sink. Yuri set the table for ten. Maya just called Lily and said she and Penelope are on their way. It looks like there's not enough chicken, but there's some ground beef. I'll start the grill if anyone wants burgers."

"I do," Dave said from the dining room.

"Me too," Sherri said, coming in right behind him.

"I'm in for burgers. I just called Maya, and she and Pen are chicken," Yuri called from the dining room.

"I'm chicken," Lily said.

"I could eat a couple of burgers and some chicken," J-D said, putting the pot on the stove. "How does this thing turn on? I've never seen anything like this."

Lily walked over and said, "Let me show you. You're going to need to know this. See the black circles on the surface; they're the heating units. You put the pot over the one closest to the size of the pot and then turn the dial for that burner on the front here, see how they are marked with a map of the surface and a heat level? For boiling water, you'll want to turn it to high."

"Like this?" J-D asked.

"Perfect! It should be at a boil in about ten minutes."

"I hate to be a nuisance," George said quietly, "but do you have any vegetarian meat substitute?"

"I think there might be a veggie burger or two," Dave said, rummaging through the fridge. "You're in luck, we have a whole stack. Anyone else want a veggie burger?"

"I would," Maya said, coming in the back door.

"Me too," said Penelope, right behind her.

After dinner, the whole crew walked through town, squeezing past destroyed vehicles and climbing over piles of rubble from bombed-out buildings where people were out, clearing the roads and moving belongings from damaged homes. They stopped and helped people load wagons and clear walkways.

Three hours later, they reached the tavern, which had, somehow, avoided damage. The mood inside was jubilant, and room was made for the newcomers to sit at the bar. William came out from behind and greeted everyone with a bear hug. When he got to George and J-D, he looked them up and down and declared, "Let us all welcome the renegade members of the Chang Gang. Yuri, get over here."

After Yuri squeezed through the crowd and hugged him, William said in his outshout-the-crowd voice, "A-C, you get over here too. Now both of you close your eyes and count down from twenty."

They did as directed and opened their eyes to find Maya and Penelope in full battle gear. They fell into their partner's arms, and William declared, "Everyone, I give you the Heroes of the Martian war!"

The resulting roar could be heard several blocks away, as witnessed by the four different groups of Lily's command, who came rushing in over the next half-hour. The final group pushed the crowd in the tavern twice capacity, resulting in the party spilling out onto the road. Yuri and Maya found George and J-D at the fringe of the crowd, arguing quietly just below the celebration volume. As they got nearer, they could make out the words "stay" from J-B and "can't" from George.

"I've got this," Maya said, putting her hand on Yuri's chest. "You stay here and let me handle it."

"Better you than me," he replied, blowing her a kiss which she caught over her shoulder as she strode to the Changs, père, and fils.

"OK, boys, what seems to be the problem here?" She said, pushing them apart and glaring at them. George cringed, and J-D stood wide-eyed and open-mouthed.

"He doesn't want to go back to the Forbidden City," George said spitting venom.

"Is that right, J-D?" she said, staring him down.

"Ye, ye, ye, yes, Ma'am." He replied looking down at his feet.

A New Origin

"You can call me Maya, or cousin if you prefer," she said soothingly. "I can make that happen for you, but I would suggest you go to Gaia City. It may take the Originites a while to forgive you. As for you, Uncle George, Yuri, and I are going to escort you back. We will be leaving in about twenty minutes. Unless, of course, you wish to stay."

"I am ready to go," George said, sticking his arms out as if expecting handcuffs.

"Put your hands down, Uncle George," Yuri said as he walked over, "We're giving you a ride, not arresting you." Then turning to Maya, "Where's your helmet? We should start walking to the train station."

"William put it behind the bar. You guys start. I'll go get it and say goodbyes," she said, squeezing through the crowd and into the tavern.

Yuri put his arms around J-D and George as they started up the road to the train station. "We have an hour layover in Gaia City, J-D. We'll get you through immigration and to the orientation center before the train up the peninsula leaves. There's still time to change your mind, Uncle George."

"I can't, Yuri. At least not yet," he said with a sigh.

Maya came running up and grabbed Yuri's hand. "There's a problem with the peninsula train so we're going to stay with Mayor Lisa and Judy for a couple of days. I'm sure you'll like them, Uncle George. We'll also have time to check out J-D's new apartment. It's where Pen used to live, and it's in the middle of downtown where all the action is. You'll love it J-D. There was something else. Oh Yeah, Judy's set up some tryouts for you, J-D. Did Yuri tell you that participating in sports is classified as a job on this planet? So you won't need to find a job to support your hobby. Your hobby will be your job!"

"I'm loving it already! Thanks, coz!"

They got off the train at six AM and walked to Lisa's house on Main Street, a block away from City Hall. They were met by the aroma of bacon, french toast, and strong coffee. Mayor Lisa and Judy were in their bath robes, along with A-C and Penelope, who had taken an earlier train and were playing with their twins in the living room. Lisa latched onto J-D and talked to him over breakfast about how he would be starting his new life. Judy engaged George, and they spent several hours discussing society, relationships, and the nearly non-existent prejudice in the realm of relationships. Yuri and Maya slipped quietly to the guest suite and only reappeared, briefly, at dinner. They were not seen again until noon when they came to lunch in civvies they had borrowed from Lisa and Judy. Fortunately, the current fashion was unisex, and Judy was a centimeter taller than Maya and the same height as Yuri.

Lunch was a strange event with Judy and George engaged in a long and energetic discussion, that they conducted in whispers, Lisa and Maya chatting over the stove, and Yuri wolfing pancakes as fast as they were made.

The train was still down, but it was warm and sunny. Lisa ordered a landau which arrived just as everyone finished their lunch. Judy looked at George and said, "Are you sure you don't want to stay?"

He sighed, "I can't, at least for now, but I'll come visit."

"Bring your friend when you do, OK," she said, hugging him.

"I'll see what I can do," he said, breaking the embrace.

The carriage ride took two hours to reach the Forbidden City. George and Yuri talked and laughed about old times, and Maya related anecdotes from her time with Yuri on the Hexagon, which made George laugh and Yuri blush. Finally, they entered the Forbidden City to the chaos of construction on the towers and lines of people standing at kiosks that were serving as customs and immigration portals.

SCENE THREE
Who Guessed Whimper?

As soon as they stopped at the gate, a family of six rushed to the carriage and started climbing on.

"Hey!" the driver shouted, "Where are your manners? Please wait for my passengers to get off."

The father pulled two of the kids off the back of the carriage and the mother the other two from the side. "I'm sorry, sir," she said contritely, "We were so anxious to get away from this evil place before our employers woke up that we didn't think. We just ran."

"I understand," he said softly. "Please allow me to take you to the city and excuse my rude behavior." Yuri and George had gotten out and were already through the gate. Maya helped the children get into the landau. When they were in and settled, she turned to the mother and asked, "What is all the commotion at those kiosks?" pointing to the ones with the long lines and shouting men.

"That's where the rich men are arguing with the customs officers."

Perplexed, Maia asked, "About what?"

"The men don't want to register their wives and children. They want to keep all the credits for themselves, and they are mad that their servants, like us, can register."

Maya couldn't hold back her smile as she hugged the young mother. "My name is Maya, and I am the commanding officer of the Gaian army. I can tell you that that is NEVER going to happen. So please tell me your name and I'll contact my friend Lisa, the mayor of Gaia City. I'll tell her you and your family are coming and she will help you get settled."

"You would do that for us?"

Maya reached into her pocket and pulled out her handheld communicator. "Hi Lisa, I'm sending you a family of six I just met. They need to get away before their employer wakes up. Sure." She handed the communicator to the woman, "You talk on here and listen from here," she said, pointing to the bottom and top of the thin rectangular plastic block.

The woman looked at Maya, who nodded.

"Hello? Yes, I can hear you, I don't know how, but I can ... My name is Lucinda, my husband is Joe, and we have four children ... How do you know that?... Yes, we did ... Thank you, thank you, thank you ...I will. Thank you again ... OK." Lucinda handed the communicator back to Maya with a look of awe. "She knew my children's names, and she said she would see us in about an hour, and that the driver knows where to take us."

"That's because you are now citizens of Gaia with all the same rights and privileges as any other citizen."

Lucinda crumpled in her arms, crying, causing a chain reaction from Joe, the kids, the driver, and herself.

"I'll look you up and Yuri and I will visit."

"You know Yuri Chang?" Joe asked drop jawed. "I *thought* I saw him walking into the courtyard with the Prime minister. I worked with him, building the Hexagon."

"I kinda do know him; he's my husband and the father of our soon-to-be child."

Lucinda hugged Maya and whispered congratulations."

"Folks," the driver said with urgency, "There's a whole bunch of people running in this direction. We gotta take off, like now!"

"Go! I'll see you soon!" Maya shouted to the quickly receding carriage.

She turned around and saw the wave of people turning left out of the entrance to the Forbidden City heading toward a sign that said Metro and realized that the train was now running. She looked back at the gates of the city where there was part in the crowd where Yuri and Lincoln were waking arm-in-arm. *Yuri, my love, can you hear me?* she messaged.

Always, anytime, anywhere you wish, he replied.

A New Origin

I've been made aware of some issues at the immigration gates that I must address. It is likely to involve some arrests and detainments. I'm likely to be engaged for some time.

How can I help?

Take George home and go talk to Josh about the museum we talked about last night. We need to make him feel like he can still be significant. I'm afraid he's going to commit suicide.

That's the plan if it's not too late. I think you're going to need to bring in the troops. You can use Five as a detainment center.

As you said, that's the plan. Be gentle with Josh.

Will do. I'll see you at William's tavern.

Maya pulled her communicator out of her jeans pocket and called Marta at Green command.

"General Maya! How can I help you?"

"Marta, it's good to hear your voice. How much of Green company are on site?"

"Everyone except the commandos. They are escorting the renegade immigrants to New Origin for orientation."

"Good. Put me on the intercom."

"You're good to go."

"Attention, Green Company. Gear up for crowd control and detention of inciting individuals. I need you at the Forbidden City gates ASAP. Bring the mobile detention cells. Do not bring lethal weapons. That is all."

Fifteen minutes later the company was formed up at the gates. The number of people exiting the city had dropped to near zero, and the lines at the kiosks had grown ten-fold. Maya stood in front of the company with a megaphone and announced, "Green company, at ease. Here's the situation. The Alpha males of the aristocratic families are refusing to register their family members, except for their firstborn sons, as citizens of Gaia. Instead, they are verbally and, in some cases, physically abusing our immigration agents. This activity is unconscionable and cannot be allowed to continue. Your job here is to remove these individuals, bring them to the detention cells, and help their families through registration and transport to orientation centers in the city. Resistant family members will be led to orientation centers on-site. Physical resistance will be responded to with stunning and removal to special orientation centers in the city. Operation Integrate begins now!"

The company responded with the efficiency of a well-programmed machine. The detention cells were assembled and were soon occupied with screaming, red-faced men cursing the women of Green Company. The on-site orientation center would only host five people, all of them adult males. The end result of the intervention was the clearing of the lines at the kiosks and the registration of fifty-five hundred new citizens.

****

Emperor Joshua the first was pacing the Dais of the throne room with his hands in his pockets, contemplating whether or not he would become Emperor Joshua last. The loss of half of his starship and three-quarters of his military to what, on the surface, appeared to be a backward planet was weighing heavily on his mood to the extent that he was clutching the syringe of cyanide in his left hand with his thumb on the plunger and the needle scratching his thigh.

"Don't do it, Josh, I know what you're thinking, and it's just not true," Yuri said, moving closer to the Dais. "There is an essential place for you on this world. Your knowledge of Human history is unsurpassed, and the future of the human race depends on not making the mistakes of our ancestors. We can only do that if we have a fundamental understanding of what those mistakes were. Remember what you told me your father said? That you needed me to keep you on the right track? Well, here I am, and I'm begging you to give me the syringe and come with me to my friend William's tavern. I promise it's the best beer ever, and I'll get just as shit-faced as you do."

"Why should I do that? You just want to get me drunk so you can humiliate me just like you did when we rushed the Frat you wanted to join," Josh said, pulling the syringe out of his pocket and holding the needle next to his carotid artery.

"Wow, wow, wow. You've got that wrong, Josh. Think hard now. Remember, you were a year ahead of me and trying to get me into your Frat, but your 'Brothers' didn't want anyone from the middle class in their elite's only club. You tried your best, but you had one beer too many and

A New Origin

passed out. While you were out, they force-fed me a half bottle of whisky, and I got stripped naked and was dragged to the soccer pitch and beaten unconscious with cricket bats. I don't know who dragged me back to the dorm, but when I woke up, you were there with a couple of medics who got me into an ambulance and to the hospital. I'm pretty sure that they made shunning me a requirement for you to stay in the Frat because, after that, every time I saw you on campus, you quickly looked back to see if I was following you."

Josh looked at Yuri with watery eyes and threw the syringe against the back wall of the throne room. He sat down at the edge of the Dais and patted the floor on his right. Yuri came over and sat next to him. He put his arm around Josh's shoulder and pulled him into a full embrace. Josh responded in kind. They spent the next two hours reminiscing and discussing the establishment of 'The Emperor Joshua the First Museum of Human History' which would occupy the Imperial Towers and Tower Two and exhibit the thousands of artifacts and artworks brought by the wealthy. Tower Five would be converted to a hostel for visitors from across the planet and, what they didn't know at the time was possible, from Earth and Mars.

EPILOGUE

The hourglass inverts
and we move from then to now
the new spring in view

Master of Ceremonies: Gentle viewers, on behalf of our cast and crew, many of whom are fourth and fifth-generation descendants of the women and men they depict, we thank you for your support. I am proud to announce the newest play in our legacy series, "Origin Renewed" which will debut next year, two years by your calendar, on the grassy plains of Greenland on our first planet of origin, Earth.

Final Curtain

ACKNOWLEDMENT

I am indebted, as always , to my wife, Jill, for her moral support while working on the book.

I would like to acknowledge my daughter Emily Rook-Koepsel for her editorial comments, her support for this project, and her enthusiastic encouragement that I should publish the book. I would also like thank the members of the Writers Workshop Osher class who read the story and made suggestions for improvements

My gratitude to publisher Krish Singh for his patience and good humor in helping me prepare *A New Origin* for publication